CITY
OF
SECRETS

ALSO BY P. J. TRACY

THE DETECTIVE MARGARET NOLAN SERIES

The Devil You Know
Desolation Canyon
Deep into the Dark

THE MONKEEWRENCH SERIES

Ice Cold Heart
The Guilty Dead
Nothing Stays Buried
The Sixth Idea
Off the Grid
Shoot to Thrill
Snow Blind
Dead Run
Live Bait
Monkeewrench

The Return of the Magi

CITY

OF

SECRETS

P. J. TRACY

MINOTAUR BOOKS
NEW YORK

First published in the United States by Minotaur Books, an imprint of St. Martin's Publishing Group

www.minotaurbooks.com

Designed by Devan Norman

The Library of Congress Cataloging-in-Publication Data is available upon request.

ISBN 978-1-250-33435-0 (hardcover)
ISBN 978-1-250-33436-7 (ebook)

First Edition: 2024

10 9 8 7 6 5 4 3 2 1

To Sugar, Ollie, and Cinnamon, my sweetest angels.
You are in my heart forever.

CITY
OF
SECRETS

Chapter One

WHEN BRUCE MESSANE'S PHONE WOKE HIM at half past midnight, he knew it couldn't possibly be good news—good news never came this late. He tried to guess what calamity was waiting for him on the other end of the line. Best-case scenario was more supply chain issues and shipping delays, a constant scourge since COVID. Worst-case scenario was a bad quarterly projection that could blow up the deal with Wilder Foods. Please, God, not that. Not now. They were so close.

Or perhaps it wasn't a company problem at all, but a death. The thought cheered him. Maybe Camille had fallen off a mountain in the Italian Alps, which would be a just and poetic end for a *former* Olympic skier and a *former* wife who'd absconded to Europe with her *former* trainer. She'd also absconded with his fourteen-year-old daughter and half of his wealth. Actually, it had been Trina's choice to decamp to Livigno with her mother, but only because her mind had been poisoned against him.

As vindictive and rapacious as Camille was, he couldn't really begrudge her choice—he'd been a miserable husband. He probably would have done the same thing in her position. But he still hated her. And paradoxically, still loved her. Or maybe he just loved the memory of the small-town Colorado girl he'd met in Aspen and married six months later. Money did strange things to people.

He fumbled for the bedside lamp in his Holmby Hills bedroom, tugged on the ridiculous tasseled pull, and illuminated a nauseatingly feminine space that raised his hackles and made his stomach burn. Too damn much brocade and gilt, too many stupid, pointless tassels, too many useless, overpriced tchotchkes that Camille referred to haughtily as decorative accents. And the hideous curtains—mustard-yellow silk trimmed with blue fringe. It was like Versailles had vomited here, and it haunted him. God, how he hated those curtains—*window treatments*—especially after he found out they'd cost him eighty thousand dollars.

He was going to gut this room—no, the whole house—and have a ceremonial bonfire in the desert somewhere as soon as the deal was inked. Replace the abominable French baroque with masculine, industrial-chic pieces in leather and steel. Erase her. He liked erasing extraneous people from his life.

Hi, Camille, thought you would enjoy this video of your shit burning. By the way, the deal just went through. A hundred million and change for a company I started with a five-thousand-dollar loan. Can you believe it? Too bad you missed the really big payday. Best wishes. Love, Bruce.

His incessantly bleating phone fragmented his revenge fantasy, and he squinted at the screen. Unknown number. He thought about muting it and going back to sleep, but the caprices of technology sometimes registered important calls as unknown numbers. And every call was important, especially now. "Bruce Messane."

"Oh, dear, you sound groggy. Did I wake you?"

Mimi. What the hell did she want? He'd erased her from his life months ago, but she kept resurfacing like a stubborn stain. "It's late."

"Never too late to hear from an old friend, is it?" she purred.

Mimi either purred or rasped. There was no middle ground with her. The purr meant she wanted something; the rasp meant she was sharpening her claws. "I have a very important early meeting—"

"I need to see you."

Bruce wiped the pearls of sweat that had erupted on his forehead. Mimi was an addiction; a flesh-and-blood manifestation of the very worst in him. She made him feel sick and weak, and she wielded her power with cunning alacrity. But that toxic part of his life was in the rearview mirror, and it had to stay there. He couldn't go back, it would ruin him. "No. Our relationship is over. It never should have happened in the first place."

Her voice transformed into that ugly, husky scraping, like bone against bone. "I gave you everything, Bruce. Everything you ever wanted, and you discarded me like a used condom when something better came along. You owe me this, so don't keep me waiting. I'll pick you up at the usual place."

He listened to the dead air of an ended call and stared at the revolting mustard curtains as if they might inform him of the right decision. Maybe just this one last time. Predictably, his lack of resolve ignited self-loathing, but the transgression would be worth it. If you'd never enjoyed the danger of sex with a psychopath, you hadn't lived.

Chapter Two

FOR THE FOURTH DAY IN A row, rain swept through downtown LA in silvery, oblique sheets, driven by a fierce wind. Overtaxed storm drains regurgitated gray water that pooled in the streets and on the sidewalks. The normally desiccated Los Angeles River—not a river at all, just a concrete flood channel cleaving the city—roiled and foamed as it raced to sea with a woeful collection of debris. It was an excellent time to dispose of a body there, Detective Margaret Nolan thought. Once it hit the Pacific, it would be gone for good.

She was mesmerized by nature's fury as she watched the slashing, sideways rain out the window of the LAPD Administration Building, colloquially known as the Glass House. All morning, overcaffeinated meteorologists who usually had nothing to talk about in Southern California prattled on about apocalyptic weather. They spoke with deranged glee, the tacit message being the End of Days was near, time to gather flora and fauna and build an ark, time to kiss your ass and life as you knew it good-bye. The sure antidote to boredom and low ratings was hyperbole.

Admittedly, the weather was strange these days, but hadn't weather always been strange? Antarctica and Death Valley had once been lush tropical forests; Europe had experienced a little ice age in the sixteenth and seventeenth centuries. Maybe it was time for SoCal to become a rain forest once again. The city founders had been aiming for that since the first Los Angeles Aqueduct had been completed in 1913. That clever piece of engineering had drained the Owens River and the Owens Lake to supply water to a new paradise at the expense of a fertile, productive valley. The destruction they'd wrought over the years could easily be administered by Mother Nature in relative minutes.

But Nolan wasn't interested in the politics of water or climate change at the moment; she was interested in her partner, Al Crawford, who was stuck between exits on the backside of a ten-car pileup on the 101. Why did people turn into abject idiots behind the wheel when it rained?

He answered before the phone rang on her end. The sound of rain pounding his car was thunderous, but it didn't drown out the aggravation in his voice, which had escalated since the last time they'd spoken. "Where are you now?"

"I'm in exactly the same spot I was when I called you twenty minutes ago. I can't even squeeze through with the gumball, it's a freaking wall-to-wall disaster, and half the assholes around me are getting out of their cars in this monsoon, like *that's* going to help . . ." He paused his rant to refill his lungs. "You're calling with a body, aren't you?"

"Culver City. Meet me there, I just texted you the address. Take deep breaths and don't kill anybody. It would look bad on your performance review."

He grunted. "I'll try my best."

"Try harder."

"Yeah. See you sometime next year." She pocketed her phone and watched a solitary figure on the plaza below fight the elements. The brave soul and his tattered blue umbrella were losing.

"Enjoying the scenery?"

Remy Beaudreau's low, smooth voice behind her startled as much as it catalyzed a furious rush of endorphins. She loved the sizzling high, but hated that she was a feeble pawn to biology in even the most inappropriate circumstances. She came from a long line of control freaks, and had probably absorbed the trait in the womb. Hormonal autopilot contravened her most basic principles.

She turned and nodded curtly; professionally. Their relationship was nebulous at the moment, but whatever it was or might become, it simply couldn't exist in the Glass House. If Captain Mendoza found out, one of them would have to leave the vaunted Homicide Special Section, and that would be sudden death. Any other position would be a significant demotion for the loser, and bitterness would ensue no matter how hard they tried to make it work.

"Good morning, Detective Beaudreau."

"I do admire your formality and restraint, Maggie," he whispered close to her ear. "I'm having some difficulty maintaining the same discipline."

His words were silky and tinged with old-money New Orleans. It wasn't fair that he could smile without smiling; that his dark, curly hair was damp and unkempt in the most alluring way; that his bespoke suit, dotted with dark water spots because he never carried an umbrella, was perfectly snug on his lean frame. Was he trying to torture her? "Behave yourself, Detective."

"Prudent, but possibly futile. I believe we're the worst-kept secret in HSS."

That deflated her, and washed away all those excellent endorphins. "Mendoza doesn't know, let's keep it that way."

"I think you might be underestimating him."

Without the love buzz, she was able to get irritated with him, just like anybody else who endeavored to ruin her day. "All the more reason for absolute propriety."

"You're right." Remy raised his hand in oath. "Absolute propriety from now on, Scout's honor. Was this our first quarrel?"

She took a beat, then covered her mouth to hide a smile from anyone who might be watching. "Hardly. It was me being sensible in response to you being incorrigible. No *way* you were a Boy Scout."

"No, but I'm always prepared."

"For what?"

"Plagues, floods, scoundrels . . . even vexed sweethearts. I hope to restore your confidence in me with dinner tonight."

Yes, please. "I'm not sure. We just got a call-out to Culver City. Body in a car."

He scanned Homicide's busy honeycomb of work cubicles. "Where's Al?"

"Stuck behind the pileup on the 101. He's meeting me there." Tensions smoothed and forgotten, Nolan's mind was free to focus on other things, like the body waiting for her. Yet it mulishly remained on Remy. They'd never spoken about what had to happen if . . . or *when* the captain found out. It was a pivotal aspect of their situation, their relationship, yet they were frolicking like spring lambs oblivious to impending slaughter. Well, maybe that was a little dramatic, but it had to be addressed at some point. Soon. Over several martinis.

"Why are you even here? I thought you'd be out all day with the Kang case."

"I thought so, too, but the disgraced Dr. Kang solved it all on his own with a fentanyl overdose, so I can't take credit for staggering virtuosity. We found over two hundred counterfeit oxys in a vitamin bottle. His patients weren't the only ones with an opioid problem."

"Sounds like he was dealing to support his habit."

"Two hundred oxys aren't for personal use," he agreed. "Although I doubt he realized they were tainted. By all accounts, he wasn't suicidal."

"Ironic that a famous plastic surgeon who lost his license by over-prescribing real opioids died from street trash."

"Life is full of irony. And fortunes change. He went from a Beverly Hills mansion to a depressing studio in Chinatown."

Fentanyl was public enemy number one; the biggest menace since meth, but far deadlier. "Kang's death makes that over two thousand ODs this year."

He grimaced. "More to come, unfortunately. There's a lot of bad product on the street right now. I showed the pills to Justin in Gang-Narc, and they're a perfect match with the four hundred thousand rainbows they just confiscated in Inglewood."

"Rainbows?"

"Bright cheery colors to attract the tween crowd."

Nolan's stomach spasmed around the chalky lemon yogurt she'd had for breakfast. "That's disgusting . . . worse than disgusting—it's evil."

"There's a high percentage of sociopaths in the drug realm."

"Do they know where it's coming from?"

"They think it's part of a cartel dump, meant to flood the market and drive down the price."

"Why would they cut into their bottom line?" His unreadable onyx eyes were distracting her, so she turned back to the window.

"Power grab. Cull the weak and take over their share of the action without a turf war. Or force alliances."

"That sounds awfully sophisticated for sociopathic thugs."

"It's a multibillion-dollar business, and the new generation *is* so-phisticated. The drug lords probably all have MBAs now."

She sighed dispiritedly. "Between the cartels, overseas suppliers, and dark web drug emporiums, it's never going to end."

Remy tapped the window. "I'm not sure this rain will, either. I hope your crime scene isn't getting washed away."

"I'm sure it's too late to worry about that, but I have to go." She turned, risked a glance at him, and maintained her self-possession. Good job. "I'll call you later."

A discreet smile lifted one corner of his mouth. "I have reservations for two at the Hotel Bel-Air at nine. If you're free."

"And if I don't make it, who is my replacement?"

"You're irreplaceable, of course, so I don't have anyone else in mind. I imagine I'll just eat at the bar and have a conversation with whoever is tending. Dr. Kang was a regular there, even after his fall from grace. Bartenders know more about their customers than they know about themselves."

"I thought the case was closed."

"Essentially, but where he acquired his stash is still a mystery I'd like to solve."

"That's Narc's job, and I'm sure the Inglewood bust gave them plenty of intelligence."

"There's no such thing as too much intelligence. And I'd like to be an asset, small as my contribution may be." He shrugged nonchalantly. "I might enjoy a change of scenery at some point, and Narc would be my first choice if I were to transfer to another division. Take care, Maggie. See you later, I hope."

She watched him saunter away, stunned by his illusory bomb-drop. Remy had been thinking about their situation, too, and he was way ahead of her, making plans. She didn't know why it surprised her. Thrilled her. Terrified her.

Chapter Three

LAPD'S METROPOLITAN DIVISION, NOT FAR FROM where Nolan was processing Remy's parting comments, was head-quartered in a squat, unassuming building that took up a good chunk of a city block on West Temple Street downtown. The inside was equally humble—no frills, just utilitarian furniture and serious people. Sam Easton liked it, because it reminded him of the military, and there was comfort in familiarity. He didn't know if that was a good thing, but the possibility of consulting for SWAT was something that made sense to him at this stage in his life. He didn't feel like a civilian, but he didn't feel like a soldier anymore, either, and this was a bridge between the two. Happiness was about finding the right transitions.

Sam also liked Captain Margolis. He wasn't ex-military, but he had the bearing, and looked the part with his grizzled buzz cut and Special Forces action-doll physique. The only difference was the absence of martial formality. Special teams in any organization had their own unique cultures, and they often existed outside the parameters of convention.

The captain ended the initial pleasantries of acquaintance and began to scan the pages of the file in front of him. "Your military record is remarkable, as are the recommendations from Detectives Nolan,

Crawford, and Beaudreau. And you've already proven yourself to be a valuable asset to LAPD. Hell, you did our job single-handedly in Death Valley."

"Nice of you to say so, sir, but I was just helping out friends, and I definitely wasn't alone up there."

"Modest, too." Margolis looked at him curiously. "You have a degree in electrical engineering. This position is part-time, and it doesn't pay much. You could do a lot better consulting for corporate or private security. Or in engineering, for that matter. If it's action you're looking for, you won't find it here, unless you start from the bottom and fight your way to the top like everyone else."

"Action is the last thing I'm looking for. I've had enough of that for several lifetimes."

Margolis's eyes probed his badly scarred face. Sam was used to the scrutiny, but it still made the rubble of his flesh itch, even though the nerves on that side had been destroyed by the IED explosion. The cicatrices were like a collective ghost limb.

"I believe you. So why are you interested in SWAT?"

It was the single question Sam could answer about himself without hesitation. "I want to continue serving in some capacity. Honestly, life feels incomplete without it."

"I understand. You're a man with a long military bloodline?"

"Yes, sir. My great-grandfather died on Normandy Beach. My grandfather was a Vietnam War hero. My father served in the first Gulf War and was a career officer until his death."

"And you earned yourself a Purple Heart in Afghanistan."

"I would have preferred to leave without the Purple Heart."

He nodded, his eyes once again tracking to his scars. "I hear you. There are other ways you can serve community and country."

"True, but I know where I need to be."

The captain sipped coffee noisily from a travel mug emblazoned with the SWAT logo. "How?"

Sam hadn't told anyone in great detail about his trip to Pennsylvania, because he didn't have the words or linguistic dexterity to explain its significance. He knew Melody understood, because she'd been there; and she knew him better than anyone except his mother.

"I recently learned that a distant cousin—Peter was his name—was wounded at Gettysburg and came home with 'soldier's fatigue.' What we now know as PTSD. Peter's case was severe. His family tied him up in the attic because they didn't know what else to do."

Margolis winced. "That's horrific. And if you'd been born earlier, that could have been you."

Sam nodded. "I went out east to visit his grave. Kneeling on the grass, making an etching of his tombstone . . . maybe this sounds crazy, but it was like I could feel the shadows and ghosts of a hundred and fifty years of family history coming to life inside. It changed me, and it clarified things."

The captain's face softened a little. "It doesn't sound crazy, it sounds powerful."

"It was, sir. I have a duty to honor those who sacrificed before me. What SWAT does isn't any different from battle except that it's on home turf. If my knowledge and experience can help your men and women stay safe, I have a duty to them, too."

"I admire your commitment, Mr. Easton." He tapped a pen on the desk. "Tell me more about your PTSD."

He was amazed by how effortless it was to chart his dark journey: the pain, the grief, the depression; the flashbacks and night terrors and paranoia; the suicidal thoughts and substance abuse. Not long ago, he couldn't talk about any of it, not even to Dr. Frolich. He was getting better.

Margolis closed the file in front of him. "The war after the war."

"Yes, sir. It will always be a part of me, but it doesn't control my life anymore."

"I think the incident in Death Valley proved that. Thank you for your candor. And for coming home and climbing out of the darkness. I know what I need to know, and we'd be lucky to have you as a part of our team."

"Thank you, sir."

"Think about it. If you decide you want the job, come back and meet some of our guys and gals from D Platoon—that's our tactical unit, but you probably know that already. Watch some exercises, sit in on some strategic sessions. If we get called out, you can come along and observe. That ought to tell you if it's the fit you're looking for."

"I'd like that that very much."

He stood and offered his hand. "It's been a pleasure. I'll be in touch."

Chapter Four

IF YOU WEREN'T FAMILIAR WITH LOS Angeles and its neighborhoods, you might think Hollywood was a magical kingdom where movie stars littered the sidewalks like jacaranda blossoms in springtime. In reality, parts of Hollywood proper were some of the scariest places in the city. A few wrong turns, and you could be in serious trouble. A lot of tourists had discovered that the hard way.

This part of Culver City was even more dangerous. It was far off the gentrified main drag, and gang culture flourished here like the noxious weeds growing from cracks in the broken sidewalks. All the houses and businesses had bars on the windows and steel grates over the doors—a deterrent maybe, but not a guarantee. Nolan drove past a shuttered pawnshop, a check-cashing outfit, and a bodega with a faded sign in Spanish promising customers the best menudo in LA. She had her doubts.

Poppy's Auto Body was a weary concrete block building surrounded by a chain-link fence and this morning, a phalanx of blue. The cynical cop in her wondered what portion of the business's income came from chopping stolen cars. The purely human part of her felt shame, and then sorrow for thinking that way. Most residents in these embattled neighborhoods were good and honest, trying to scrape out a living in a war zone. They were victims of a rotting culture of violence—domestic terrorism, really—that wouldn't go away no matter how many gangsters the LAPD locked up.

A half-dozen squads were blocking the street, and the uniforms setting up a cordon and stringing tape looked cold and miserable. At least the driving rain was keeping the lookie-loos at bay, but she had a feeling the absence of street life had more to do with the heavy police presence than inclement weather. If you talked to cops, you might not live long enough to see the sun rise again.

Nolan pulled on a slicker, grabbed her umbrella, and stepped out of the car and into a puddle the size of Lake Tahoe. She hoped her new Timberland hikers would survive the trauma.

The Field Investigation Unit—the unwieldly name of what they all referred to as Crime Scene—was already on-site, erecting a tent over a late-model BMW sedan that had been relieved of its wheels. It didn't belong in this zip code, and especially not in this neighborhood, unless it belonged to a banger. If not for the dead body behind the wheel, the Beemer would probably be gone, too. Even thieves had the sense not to steal a car with a corpse in it.

She signed in with a young officer named Gonzales, who was trying hard not to notice the rain sluicing off his plastic-covered hat and down his face. In her Timberlands, she was six feet, but he was taller. "Some weather for the first week in December."

"It's crazy. But maybe it'll break the drought."

Nolan wished she could be so positive. "Who's the first responder?"

"I am, Detective." He jerked a thumb in the direction of the body shop. "Poppy called it in."

So Poppy was a real person. "You know him?"

He nodded. "I'm from the neighborhood. His place has been here as long as I can remember. Poppy's a sweet old guy, but he loses his English when he's upset. How's your Spanish?"

"Passable, but not good enough to interview a witness with any accuracy."

"Let me know when you want to talk to him and I'll help you out."

"I appreciate that, Officer. Get someone to spell you and take a break. I hope you have a thermos of hot coffee in your squad."

"I do, ma'am. Thank you."

"Canvass?"

"Sergeant Acosta is organizing it."

"Good." She folded her umbrella and ducked under the yellow tape. In that short time without cover, icy rain breached the neck of her slicker and soaked through the collar of her silk blouse. Damn weather was ruining her wardrobe *and* her crime scene.

Roscoe Miles, lead tech and dilettante filmmaker, was overseeing the construction project. The wind was making it an onerous task. The dead man was visible through the open driver's side window, and he definitely wasn't a banger.

"Hey, Maggie. Where's your right-hand man?"

"Snarled in traffic, but he's on his way."

He gestured to the car. "This is a mess. Everything is soaked inside and out. We can't lift prints until everything dries out, and it's not going to impound until we work it on-site."

"Can you get a generator and some heaters or fans?"

"Working on it."

"You never disappoint, Ross." She peered inside. No outward signs of a struggle. The man was mid to late fifties, she guessed; well-dressed, as she'd expected. His abundant, artfully graying hair was plastered to his skull. A droplet of water trickled down his artificially tight, blanched cheek, and dripped on the front of his sodden cashmere sweater. The small hole in the middle of his forehead was clean, scoured of blood by the rain. From the size and minimal damage, most likely a .22. "He saw it coming."

"Yeah. Poor bastard. Carjacking?"

"Possible, but those assholes usually carry bigger pieces. And his window is down. It's been too cold and rainy for that all week, so there was another reason it was open, and it wasn't to greet a carjacker."

Ross brightened. "Maybe he knew his killer. 'Hi, Bill, how's it going . . . hey, what's with the gun?'"

"Nice dialogue. Is that part of the new script?"

He blushed. "No, but it might be a good addition."

Nolan's mind shuffled through various scenarios, chief among them drug or prostitute seeking, then filed them in the mental hard drive for later retrieval. "In the script, you might want to add the part about a big, fancy car in a bad part of town, parked on the curb like it belongs here. Which it doesn't."

Ross nodded in agreement. "It's pretty unlikely he was bringing it to Poppy's for body work. So why was he here?"

"That's the question. And probably the answer. He knew he was putting his life in danger. Risk-reward, and he lost the bet."

Ross shrugged. "He could have been counting on losing the bet. There's suicide by cop, is there suicide by criminal?"

Nolan raised a brow. "Unique outlook. That would be a good addition to the script, too."

He looked at the car with a wistful expression. "It would have to be a junkier car, though. If I was driving an 8 Series, I wouldn't kill myself."

"Rich people have problems like everybody else. Did you get photos and video yet?"

"Yeah, have at it, Maggie."

She slipped on gloves and opened the door carefully. His seat belt was fastened, but his designer alligator-skin belt wasn't. Getting ready to party? Already finished and got whacked before he could pull himself together?

She manipulated his arm. He was cold and stiff, but rigor hadn't set in yet. This hadn't happened in broad daylight, so they had a ru-dimentary time frame. Dr. Weil would narrow it down.

She reached behind his head and found no exit wound, so they would also have a bullet to work with. He wasn't wearing a watch, but there was a tan line where one had been. His ring finger didn't have a ring or a tan line. Divorced, or maybe an avowed bachelor. Whatever jewelry he'd been wearing, it would show up in a pawnshop soon, possibly the one she'd passed on her way here.

Whereas criminals had no problem groping corpses for treasure, she always had to steel herself for the gruesome task. The worst was going through the pockets, especially the pants pockets. It was too intimate, too much a violation of something that had once been a life, but it had to be done. In this poor soul's pockets, she found nothing but lint and a ticket from Beverly Hills Cleaners on Pico Boulevard.

She ducked out and circled to the passenger's side. The con-sole—in her experience, a repository of all useless things you were too lazy to throw out—was nearly empty. Just a box of cinnamon Tic Tacs, a comb, and a pen from Broadway Dental Associates. The contents of the glove box were equally scant, yielding a tire pressure gauge and a mini flashlight. No wallet, no phone, no paperwork, no jewelry. No surprise.

"He was cleaned out," she said to Ross. "I didn't see a key fob."

"It's push-button ignition, maybe he forgot it."

"You need it to lock the doors. Nobody goes anywhere without the fob in LA."

"Yeah, you're right."

"It's weird they took it and not the car. Dead body notwith-standing."

Ross folded his arms across his chest and scratched the blond stubble on his jaw. "The fob wouldn't work on any other car, but maybe they thought it would. Never underestimate the stupidity of criminals."

"Or maybe they took the fob because it had other keys on it. Like a house key. They have his wallet and registration, so they know where he lives. But we don't. I'm going to run his plates, be right back."

As she walked to the car, she saw Al getting out of his Buick. He was wearing a foul weather windbreaker and his frowny, pissed-off face. Maybe it was because his tiny umbrella had unicorns on it. She ducked behind a squad and surreptitiously snapped a couple photos before greeting him.

"You made it here quick, considering."

"I had to shoot a few people. You'd be amazed how fast the rest of them got out of my way."

Nolan bit her lip on a smile. "Did you also shoot a schoolgirl for her umbrella?"

He glowered at her. "It was the only damned umbrella I could find. Corinne's niece forgot it last week."

"It's a good story, but you'd better ditch it, or you're going to be the butt of every joke for the next year."

"Screw everybody, my comfort is worth more than my pride."

"I've got another one in the car. It's black. Very manly."

He let out a relieved breath. "Thank God."

"Hop in, I'm about to run our vic's plates. I'll fill you in while we wait."

Chapter Five

CYNTHIA JACKSON WAS SWEATING PROFUSELY, AND it wasn't the benign, purifying kind that came from a good workout or good sex—it was the sticky, rank sweat of fear. She could smell herself, and that meant everybody else would, too. She imagined walking back into the boardroom wafting body odor; imagined the noses wrinkling, the stomachs turning, the eyes rolling.

The chief financial officer obviously hasn't showered this week. We'll definitely have to replace her with someone more judicious about personal hygiene.

Jesus, what a disaster.

"Bruce, goddammit, where the hell are you?" she whisper-hissed into the phone. "Wilder and his rabid pack of Ivy League lawyers have been waiting for half an hour, and they're pissed. *Call me.*"

Cynthia slammed her phone down, and scrambled in her desk drawer for one of the many packs of sanitizing wipes she always kept there. During the pandemic, she'd become compulsive about sterilizing every surface in her office regularly, and especially if anybody touched something or even breathed on it. The virus had finally limped away, but her obsession hadn't. If anything, it had escalated.

It bothered her, especially with her family history of mental illness, but if she'd truly inherited the crazy gene, it was serving a purpose. She hadn't had a cold in three years.

She unbuttoned her blouse, swabbed her armpits, and sniffed. To her dismay, the odor had leeched into her embroidered La Perla bra, the one Bruce had given her. It had to go. Her suit jacket would conceal her unrestrained double-D cups well enough.

At the very moment she freed her splendidly augmented breasts, Tim, the company's general counsel, burst into her office. He gawped for a moment, then turned away.

"What the fuck, Tim? Knock on the goddamn door."

"How the hell was I supposed to know you'd be half-naked? What are you doing? This is *serious,* Cyndi! Did you reach Bruce?"

She rebuttoned her blouse with trembling hands. "No. Just get back in there, look grim, and tell them I'm on the phone with him. I'll handle the rest, just follow my lead."

"You're going to lie?"

"Of course, I'm going to lie! What else am I supposed to do?"

He exited, muttering a string of expletives.

The temperature in the boardroom was arctic when she reentered fully clothed, sans bra, with a fresh application of lipstick and some powder to absorb the nervous shine on her face. The board members looked like startled deer, eyes following her every move with apprehension. Wilder and his entourage all wore imperious, impatient expressions. She'd seen that look a million times as a woman rising up the corporate ladder. The doubt. The skepticism. The arrogant lift of chins. They were all such pricks. And Montserrat De Leon, Wilder's newest pet lawyer, was a ravening bitch—the most superior and dismissive of them all. So much for gender solidarity.

She hated the woman for her European hauteur, her looks, her Oxford *and* Harvard law degrees. Most of all, she hated the way men tripped over their dicks trying to curry her favor. But Cynthia would put them all in their place, and if any of them had souls, they'd feel like dogshit.

She manufactured some crocodile tears and took a deep, somber breath. "Ladies and gentlemen, I'm afraid I have some very unfortunate news. Mr. Messane is dealing with a family emergency and sends his deepest apologies."

"His daughter is overseas," Tim offered gravely.

Perfect. The inference was ominous, but vague; nothing that could be confirmed or discredited. "Since you've all made the trip to Los Angeles, and everyone but Mr. Messane is present, we're prepared to present the data you requested. I suggest we continue the meeting."

Wilder stood, his bloated, ruddy face now scarlet. His suit, his tie, his multiple plastic surgeries didn't hide the ugliness within.

"I'm sorry for Mr. Messane's troubles," he said in a stentorian voice meant to intimidate. "I truly am, but we will not proceed without the company's president and CEO. We'll pick this up in the future, when his situation has stabilized."

Future? There *was* no future without this deal. Not for any of them. "We can at least present the current—"

"The language in the letter of intent is very clear on this, Ms. Jackson, I made sure of that," De Leon interrupted crisply. "We'll speak again when Mr. Messane is available."

Cynthia watched her close her polished leather briefcase. It looked like fine lamb or kid, but was probably crafted from the flesh of men she'd torn apart. "Of course, Ms. De Leon. We'll reschedule at the soonest possible date. And again, many apologies for the inconvenience. I'll walk you all out."

Wilder brushed her offer aside with the flap of a fat hand. "That's not necessary, Miss Jackson, we'll find our way. Good day."

Miss? Cynthia was grinding her teeth so hard, she could hear them squeak. What a monumental, condescending asshole. She would tell him exactly what she thought of him after the deal was done. When they were gone, she stormed toward the door. "Keep trying to reach Bruce."

Tim jumped out of his chair and intercepted her. "Where do you think you're going?"

"I'm going to try to find him, you fucking moron!"

Chapter Six

CRAWFORD TUCKED HIS PHONE BACK IN his pocket. "Beverly Hills is sending a car to check out Messane's place. You finding anything on this guy?"

Nolan scrolled through the Google search on her phone. What did cops do before smart phones and car computers? Unfortunately, the crime rate always seemed to pace advancements in technology, and the game of whack-a-mole continued as it always had. There was a conspiracy theory in there somewhere.

"According to an article in a business journal, Bruce Messane was 'a marketing savant who forever transformed the way our furry families live and eat.'"

"Huh?"

"He was the co-founder of Peppy Pets. Current president and CEO."

He whistled. "Explains the address in Holmby Hills. So, what's a guy who made a fortune on overpriced organic pet food doing here?"

"Drugs or prostitutes come to mind. Actually, it's the only thing that comes to mind."

"He could afford concierge service for either of those things."

"Maybe he liked cheap thrills."

Crawford watched fat, juicy raindrops splatting on the windshield. "Think this is a biblical event?"

"Yeah. God is pissed at us for using too much water."

"That's what Reverend Bandy says."

She glanced at him. "Corinne is still listening to the podcast preacher?"

"Every Sunday. She's catching up on the archives now. Drives me a little crazy, but it gives her peace."

"You're that hard to live with?"

"Apparently." He opened his door on Armageddon. "Thanks for the manly umbrella."

"The sadist in me wishes I hadn't mentioned it."

Nolan was surprised to see a generator rumbling outside the tent when they returned. Ross was crouched by the car, aiming a loud, industrial snail fan.

"Where did this come from?" she had to shout. "I didn't see anybody off-loading equipment."

He spun in his crouch, gave Crawford a little salute, and switched off the fan. "Gonzales set us up. He talked to Poppy, and the old guy brought out what he had in his shop, otherwise we'd still be waiting." He smiled slyly. "I'm taking Gonzales out for a drink later to thank him."

"I hear workplace romances can work out occasionally," Crawford said cheerfully.

"It's just a drink."

"That's how it all starts. Isn't that right, Maggie?"

She eviscerated him with a look.

Ross watched them curiously. "Am I missing out on something?"

"Absolutely nothing at all, unless you didn't realize that Al can be a pain in the ass," she snapped, then regretted her defensiveness, because Ross was very intrigued now. From a young age, her mother had always told her that her rare combination of strawberry-blond hair and pale skin made her a genetic tinderbox and her temper should be managed early. It was anecdotal bullshit, of course, but Emily Nolan had been right about one thing: a short fuse got you into trouble more often than not.

"If you say so, Maggie. Did you get an ID?"

"Bruce Messane." Nolan watched his face crumple. "What, you know him?"

"Of him. He's the Peppy Pets guy. He formed the company because his cats died from tainted food. Really sad."

"How the hell do you know this?" Crawford asked.

"The story is on the back of every bag of dry food. Man, I hope the company doesn't go under. My cats won't eat anything else."

"I think it's too big to fail," Nolan reassured him.

"I hope so, otherwise it's back to cooking a chicken every week."

"That's probably cheaper." She glanced at Al, who seemed mystified by the exchange. He'd never owned a pet in his life.

"I'm going to check out the scene while you two discuss cat food."

While he busied himself with Messane, and Ross resumed his examination of the car, Nolan replayed the scenarios she'd docked earlier. Drug deal gone bad. Possible. Encounter with a prostitute, maybe a regular, also possible. The pimp realized Messane was worth more dead than alive and took his keys straight to Holmby Hills for a little late-night shopping. No, that didn't feel right. Too thoughtful for street scum. And too risky. "Am I off my nut, thinking this is more complicated than it looks, Al?"

"No. It's weird he was here. Weird his window is open. Weird he got a single twenty-two to the head. This doesn't look like the sloppy work of a hopped-up shitbag."

"You're going straight for a hit?"

"Just throwing it in the mix. There are no signs of violence."

"Aside from him getting killed."

"Yeah, there is that. The unbuckled belt says he was here for action.

The open window says he wasn't afraid of whoever was approaching him. I don't think he was a stranger here. Phone records are a good place to start."

"I'll get Ike on that, and have him search for next of kin, too."

"Check this out, you two." Ross rose to his feet and gestured to the rear quarter panel of the car. "Oily smudges, probably from when the wheels were boosted. I didn't notice them before because of all the water beading, but the fan took care of that."

Nolan could see them clearly now, too. "Could be fingerprint gold."

"Yeah. And I'm guessing those prints are going to match a record."

Crawford cocked his head. "If the thief was the killer and he wasn't wearing gloves, that is gold. How long before you can dust?"

"Give it another half hour with the fan on."

Nolan searched the uniforms on the sidewalk and street. "Where's your happy-hour date, Ross? He offered to be our interpreter."

"It's not a date."

"Nothing sexier than a bilingual man," Crawford remarked drolly.

Chapter Seven

POPPY RIVERA WAS SITTING BEHIND A dented metal desk when they entered his shop to the accompaniment of a tarnished bell on the door. A real bell, not a soulless electronic one. It was a comforting sound that brought back memories from Nolan's childhood. No matter what country had been home to her transient Army family, every small business seemed to have one.

The place was respectably clean for what it was, but the powerful smell of gasoline, solvents, and paint would linger in this small building long after the business and its owner were gone. She couldn't imagine breathing this toxic air day in and day out.

Poppy was fit and strong for an old man, but there was a lassitude in his slumped shoulders, as if he'd been carrying a lot of bad weight that was finally crushing him. His eyes were rheumy, and devoid of hope, Nolan thought. The world around his modest business had changed for the worse over the years, and he knew he wouldn't live long enough to see things improve.

Introductions were made, coffee was offered and politely declined, and he apologized for not having extra chairs.

Crawford was admiring the vintage automotive memorabilia

scattered around the small space. "How long have you owned your shop, Mr. Rivera?"

His mournful eyes came to life a little. "Since 1990."

"That's quite an accomplishment. Something to be proud of."

"Thank you. Hard work, but honest work."

Nolan opened her notepad. "Can you tell us about this morning, Mr. Rivera? When you arrived?"

He reflexively began fiddling with the crucifix around his neck and started speaking to Gonzales in rapid-fire Spanish.

"He says he arrived around seven to open and knew something bad had happened when he saw the expensive car without wheels." Gonzales paused and listened as Poppy continued his story. "He was afraid, and didn't want to get involved, because the only people who drive cars like that around here are the narcos. You turn the other cheek with them. But then he saw the dead man inside, and called 911 right away."

"Had you ever seen the man before?"

Poppy understood and shook his head vehemently. "No, ma'am. No rich gringos here ever, not that I see." He blushed profusely. "Sorry, I don't mean gringo, I mean . . ." He threw up his hands in frustration. "I don't know what to call people no more."

"It's okay, Mr. Rivera."

"Thank you. Sorry." He launched into another fusillade of Spanish.

"This used to be a nice neighborhood," Gonzales related. "Families and kids who weren't afraid to play in the streets, they would have ball games until midnight in the summers. Now people hide in their houses, everything is ruined."

"*La muerte está en todas partes*," Poppy concluded darkly.

Death was everywhere. Nolan didn't need a translator for that. It said something about her job that she had no trouble understanding that bit of Spanish. "Do you have security cameras, Mr. Rivera? Anything that would show the street?"

He shook his head. "They get wrecked, they get stolen. I give up a long time ago."

"Have you noticed anything unusual around here lately? Activity or people you haven't seen before?" Crawford asked.

Poppy looked to Gonzales for help. As he listened, his face darkened, and his words came faster and more fervently.

"He says there are new narcos and buchonas every day."

"Buchonas?"

"Girlfriends. Flamboyant ones," Gonzales clarified.

Poppy went on another roll, angrier than the last.

"The way they dress and look, they're bragging about being with murderers and drug dealers. But nobody does anything. The police don't even come here anymore."

A damning truth, Nolan thought. But there was something about his demeanor, his expression, that had shifted. She realized he wasn't just angry, he was terrified. "We're trying, Mr. Rivera."

He sagged in his chair like a battered, old boxer after his final fight. But his eyes pierced hers. "*Ángel de la muerte* is here. The angel of death."

She looked at Gonzales. "Does he mean that literally?"

"It's just an expression."

Poppy stood suddenly. "Okay? I have work."

He wouldn't be saying anything more, Nolan knew that much. "Yes, okay, thank you for your time, Mr. Rivera. Also, for the fan and generator. It was very helpful."

"*De nada. Por favor cuidadmente.*"

The exhortation to stay safe seemed ominous in this environment, and Nolan felt a chill tickle her spine. "You, too, Mr. Rivera."

She took a deep breath of cleansing fresh air when they stepped outside, but had a feeling the chemicals she'd inhaled were going to coat her throat and stay in her nose for days, much like the odors of advanced decomposition. At least Bruce Messane had spared her the double assault by being killed relatively recently.

The rain had eased, but the sky was still ashen, and a mass of menacing clouds boiled on the western horizon. The latest weather report said it was moving north, up into the Sierras, where the torrential rain would turn into feet of snow. And people thought California had perfect weather all the time. Those idealistic souls didn't realize the state was big enough to have multiple climates.

The coroner's van had arrived with stout Dr. Otto Weil—a sternly Teutonic, older gent Nolan liked and respected immensely. He'd been particularly heroic in their last few cases, bumping their bodies to the top of his long to-do list and saving lives in the process.

He was consulting with Ross in the shelter of the tent while techs swarmed in and around the car, dusting, tweezing up evidence, and placing markers. The fan had done its job. "What was your impression of the interview, Officer Gonzales?"

"I think Poppy is having problems. He didn't say as much, but he's scared. I don't know how anybody could stay in business here without being under the thumb of the gangs. You pay for protection, or something bad will happen to you or your family. You don't think the murder is gang-related, do you?"

Nolan shook her head. "No, but he may have been caught in the figurative crossfire. Only the bangers drive expensive cars here, and they're not the lowly street soldiers. That could have made him a target if there's some bad blood running. Shoot first, then see who you killed later."

"I'll keep my eyes and ears open." Gonzales reached under his slicker and gave them both cards. "Let me know if there's anything else I can do to help."

"We appreciate it, Officer. Do you still have family here?"

"They're in a small town in East Texas now. And happy to be there."

"Thanks for your help. You stay safe, too."

Chapter Eight

BRUCE'S HOUSE WAS THE MOST OBVIOUS place to start. But Cynthia hadn't considered the gate because her head was a mess and she wasn't thinking clearly. She had his key so she could let herself in when his fantasy required it, but he'd never given her a remote or the code for the gate. He'd never given her anything except the La Perla bra and matching panties, which established clear boundaries. And she was fine with that. There was no circumstance in which she would even entertain a serious relationship with him. Too much baggage, too many neuroses, and he was sometimes kinkier than she liked. She enjoyed handcuffs or a blindfold on occasion, but when he'd brought out the gas mask and that disgusting costume . . .

She shivered in revulsion as the windshield wipers thunked a prestissimo tempo that drilled into her brain, triggering the prodromes of a migraine. She opened her window and stuck her arm out in the relentless rain to press the call button. He wasn't answering his phone, but he might answer this.

He didn't. If he'd gone off on one of his sex benders before the most important meeting of their lives, she was going to kill him. She swept water from the sleeve of her Burberry trench and leaned back against the seat, considering her next move, then slammed her hand against the steering wheel and cursed. She couldn't scale the gate or the fence, especially not in a suit and heels; especially not in the rain. And the fence encircled the entirety of the property with no breaks or low spots. Bruce had told her the estate was built by a famous mobster in the heyday of Prohibition, and the contractor was supposedly buried somewhere on the property because he'd tried to skimp on the fence.

But there was a keypad on the stone column, and she could at least try that. Bruce wasn't particularly security minded—he was that arrogant—so he probably used something obvious, like his birth date. Or his daughter's.

She unfurled her umbrella as she got out of the car and scowled at her new suede Pradas, instantly soaked through by the standing water. That bastard had destroyed her bra and her shoes in less than an hour. And maybe her life.

Trembling from the cold, her frayed nerves, and a growing anger, she punched 1024 in the pad—his birthday. Nothing. She knew his daughter was born on June 11, so she tried that. No, of course that wasn't it, he didn't even like her. Then she pressed the call button over and over. Son of a bitch.

She was about to retreat to the car, defeated by an ugly, florid piece of metal, when she remembered he actually *had* given her something besides lingerie: his house alarm code. Sometimes he liked to wait for her in the bedroom, pretend she was a home invader, and beg for his life. Why hadn't she seen how pathetic, how damaged he was?

Cynthia pressed 6666—and praise the lord or maybe the devil in this case, the gate motor whirred and creaked open. For all his psychological complications, he truly was simple. Like all men. She piloted her Maserati up the winding drive and parked under the porte cochere. The faux chateau wasn't as large as its neighbors, but it was still ridiculously over the top, even for Holmby Hills. Today, she appreciated this pretentious architectural element.

The massive, carved front door was locked, but the security system wasn't armed. That was strange, because it meant he was probably home. So why wasn't he answering? She stepped in and shouted his name, then noticed a utilitarian pair of boots and muddy footprints despoiling the marble foyer floor. He must have been out in his stupid rose garden, covering them to spare the precious blooms from the storm. He cared more about them than any human.

Her thoughts stuttered. Bruce was an obsessive clean-freak. The man she knew would rather die than allow mud to ruin his marble. He would have left his shoes outside.

Suddenly, the silent house took on a menacing presence. Her neck prickled, her heart rate accelerated, and a soft, slumbering voice rose from the deepest recesses of her subconscious. *Something is wrong. What if he had an accident or a medical emergency? What if he was dead?*

Ohmygod. He couldn't be dead, don't let him be dead. She careened through the main level, calling his name, imploring him to answer. Then she ran up the broad, curving staircase toward his bedroom, propelled by panic. People died from heart attacks all the time, and Bruce was a good candidate, with all the stress and excesses.

His bed was empty and unmade. The bathroom was empty, too. She half sat, half collapsed on the window seat and rubbed her temples, trying to banish the drumming in her skull that kept cadence with the rain against the windows. Beyond the bay windows was the rose garden. The plants hadn't been covered.

What about the muddy footprints? They were still wet, weren't they?

Fear momentarily paralyzed her. What if his home invasion fantasy had come true? And what if those boots belonged to them and they were still here?

Get the hell out of here and call the police.

Cynthia's subconscious didn't have to tell her twice. She fled the bedroom, unaware of the pair of eyes watching her through the louvers of the closet door.

Chapter Nine

NOLAN THOUGHT THAT OTTO WEIL WAS looking particularly amiable for a man who generally preferred the company of the dead over the living. If not for the grim backdrop, he and Ross could have been discussing the Rams' win on Thursday night football. Or maybe that's exactly what they were doing.

Weil paused the conversation as she and Al approached. His heavy jowls lifted with a restrained smile, and his glacial blue eyes seemed almost merry. "Detectives. I must say I'm pleasantly surprised. This is the first case you've handled in some time where the cause of death appears to be evident." He lifted a shaggy gray brow. "Of course, looks can be deceiving. The scene itself is enigmatic; contradictory and pedestrian at the same time. You and Detective Crawford have undoubtedly come up with a preliminary theory based on your observations."

Wow, Weil was really in a good mood. She'd never heard him say that many consecutive words not directly related to autopsy results since she'd known him. "We have some compass points, but we know you'll help us home in on the right one. We're particularly interested in toxicology, and signs of drug abuse or sexual activity."

"Yes, I see how you might be. A logical interpretation of what we see before us."

"Any idea when you might be able to get him on the table, Doc?" Crawford asked politely without sounding too desperate.

"I will make time today." He glanced up at the tarnished gray sky. "I understand they call this climatological phenomenon an atmospheric river. The English language is so descriptively specialized. Quite beautiful." He returned his attention to them, all business now. "Are you finished with the body?"

"He's all yours."

"Very good. I'll be in contact, Detectives." Weil retreated to his default personality and his van to retrieve his assistants and less pleasant things, like a gurney and a body bag.

"I've never seen the doc so perky," Crawford said to Ross under his breath.

"His youngest daughter, who's not that young, is getting married over Christmas."

"That's obviously a good thing."

"He's hoping for a grandkid."

Nolan had never even considered that Weil had a family, but of course he did. It was nice to see the human side of him, even if it had only made a brief foray into their professional domain. "Ross, tell your team to pay close attention to the passenger's side. There may have been someone with him."

"You got it, Maggie. And I'll run the prints for you right away, too. We got some nice ones."

Crawford clapped him on the shoulder. "Thanks, buddy. Have a good date."

"It's *not* a date."

"Gonzales isn't just bilingual, he's sharp, so look alive."

Ross glowered at him. "Maggie's right, you are a pain in the ass."

She coughed to cover a laugh, and excused herself when her phone rang. It was Ike Bondi, the department's enfant terrible. He was a stellar detective, but his considerable cyber skills had taken him off the active-duty roster and into a private office where he enjoyed little to no supervision. He was free to traverse the murky terrain of electronic legality while drinking his Jack Daniel's in peace, which he did often. "Ike, what's up?"

"The ball is rolling on phone records. And Messane's only living family is a fourteen-year-old daughter named Katrina, currently living with her mother in northern Italy. That would be Camille Travanti, ex-wife, and apropos of nothing, an Olympic silver medalist in the Super-G. Very ugly divorce a few years ago, if you believe the tabloids."

"How so?"

"The usual shit divorce attorneys march out. Both sides claimed emotional abuse, child neglect, financial indiscretions—hell, probably crimes against humanity. They were married for fifteen years, and she didn't earn for most of that time, so she got half of what he was worth, around twenty mil. No prenup."

"Fair and square in the eyes of the law."

"Yeah. The only one who really lost out was the daughter."

"True." Nolan tried to imagine herself and her brother, Max, as children of an acrimonious divorce, and what impact it may have had on their lives. It was beyond her speculative capabilities. Colonel York and Emily Nolan had undoubtedly experienced their share of marital friction in their forty years together, but they had always been devoted to each other. That was probably the only thing that had gotten them through Max's death in Afghanistan.

"It took me about two minutes to track this down. I hope you have something more exciting for me to do."

"Start looking at his phone records when they come in."

"That's more boring than trying to find next of kin," he complained. "Anything in particular I should be looking for?"

"Not yet, which will make it less boring. A genius like you could find a pattern and solve this thing before we even get back."

He snorted. "You have such a silver tongue, Maggie. I like it. That's not sexual harassment, is it?"

"Probably."

"I just texted you Travanti's number."

"Thanks, Ike. Hey, how's Chance doing?" His dog was the center of his universe, and the golden retriever had just been diagnosed with epilepsy.

"Great, the meds are working. Thanks for asking."

Nolan wasn't kissing up to pave the way for big asks in the future, and hoped he didn't think she was. She really did care, and not just about the dog. If anything happened to Chance, Ike might plunge into the desolate abyss where his demons cavorted, and she liked him too much to see that happen again. "So glad to hear that. See you later."

She looked at Crawford. "Next of kin is in Italy. I've never had to do a long-distance notification before."

"It's a gift, Mags. We don't have to look anyone in the eye. Who's the survivor?"

"A fourteen-year-old daughter in the care of her mother, his ex. She'll have to break the bad news to her."

"Poor kid."

Chapter Ten

NOLAN STARTED THE SEDAN AND CRANKED the heat.
The windows fogged to opaque briefly, then coincidentally cleared just
as Camille Travanti's sunny voice chirped *pronto* through the Bluetooth speaker. The background noise was festive, and she imagined an
après ski party in some fabulous chalet in the Italian Alps. But when
she introduced herself and Al as LAPD detectives, the sun set.

"It's something with Bruce, isn't it?"

She sounded angry, as if she'd been expecting trouble from him.
He didn't have a record, but he'd obviously been a source of angst
verging on law enforcement intervention. Maybe the accusations in
the divorce proceedings had been more truth than attorney fiction.
"I'm very sorry to have to pass along this news, Ms. Travanti, but Mr.
Messane is dead."

She let out a strangled sound. "Oh, God. Oh, God."

Nolan heard the clacking of heels and a door close, muting the
party sounds.

"What happened? Was it a heart attack?"

"He was shot."

"*Murdered?* No, no. That can't be right." Her voice cracked and
she started sobbing.

Denial was a common response, whatever the status of your relation-ship with the victim. Many times, estranged friends, lovers, or relatives took the news the hardest, because unresolved issues would remain that way forever. "I'm sorry, ma'am." She glanced at Al. *Long-distance notifi-cations are just as bad after all,* his expression seemed to say.

"Where? What happened?"

"He was parked in a bad part of Culver City, which seemed strange to us. He was also robbed. Do you know of any reason he would have been there?"

Her short, shallow gasps filled the car. "I have no idea, we weren't on speaking terms unless it was something to do with our daughter." The sobs intensified. "How am I going to tell her?"

Nolan felt her slipping into a new, painful reality, and it was time to bring her out before she was lost to them. Offering a sense of pur-pose, an opportunity to lube the wheels of justice, usually sufficed. "I know this is a terrible time, but may I ask you some questions? Your answers could help us with the investigation."

She struggled for composure with marginal success. "Whatever I can do to help."

"Thank you. Can you think of anyone who may have wanted to harm him?"

"No! You don't think this was a carjacking?"

Nolan didn't, but that wasn't something Camille Travanti needed to know. "We have to cover everything, ma'am."

"Yes. Of course." She sniffled, then blew her nose loudly. "Bruce never had any enemies that I knew of. He was very successful, but he never stepped on necks to get ahead."

"We understand you were married for fifteen years. In that time, did Mr. Messane have any issues with drug use?"

"There were *drugs* on him?"

"No, ma'am, but compiling a personal history is an important part of our job."

Her sigh was dense with anxiety. "Stupid question. He was robbed, drugs would have been the first thing they took. I'm not thinking straight."

"It's okay, Ms. Travanti, nobody is ever prepared for this kind of shock. But can you tell us if were drugs were ever a problem?"

"No. He was prescribed pain pills for some surgeries, but he didn't abuse them. To my knowledge, at least. Bruce was good at hiding things, though. At least for a while."

Crawford's brows jumped up his forehead. "What sorts of things, Ms. Travanti?"

She took a trembling breath, no doubt regretting her impulsive frankness. "This is in confidence, right? Trina can *never* know."

"Of course. You have our word."

"Bruce wasn't a drug addict, he was a sex addict. And I mean that in a purely clinical way. It was a crippling obsession, and just as destructive as any other addiction. He went to treatment, we both went to counseling, but it never helped."

"Thank you for being honest with us, Ms. Travanti. I have to ask, did he frequent prostitutes?"

"Certainly not. Sex addiction isn't really about sex, it's about building self-image and personal value. He had a horrific childhood, and it was his way of self-medicating past issues. An endorphin rush is better than any drug, at least temporarily. That's why the behavior is compulsive." Her voice hitched. "Poor Bruce. I was so angry with him for so long, but I finally understood that he hurt everybody he loved because pain was all he ever received as a boy. It was his shining example of how to treat others."

Nolan felt her stomach twist. "So he had relationships, Ms. Travanti?"

She scoffed through her tears. "Highly dysfunctional ones, but yes."

"Would you happen to know of any of his previous . . . uh . . ."

"Lovers? I have no idea who they were. I never wanted to know. Are we finished? I really have to go now."

"Yes, thank you for your time—"

"Trina and I will fly back as soon as we can."

The grating beep-beep-beep of a disconnected call echoed in the car until Nolan cut the Bluetooth. "That sucked in a way I didn't expect."

Crawford glanced at her. "I hear you. So, a sex addict. That's high-risk behavior, and it fits with your cheap thrills theory, Maggie."

"But not with prostitutes, according to her."

"Doesn't matter, he and his partner could have been turned on by assignations in dangerous places. If it's all about the endorphins, that's a double shot of them." His phone chirruped inside his coat. He answered, listened, and Nolan watched his face shuffle through a deck of expressions.

"Where is she?" he asked. "Okay, we'll go talk to her before we head over. Seal off the scene and get a detective and Crime Scene there. Thanks."

He tossed his phone on the dashboard. "That was Beverly Hills. Messane's house and gate were open, the door was unlocked, and the alarm wasn't set. The place is loaded with treasure, but no signs of robbery they could see. While they were searching, dispatch got a panicky call from one of his colleagues. She went to his house looking for him this morning, and got spooked."

"Why?"

"She thought maybe home invasion. There were boots and fresh, muddy footprints in the foyer, and we know they don't belong to Messane."

Nolan tapped her cold, stiff fingers on the steering wheel, wishing she'd had the forethought to wear gloves. "Where is the colleague now?"

"Back at Peppy Pets headquarters in Tarzana."

Nolan pulled away from the curb, the scene, and Poppy's angel of death. Her chances of dinner at the Bel-Air weren't looking great.

Chapter Eleven

REMY SCROLLED THROUGH HIS PHONE'S CONTACT list and tapped "Ringo." Confidential informants dwelled below the scum line, so you never knew if they would have the same number the next time you tried to call them; if they were in jail; or if they were even still alive. But Ringo was a survivor and an avaricious cockroach, which made him reasonably dependable. At least as far as CIs went. Froggy had been more reliable, but he'd had an unfortunate encounter with the Monster of Miracle Mile six months ago. It was a wicked twist that he'd met his end trying to help Remy catch that butcher of women.

Ringo answered with a genial, "Hey, man, I can't do business with you right now, things are too hot."

"Good morning to you, too, Ringo. When things are hot, that's exactly when you want to do business with me."

His pause was long. "It's gonna cost you extra. Hazard pay."

"I'll be at the Pantry in fifteen minutes. I know how much you enjoy their waffles."

"Ah, shit, it's raining again, and I don't have a car these days," he whined.

"Your problem, not mine. I'm sure you can find an umbrella to steal on your way."

"You're cold, man."

"I can pick you up."

"*Hell* no, there are eyes everywhere, you want me to get my ass capped?"

Remy didn't particularly care, but kept the uncharitable sentiment to himself. "See you soon."

"A hundred or no deal. The extra is for hazard pay *and* for walking ten blocks in this fucking rain."

"I'll tell you what your information is worth when you give it to me."

"Ice cold," he grumped.

When Remy arrived at the Original Pantry Café, a wet, bedraggled Ringo was already there, sitting at a table farthest from the door and street-side windows. He wore a Dodgers cap and a frayed, dumpster-chic corduroy jacket that hung flaccidly over his skeletal frame. One of his eyes was swollen and purple.

"What happened to you?"

"Told you things were hot. I already ordered. Got you a coffee."

"How very considerate." Remy shed his trench coat and sat across from him as a waiter appeared with a stack of waffles entombed in gloppy red strawberry sauce that reminded him of congealing blood. Ringo gilded the lily by pouring a reservoir of blueberry syrup over the abomination, then tucked into it with the zeal of a starving predator.

"So, what do you want?" he asked, spraying bits of red and blue waffle on the table.

Remy inched his chair back with unconcealed disgust. "Do you know anything about Kang?"

"Never heard of it. Nothing on the streets called kang around here."

Ringo obviously didn't watch the news. "Kang isn't a drug, he was a doctor. He just died of a fentanyl overdose. Asian, about five-nine, mid-forties. Have you seen him around?"

He snorted out a laugh. "You think a guy with his own prescription pad is going to be scratching around my turf?"

"I'm not talking about buying, I'm talking about selling. He was holding enough, and he was desperate for money."

"The Triad doesn't operate here."

The Triad was an Asian syndicate. Distributing drugs was an extremely segregated vocation. "I doubt he was connected to the Triad. I'm talking small-fry freelance."

"Nah, man, ain't seen him. Ain't seen no Asians buying or selling around here."

Remy flagged the harried waiter for a refill. "Rainbows killed him. I hear there's a lot of them on the street right now. You know anything about that?"

He wiped his mouth with his sleeve, looking around the room circumspectly. "Maybe."

"Maybe isn't worth a hundred bucks. Tell me why things are hot. I assume it has something to do with your eye. Who did you piss off?"

"I don't know."

"If you don't start talking, I'm out of here."

"I'm serious, I don't know! There's some strange shit going on out there. Bad juju."

Remy poured a plastic container of fake cream and a packet of sugar in his coffee. It was the only way to make the caffeinated dishwater palatable. "I'm listening."

"Okay, okay, okay. I get my product from a certain guy. And this certain guy stopped answering his phone, so I ask around. Nobody else has heard from him, either. I figure maybe he ran into trouble and rabbited, so I start shopping for a new wholesaler."

Remy smirked at the term. "And did you find a new 'wholesaler'?"

"A new wholesaler found me." He touched his eye gingerly and winced. "Some nasty-ass cholo with tattoos all over his face corners me in an alley and told me I was doing business with him from now on. He gives me a beat-down, then shows me rainbows and said he'd be back to make arrangements. Word is, he's pissing all over everyone's territory. Trust me, there's a war coming."

"If you're selling fentanyl, Ringo, our relationship is going to change in a hurry."

"I told you, he just showed me! I won't sell that shit, I'm not going to kill a bunch of people!"

"That's heartwarming. You're a true American hero."

He scowled and finished off his waffles. "This motherfucker is scary, and he's somebody big."

"How do you know?"

"I can just tell. You could, too, if you ever ran into him. Some kind of jefe for sure. Nobody wants to deal with him, but the boss isn't gonna give us a choice, so I'm pulling up stakes and relocating far the hell away from here until things cool down. My buddy Chick in Culver City got a visit, too. He says the dude is the angel of death, that all this rain and shit is a sign the devil is coming for us. Like in Revelations."

"Maybe God doesn't want you to be a drug dealer anymore."

"Hey, a man's gotta make a living, honest or not."

Remy watched him scrape his plate, licking the last bit of bicolored syrup from his fork. Ringo was repugnant, irredeemable, and a menace, but he was useful. Consorting with evil to exterminate greater evil was an existential conflict of the job—hell, of the world—but it was getting more difficult to justify. He knew Maggie had something to do with his evolving perspective. When you cared about somebody, you also cared if society was going to shit. "Did this angel of death schedule a meet to discuss terms?"

Ringo leaned back in his chair, happily sated. "No. He'll just show up like a fucking goblin again . . . nah, he'll probably send somebody else. But I won't be here. I don't know nothing else."

Remy believed him. Like all dope pushers, Ringo was cagey, but he wasn't smart enough to tell a convincing lie or withhold information. He stood and threw a hundred on the table. "Thanks, Ringo, you're a credit to your profession."

"And you're a smart-ass."

"You got the joke, there's hope for you yet. Watch your back, get out of town."

"Got a bus ticket already. Hey, what about the check?"

"Keep the change."

Chapter Twelve

DR. ROME BECHTOLD WAS GOING TO get in shape if it killed him, and it just might. He'd only done twenty minutes on the elliptical, but his heart and lungs felt like coals searing through his chest wall, and sweat rained down his face, pacing the storm outside. Every cell screamed for him to stop, but he couldn't. The harder he pushed, the faster he'd transform his bloated body. And maybe—just maybe—he could salvage his marriage.

It was an idiotic, juvenile way to think—the troubles between them went deeper than his slack muscles and ever-expanding girth. Which is why he'd signed up for a webinar with a famous relationship guru, was starting a three-day seaweed cleanse tomorrow, and going to guided meditation classes twice a week. Visualize success. He was going to transform himself into a fully refurbished man inside and out, and Nicole would have no choice but to take notice of her new and improved husband, his commitment to their marriage and his health. Then she would invite him back and he could get rid of this rental and all the bad memories that went with it.

We've grown apart, Rome. I think we need some time away from each other. There's a nice house for rent nearby, I think you'd like it.

Grown apart. The words tormented him. He had no idea what

the vague, catchall phrase meant, but he deeply feared it was a soft-ball way of saying things were over. Irrevocably, irretrievably over. A friend had told him as much.

If she kicked you out of your own house and won't go to marriage counseling, she's obviously not interested in reconciliation. I don't mean to bring you down, but don't be surprised if you get served with divorce papers when you're least expecting it. This is like guerilla warfare—you have to be prepared for anything.

Those words haunted him, too, but Rome couldn't believe they were true. Some people just had an aversion to outside help, and Nicole had always been extremely private. The onus was on him to close the gap between them. He'd done it before, he could do it again. He cranked up the tension on the hateful machine he would learn to love one drop of sweat at a time. He wasn't going down without a fight.

He deflected his thoughts from the burning physical and psychic pain and focused on the ceaseless curtain of rain out the window; the cars splashing through standing water on his Santa Monica street; the palms bowing to the wind. The weather seemed to be all or nothing lately. It was an analog to his life.

The clatter of toenails on the wooden floor and Addison's soft woof made him smile. It also gave him an excuse to pause his labors. "What is it, Addy? Come here, boy."

Tongue lolling, he waddled over on stubby corgi legs. He was overweight by even the most lenient veterinary standards, but the little chap was almost fourteen, and he wasn't going to starve a senior citizen. Quality of life was more important than quantity after a certain point. "We can't go for a walk until the rain stops. It's not fit for man nor beast out there."

Addison whined.

"Come on, old trooper, let's try a bowl of that new diet food. We'll get in shape together, what do you say?" Rome mopped his face with a towel and followed him to the kitchen. The dog flopped down on

his considerable belly in front of the cupboard where the magic food
fairy lived. A cup of Peppy Pets new Senior Slim blend for the pup,
a bottle of Gatorade for him. Or should he should start the seaweed
cleanse today? There was no reason to put it off. He knew it was going
to hurt, so better to face it sooner rather than later.

His phone buzzed on the kitchen counter, and he frowned at the
unknown number. Another telemarketing scam, they were relentless. He dismissed the call and fed Addy, but the phone rang again.
"Take me off your list, and don't call back."

"Check your text messages," a chilling, AI-modulated voice whispered.

Rome's blood turned to icy slush. Even scammers didn't go this
far. Did they? His phone beeped a text alert from the same number.

"Did you get it, Mr. Bechtold?"

"Who are you?"

"Open it," the warped voice was louder, demanding.

"Listen, you son of a bitch—"

"Open it NOW."

Rome sank to a stool at the kitchen counter, his finger poised over
the message. A sickening prescience warned him that if he opened
it, the earth would crack open and swallow him. He pinched his eyes
shut briefly, tapped on it, and almost vomited when he saw a photo
of Nicole bound, blindfolded, and gagged in a dark room. Dear sweet
Jesus, this couldn't be happening, no, it *wasn't* happening, it was a
waking nightmare . . .

*Why do you think it's a nightmare? The world is a nightmare . . .
LA is a nightmare . . .*

"Don't hurt her! Don't you dare hurt her!"

"That's up to you. We'll take good care of her unless you call the
cops. If you do that, she's dead."

"Where is she? Let me talk to her!"

"I'll be in touch soon."

"Wait, wait! I can get money! Whatever you want—"

The call ended, along with Rome's hope for something better on the near horizon. What were the statistics on victims surviving a kidnapping? He didn't know and he didn't dare look, because it might paralyze him, and right now, he needed to liquidate some funds so he'd be ready when they called back with the ransom demand. What did they want? A million? Two? He didn't care. All or nothing.

No, no, NO, that wasn't right. He wasn't going to wait for them to be in touch, he had to be proactive, the trail was still hot. He had to find her. Find *them*. The call could be traced.

Not without the cops. And if you call the cops, she's dead.

He believed the robotic voice. And what if he did manage to find her on his own? Storm in with his peashooter handgun against God knew what firepower and how many captors? He was a fat, retired veterinarian who didn't even know how to clean his gun. He needed a goddamned private army for this. He could afford one, but he didn't know where to begin. Actually, he did have people he could call, but what if those bastards were watching him? Bugging his phone? He couldn't put friends in danger. He had to get a prepaid phone. Now was the time for extreme paranoia.

For all his manically formed, grandiose plans, Rome just wanted to sink to the floor next to Addison, weep into his fur, and die there next to his aging dog. As successful as he was, he'd never been a confident, self-assured man. Not like Bruce. And conflict made him even weaker. Which probably had something to do with his foundering marriage. He needed to be a real man, a strong man, for Nicole.

Be her hero.

He started pacing, trying to focus his scrambled thoughts. It was Wednesday, and Nicole always stayed home on Wednesdays to recharge her chakras, whatever they were; it was an inviolate part of her life's ritual. So that's where they'd abducted her. It was a place to start. There might be clues even he could decipher.

"Want to go home, Addy?"

He rose awkwardly to his feet and barked softly.

He knew the word "home." Dogs missed their people, and he believed they missed their places just as much. His eyes filled with tears. "Hang tight, old trooper, I just need a few things, then we can go home."

As he packed up his computer and gun, he wondered if there was a way this could possibly end well. But speculation was pointless, it was time for action. All or nothing.

Chapter Thirteen

AS SAM PULLED UP TO HIS modest Mar Vista house, he was touched but not surprised to see Melody's green VW Beetle parked on his curb. She understood the significance of his meeting today, and she was here to celebrate or commiserate, whichever was required. That's what best friends—and now, lovers—did for one another.

After his wife had been killed, home stopped feeling like a big hug and started feeling like a condemnation. In a convoluted way, he felt responsible for her death, and every tiny thing, from the pillows on his sofa to the dishes in the cupboard, reminded him that he'd failed Yuki miserably.

But Melody had changed that, along with his vision of the future. It had been uncertain for such a long time that it wasn't something he ever allowed himself to think about. But now he could feel himself planting roots again; feel a connection to life and the world which hadn't existed before her.

Sam pulled his grandfather's Shelby Mustang into the garage and listened to the ticking of the engine as it cooled down. It no longer seemed like an ominous countdown, but a hopeful measure of time moving forward.

He unrolled a chamois and wiped down the car he cherished for the memories, not its beauty or value, both of which were significant. It was a meditative process, and he liked feeling the smooth terrain of the body beneath the lambskin. He knew every contour by heart. But this was just a temporary measure. It would need a good wash and polish when it stopped raining. If it ever stopped raining.

Melody was in the kitchen, wearing a ridiculous Pokémon apron and a smile big enough to activate the single dimple in her left cheek. Her vibrant green eyes were wide in anticipation, and she twisted her long, blond braid nervously. She looked like a winsome little girl, except for the tattoos that decorated her arms, along with old scars from needles. They'd both come a long way together.

She gave him a look of faux disapproval. "What's so funny?"

"The apron. Very ironic for a punk rock guitarist who favors clothing with skull themes. What does your shiny new psych degree say about your choice?"

"It says I bought it to make you laugh."

"Mission accomplished."

She clapped her hands together anxiously. "How did it go?"

"Great." Sam embraced her, and pecked her perfect little nose.

"I knew it would! Tell me!"

"Not until you tell me why it smells like Christmas morning in here. Cinnamon and spice and everything nice. I'm swooning."

"I'm baking a coffee cake. And not cheater coffee cake with boxed mix, a real one with yeast and everything."

"I didn't realize you were an up-and-coming culinary dynamo."

"I would reserve judgment if I were you. It looks weird."

Sam peered into the oven. "It looks perfect to me."

"Because you don't know what it's supposed to look like. Sit down. I have a pitcher of mimosas in the fridge. Spill it, Sam."

Six months ago, he'd devoutly believed he was cursed. Not because he'd almost been killed in Afghanistan, but because he'd survived. It frightened him to think of how close he'd come to missing all the moments like this one that had turned a death wish into hope. One day, he would tell this extraordinary woman that she'd saved his life, although he suspected she knew that.

"You baked me a coffee cake from scratch, you made my favorite breakfast drink, and you bought an ironic apron just to make me laugh. You're way out of my league." He lifted his flute in a toast. "May you never realize it."

She blushed profusely. "Stop being silly and *tell* me!"

They drank prosecco and orange juice in the kitchen that smelled like Christmas while he relayed his morning at Metro. She listened intently and topped off their mimosas when he was finished.

"I'm so happy for you, Sam! When do you start?"

He took a sip and felt the bubbles working their way into his blood. He still loved to drink, but he wasn't using alcohol to kill the pain anymore. "Margolis wants me to think about it before I say yes."

"Do you need to think about it?"

"I don't know if I need to, but I should. It's a big leap for a man who's been taking micro steps for a long time."

Her attentive posture relaxed, and she absently traced circles around a patch of sun on the table with a black-tipped nail. "Does it feel right?"

"Not as right as these mimosas."

She bumped his arm. "Be serious."

"It feels like the perfect transition from where I'm at now to where I want to be."

"And where is that?"

Sam studied her face. It was beautiful, serene, unlined; if you didn't know her history, you might even say innocent. She had an unenviable past, but she wasn't burdened by it. That's where he wanted to be. "In a place where I'm never looking over my shoulder, I'm always looking ahead."

She tipped her head, her expression poignant. "Seems to me, you're already there, Sam." The timer dispelled the heady moment, and she scurried to the oven to assess her efforts.

"Is it done?"

She shrugged uncertainly. "The toothpick says so."

"Toothpicks never lie. Does it still look weird?"

"Weirder."

"But it smells fantastic, and I'm starving."

"It has to cool for a while before we can eat it."

"How long?"

"The recipe says at least half an hour."

He let out a dramatic sigh. "That's a lot of time to kill. What should we do while we wait?"

"I guess we could do the dishes." She giggled at his expression. "Not what you had in mind?"

"I've never minded a sink full of dishes when there was something better to do—"

His phone buzzed on the table and Melody glanced at the display. "I guess you should talk to your mother while you wait." She snickered wickedly and flounced off down the hall.

"You're as cute as a button," he called after her.

"What's so cute about buttons?"

Good question. "Hi, Mom."

"Hello, dear, how was your meeting today?"

"They offered me the position. In fact, I'm celebrating with a mimosa now. But I'm going to take a little time to think about it."

"Good. You promised me this wouldn't be dangerous. I'm holding you to it," she said sternly.

"It won't be dangerous, Mom, it's like a desk job with testosterone. What are you doing today? It's not great golf weather."

"I'm still going to the club. We're having a luncheon to finalize last-minute details for the holiday party. It's December thirteenth, I hope you can make it, so many people would love to see you."

Short of public execution, it was the last thing on earth he wanted to subject himself to, but he'd do it for her. "I'll put it on my calendar."

"Wonderful! And won't you bring Melody? It's about time we met."

"I'll ask her. Anything else on the agenda besides day drinking?"

She snickered, and responded with a riposte of her own. "Night drinking. I'm dining with the Carlisles, they're just back from Aruba. Arnie has a new film coming out in the spring."

"Do you plan to sleep at some point?"

"Don't be ridiculous, Sam."

It wasn't clear if that was a yes or no. Vivian Easton was a born and bred socialite from an old, illustrious California family, known for her stamina and boundless enthusiasm for *la vida bella*. Her marriage into the military seemed like an odd pairing, probably meant to horrify her domineering parents, but their love and devotion to each other had been incontrovertible. After his father's premature death, there was a time when he thought her light was forever extinguished. But she'd eventually emerged more vibrant than ever, and life once again swirled around her in neon colors. If your social calendar was bursting at the seams, you couldn't retreat into grief. "Say hello to the Carlisles for me."

"I will. Sam, I just got the strangest call."

"From who?"

"Whom."

He smiled at her correction. Vivian Easton had no tolerance for lazy grammar, slang, or any other abuse of the English language. "From whom."

"Rome Bechtold. You remember him."

"Of course. Great guy, great wife. What was strange about it?"

She sighed expansively. "Well, he and Nicole are separated, and

I know he's been having difficulties with it, but he . . . he sounded so . . . odd. Paranoid. Quite untethered, really, and he's a very stable person."

Rome was definitely the most stable of all her friends—not remotely eccentric or spoiled, just a regular, self-made man without a hint of conceit. "What did he say?"

"Well, not much of anything frankly, he was quite evasive. He just said he needed some advice and asked me if you would meet with him today, that it was an emergency. I hope he's all right. I'm not sure what to think of it."

"Give me his number, I'll get ahold of him right away."

"Thank you, Sam. I know he'll appreciate it. And you must let me know what's wrong. I'm really a bit concerned."

"I will, Mom."

"Go back to celebrating, dear. I love you."

"Love you, too."

Sam ended the call and finished his mimosa. Very strange indeed.

Chapter Fourteen

CYNTHIA JACKSON WAS A PRETTY WOMAN with polished chestnut hair. She was certainly in her forties, but clearly spent time and money battling wrinkles and gravity to great effect. Perhaps most remarkable about her appearance were her breasts, hovering over her lithe frame like twin zeppelins. Nolan knew genetics weren't involved. It was a catty thought, but truth was truth, in justice and boobs.

She was weeping bitterly, her smooth face contorting like a reflection in a warped mirror. Her hands shook violently as she dug in her desk for a packet of tissues. More the reaction of someone who'd lost a loved one, not a colleague. It definitely begged a question.

"I'm sorry, ma'am. You two were close?"

She wiped her eyes, smearing her mascara into raccoon rings. "We worked together for six years. Do you know who's responsible?"

Jackson had skirted around the question and changed the subject, which was enough of an answer for Nolan. "Not yet, ma'am. We're hoping you can help us."

"I hope so, too."

"You went to Mr. Messane's house when he didn't show up for work, correct?"

"Yes."

"Is that something you would normally do if you couldn't reach him?"

"It's never happened before. This company was his life, and Bruce was always available at any hour. But he wasn't answering his phone, and he missed an extremely important meeting with a potential buyer this morning. I knew something was wrong. Just not . . . this."

"Potential buyer? Of Peppy Pets?"

"Yes. We have a letter of intent from Wilder Foods."

Nolan knew Wilder Foods. It was a megalithic, publicly traded corporation, their marques vast and varied. Any kitchen cupboard would probably stock at least five of their brands at any given time. "What time did you arrive at his residence?"

"About nine thirty."

"Please take us through everything from the beginning. Little details matter."

Her sigh was halting. "I pulled up to the gate, and it was closed, as I expected. I tried him several times from the call box, but there was no answer. When I drove in, everything looked normal. The house was locked, but the alarm wasn't set, so I assumed he was home. When I walked in, I saw muddy footprints in the foyer that were still wet. And a pair of boots."

"What kind of boots?"

"Lightweight hikers, nothing special. I assumed they were Bruce's, so I didn't think much of it at first, then it occurred to me it was unlike him to leave such a mess." She shivered. "Someone was there this morning, and you're telling me it wasn't Bruce."

Nolan kept her expression impassive. Interviewing witnesses was like slowly unwrapping a gift, hoping there was a gold nugget inside instead of a lump of coal. "You obviously have full access to his home if you were able to get in through a closed gate and a locked door."

Her cheeks flared and she lowered her eyes. "I was able to guess the gate code. And I have a house key."

"You didn't know that the alarm wouldn't be set, so you must know that code as well."

"Yes."

"What security company did he use?"

"ADT."

Crawford leaned forward, bracing his elbows on his knees. "Ms. Jackson, why don't you tell us more about your relationship? We're not judging here."

She put her head in her hands and her shoulders shook with a fresh volley of sobs. "We were intimate occasionally. In the past. But it was never serious. Bruce wasn't relationship material."

Camille Travanti had explained why. Nolan added that juicy detail to her notes, wondering why her grief was so outsized for a man she claimed was a sporadic roll in the hay. It only made sense if she'd truly loved him, or if she'd killed him. "He didn't ask you to return his key and he didn't change the alarm code. Seems like perhaps your relationship wasn't completely over."

She shook her head firmly. "No, it was definitely over. But I think Bruce was hoping that might change."

"We'll take you at your word. Did you search the house?"

"Yes. But when it was clear he wasn't home, I thought about the footprints, and all the recent home invasions. I got scared that someone might still be there. I got out as fast as I could. I don't even remember if I closed the front door."

"It was smart to leave and call the police."

"Did they find anything?"

"We can't share any details of the investigation," Crawford apologized. "Did Mr. Messane have any personal or professional problems that you were aware of?"

"No. He was happier than I've ever seen him. He was selling the company for a substantial amount. The contract stipulates he stay on for a year to facilitate a succession plan, then he was looking forward to retirement. He wanted to spend more time at his beach house in Malibu."

"What's a substantial amount?"

"A little over a hundred million dollars."

Nolan had to work to maintain her poker face. A hundred million definitely qualified as substantial. And money was an enduring motive for murder. "Would anybody profit from his death?"

"Nobody," she said despondently. "There's a kill switch on the contract."

"What does that mean?"

"If he died or became incapacitated before the closing, the deal is null and void and Wilder walks away. Bruce made Peppy Pets the success it is. Without him, the company loses value. It's pretty standard."

"Did he own the company outright?"

"He owns seventy percent. I own fifteen, and so does our general counsel, Tim Geiger."

"So, you and Mr. Geiger had a lot to gain from the sale."

She sagged in her chair, defeated. "Yes."

Nolan suspected the tears were more for her financial statement than for Bruce Messane. The outsized grief made sense now. Jackson and Geiger wouldn't kill the golden goose, but an heir might. "Do you know who inherits his shares?"

"The majority of his holdings revert to his former partner and co-founder upon his death; it was part of the buyout deal a couple years back. I don't know who gets the rest, but I imagine his daughter, Katrina."

"It seems strange to give your ex-partner a reason to kill you, doesn't it?"

Her hands fluttered at her ample bosom in disbelief. "Dr. Bechtold would never kill Bruce! They were friends since childhood, and the parting was amicable. At the time, Bruce didn't have the liquidity to pay full market value, so the shares sweetened the package."

"It would only be sweet if Mr. Messane died," Crawford pressed her.

"Money wasn't the purpose of their agreement. Peppy Pets was their baby, and neither of them wanted to see control of the company fall into outside hands if something were to happen to Bruce."

"But Mr. Messane *was* selling to outside hands."

"Contractually, any sale was Bruce's prerogative—"

"I imagine that didn't sit well with Dr. Bechtold."

"Wilder Foods is a good company. And the sale would have been very favorable to Dr. Bechtold. He would receive the funds he deferred, plus a bonus." She shook her head sullenly. "There are no winners here, only losers."

"You mentioned liquidity issues a few years back. The company was in trouble?" Crawford asked.

She shifted in her chair uncomfortably. "It wasn't the best time for anyone during the pandemic. But Bruce really turned it around."

"Do you have contact information for Dr. Bechtold?"

"Yes, of course. He's such a kind man, he would never kill Bruce," she repeated. "I don't think he would even kill a spider. He's a veterinarian, and the mission of Peppy Pets was his passion; building the brand and growing the company was Bruce's. They were a good team. We were all sorry when Rome left, but he didn't have the stomach or stamina for big business." She jiggled her mouse. "I'll print out his contact details for you now."

"Thank you, Ms. Jackson. We'll also need to take Mr. Messane's computer. Can you show us to his office?"

* * *

Bruce Messane had favored minimalism in the extreme. The room had a bleached look, drained of color or any interest. Not so different from his corpse, Nolan thought grimly. There wasn't a filing cabinet, bookcase, or credenza; not a single piece of art hanging on the white walls. A stark blond wood table sat precisely in the center of a pale, monochrome rug, and bore none of the signs of industry, like paperwork, pens, or folders. Nothing except a computer. Didn't everyone have a family photo on their desk? A tchotchke or two? Wasn't everybody's computer monitor studded with sticky note reminders?

The room felt ghostly to Nolan, like his spirit had fled his mortal shell and come here to do some housekeeping. She knew he had to have a personality—everyone did—but it wasn't present here. Or maybe his personality was as bleached as his office.

While Crawford tagged and bagged his hard drive, she toured the bleak, unrelieved landscape. "This place says something about him, but I'm not sure what."

He looked around the room, trying without success to find an interesting place for his eyes to land. "It says to me that he was an obsessive control freak. Maybe his head was such a mess, he kept his environment simple. Personally, I'd miss the clutter."

"Your desk isn't cluttered, Al, it's a disaster."

"You're one to talk. So, nobody here had a reason to kill Messane. Neither did Bechtold. Everybody gained from the sale."

"Money isn't the only motive to kill."

"Jackson?"

"We have to look at her. Messane would have set his alarm before he left for Culver City, which was well before she arrived, don't you think?"

"Yeah, but he could have forgotten, or thought he wouldn't be gone long."

"Right, so I want to know when it was armed and disarmed. If he set it when he left, either Jackson is lying to us about it being off when she got there, or there really was an intruder, and they knew the code, too."

He hiked a brow at her. "Easy enough to check with ADT. But I really don't see her as the killer. Why would she set up this whole dog and pony show, confess to being an ex-lover, and make herself a person of interest when she didn't have to?"

"It wouldn't be the first time a killer got busted because they tried too hard to cover their tracks."

Chapter Fifteen

REMY WAS SITTING AT A PICNIC table in a car-wash parking lot on Olympic Boulevard, enjoying succulent tongue tacos with Justin Taggert. Food trucks and stalls at car washes were a remarkable Los Angeles phenomenon. If you were able to overlook the lack of ambience, you would be rewarded with some of the best street food north of the border or some of the best barbeque outside Texas.

Justin was six-four, with a prison build and neck tattoos that crawled down his broad shoulders to color both his arms. He was as intimidating as any of the human rubbish he pursued, but the most sinister part of his past was probably a few frat parties at UCLA, where he'd earned a criminal justice degree.

"Do you miss undercover work, Juice?"

He slurped Pepsi noisily through a straw. It was imperative to acquire bad manners when working UC. "No way. I mean, sure, it's a huge rush, but half the time, you're scared shitless. Job is dangerous enough as it is without embedding with a bunch of psychos. I want to watch my kids grow up and have rug rats of their own."

"Heeding the self-preservation instinct is a surprisingly rare quality. You have your priorities in the correct order."

"What about you? Seeing any little Remys in your future?"

"Children have never been a goal, but it's not something you should dismiss out of hand, is it?"

Justin laughed. "I love the way you can talk your way around anything. I hope things work out with Maggie, she's a diamond."

"I don't know what you're talking about, Juice."

"Seriously? You two have sex every time you look at each other."

Remy sighed. "That obvious?"

"Yeah, but consider my mouth wired shut." He crumpled his foil wrapper and executed a perfect, three-point shot into the trash barrel. "Thanks for the heads-up on Kang and the ghoul with the rainbows."

"I'll pass along your gratitude the next time I see Ringo."

"Honestly, I thought he got killed last month."

"It wouldn't be so easy to get rid of him, he's got the half-life of a plutonium isotope. So, has the angel of death arrived in LA?"

Justin was watching a Range Rover get the full beauty treatment at one of the detailing stations. "I'd say so. Word is, Los Zetas is back."

Remy's brows peaked. Los Zetas was founded by deserters from the Mexican special forces, initially serving as an enforcement arm of the Gulf Cartel before breaking away to form their own syndicate. They were distinguished by their atrocities, horrific even by cartel standards. To the relief of the civilized world, infighting and multiple arrests south of the border took out central command and they ultimately splintered and became a footnote. Or so he'd thought. "Didn't they burn out years ago?"

"Yeah, but they recently reconstituted as LZ2 and started creeping north like poisonous vines. And they're more sadistic than ever. I won't even tell you about the last massacre in Juarez, because you won't sleep for a year."

Remy didn't need to hear it. He knew enough, and his imagination filled in the rest. His second tongue taco would go uneaten. "All bad things seem to reconstitute, don't they? It's like the Hydra."

"Exactly. We just have to keep chopping off heads. There's no such thing as a death blow to the cartels without intelligent government policy, and that ain't ever gonna happen. Really pisses me off."

"On a positive note, you have job security."

Justin snuffled ruefully. "We all have it, don't we?"

"Until the human race rediscovers its collective soul."

"Could Ringo ID this guy?"

"I'm sure he could, but I don't know if he would. He's scared and leaving town for a while. Did the Inglewood bust give you anything?"

"Enough intel to petition a warrant on a warehouse in Anaheim."

"When does it go down?"

"Tonight. We're organizing with Metro now. Hey, speaking of which, I just talked to Margolis. He told me Sam Easton was in this morning, discussing a consulting position. He's perfect for the job, I hope he goes for it."

Good for you, Sam. "I hope so, too."

Chapter Sixteen

MONTSERRAT DE LEON WAS FURIOUS THEY'D made a cross-country trip for nothing, although Bruce Messane wasn't to blame for a family emergency, or the timing of it. Still, the entire morning left a taste in her mouth almost as foul as Wilder's personality.

She took a seat across from him on his Citation Longitude and stretched out her long, tanned legs. It wasn't meant to be provocative—she was simply stiff from hours of sitting—but he would take it that way. Most men in his position were shameless leches, because they were used to getting whatever they wanted, whenever they wanted it.

Predictably, his eyes abandoned her legs when a pretty, fawning flight attendant delivered two flutes of champagne. While he engaged her in flirty banter, she sipped contentedly as Los Angeles shrank beneath them, then disappeared entirely beneath the clouds.

"Would you like me to bring the bottle, Mr. Wilder?"

"Please do, Katya."

Montserrat regarded him with cool amusement. "Celebrating already, Mr. Wilder?"

He grunted churlishly. "Hardly. This was a waste of time and jet fuel, and I don't look favorably on either. Whatever Messane's emergency is, somebody better be dead."

"That's a rather heartless thing to say."

He ignored her. "And I didn't like Cynthia Jackson's demeanor, either. She seemed desperate. And when CFOs are desperate, I get worried."

"The entire company was thoroughly vetted over the course of months. Nobody can escape the scrutiny of your team. I think she's simply anxious to acquire her share. And who can blame her?"

He changed the subject with an oily smile. "Should we discuss further over dinner at Per Se? I have reservations for this evening."

"Thank you for the invitation, Mr. Wilder, but I'll be working well into the night. I'm behind on another project."

He swirled his glass, unfazed by the rejection. "Another time, then."

"There is something I wanted to discuss with you, though. Just between us."

"What is it?"

She leaned forward confidentially. He responded in kind. His currant-sized eyes glittered in anticipation. He was probably expecting a sexual proposition. Such a dreamer. Of course, you couldn't build an empire if you didn't dream.

"I'm considering parting ways with Rothschild Smythe. I've been offered a partnership in my uncle's firm in Madrid."

Wilder deflated. "I can't believe you would leave New York," he blustered. "It's the place to be, and I have it on good authority that you're on the partnership track there. If you're dissatisfied with your current arrangement, perhaps general counsel of Wilder Foods would be more to your liking."

"That's very flattering, but New York isn't home. I haven't made my final decision, but regardless, I will of course see this deal through to the end." She watched his meaty lower lip jut out in a hideous pout. Laughter bubbled in her throat, but she kept it there.

He regarded his glass, took a savoring sip of the good life. "I would hate to see you leave, but home is home, I understand that. We all go back to our roots eventually."

Wilder's roots were in a small town in Oklahoma, and she didn't see him ever leaving New York. Nobody would care who he was in a dusty outpost, and even if they did, the population was far too small and provincial to slake his thirst for sycophants. He craved that more than women. "I knew you would understand."

"Yes, but keep my offer in mind. You would be a brilliant addition to the Wilder family. And I quite like the idea of having you all to myself."

Of course you do, you pig.

Chapter Seventeen

NOLAN GAVE IKE'S OFFICE DOOR A courtesy rap before she walked in. He was in typical form, hunched over his keyboard, gnawing on a piece of red licorice, raking his dark hair with his fingers like he meant to rip it out. The Jack Daniel's bottle was nowhere in sight, which she took as a positive sign, especially since it was barely noon. "Got a computer for you, Ike."

He looked up with bloodshot eyes and grinned. "Outstanding! I need a new toy to play with." He moved a teetering stack of files off his desk and onto a chair to make room for the drive and an auxiliary monitor. "Did you reach the ex?"

"Yeah."

"Enlightening?"

She lifted a shoulder ambivalently. "She told me Bruce Messane was a sex addict."

Ike's brows rose. "For real?"

"Pathologically, out-of-control for real."

"That's interesting, because I'm looking through his phone records now, and he got a call from an untraceable number at half past midnight. It's out of service; a throwaway. Nothing after that until his office lit up his phone this morning. Booty call from a homicidal lover?"

"It fits. Did that number contact him before?"

He shook his head. "It was a one-off. And here's a weird thing: he got a lot of calls from different untraceable numbers. Most people never hear from a burner phone in their lifetimes."

She sat down on the remaining chair not occupied by files. "I'm sure secrecy is part of the culture. Messane was a prominent person, it stands to reason some of his partners were, too, and if they were married, discretion would be paramount."

"Makes sense. Jesus, what a way to live."

Nolan wondered if he was referencing his own addiction, at least on a subconscious level. She declined his offer of licorice from an LAPD mug stuffed with it. "No, thanks. You know that's just an extruded sugar and starch paste, right?"

"It's raspberry, so I figure I'm getting a few servings of fruit, too."

She could have pointed out that the stuff had never seen a real raspberry, but he already knew that. "We need to find his phone."

"All over that, Mags. But you know the chances of it being on or intact are about zero."

"While I breathe, I hope."

"*Dum spiro spero.* Good attitude."

"And nice Latin. You're not just another pretty face."

Ike waggled his brows. "That's what all the girls say. Canvass reports in yet?"

"Hear no evil, see no evil, just like you'd expect. People are terrified in that neighborhood, and it's getting worse according to the business owner we talked to. Ike, if you can get to Messane's computer right away, we'll take over the records."

"Sure thing. Anything specific you want me to focus on?"

"Phone might not be the only way he communicated with his

killer, especially if it's a sex thing, so look at his emails first. It's his work computer, so they might just be business, but people get reckless. Messane was also in the middle of a big deal to sell Peppy Pets for a hundred mil, so keep an eye out for anything off there, too."

Ike scratched some notes in what looked like a mangled combination of hieroglyphics and cuneiform. "I'd kill for less. What about a home computer? That's the best bet for personal stuff."

"We're headed there next."

* * *

Nolan found her partner at his desk, engrossed in whatever was on his computer screen. "Are you looking at phone records, or watching cat videos again?"

He smirked at her. "We got a hit on those oily prints on the body of the Beemer. Ty Mattison, low-level runner for the Shoreline Crips, with a jacket as long as you'd figure."

"Murder?"

"Drugs charges, B and E, stolen property, but nothing violent. A real peach of a felon."

"Culver City is out of his territory. That was risky."

"Desperation knows no boundaries. The idiot just got paroled last week, I'm sure he was looking to improve his financial situation after two years of unemployment. Venice will give us a call when they pick him up." He stood and shrugged into his windbreaker. "Next stop, Holmby Hills."

Chapter Eighteen

THE RAIN HAD FINALLY STOPPED BY the time they arrived at Messane's house. The driveway was cluttered with official vehicles, so Nolan parked on the street beneath a eucalyptus tree that was shedding water from its dusky, sickle-shaped leaves. Al was gazing up through the windshield, fascinated by something.

"Is that actually a tiny piece of blue sky, or am I hallucinating?"

"It's real. I heard the storm front is veering north. The Sierras are supposed to get seven feet of snow tonight."

"How is that even possible?"

"Anything is possible in the mountains."

He returned his eyes to ground level. "Doesn't Remy have a place up in Big Bear?"

"It's a ski lodge. And it belongs to his family."

"How many houses does his family own?"

"Just two in California."

He snorted. "Just a Bel Air mansion and a ski lodge in Big Bear. That's damn near living below the poverty line. You could do so much better."

Nolan hadn't planned on confronting Al about his insolence in the middle of a case, but her supposedly genetic ire was unpredictable. "Al, I love you, but you've got to keep your mouth shut around people. Remy thinks the captain already knows, and even a few innocent whispers could force his hand. And that means you lose a partner."

His expression fluctuated between apology and shock. "Jesus, Maggie, I'm sorry, I wasn't thinking."

In her experience, men rarely did. Except Remy. He thought a lot; sometimes too much. "Don't feel bad, I had to have a stern word with Remy this morning, too. Do men ever grow up?"

"Corinne doesn't think so."

The wisdom of the sisterhood was immutable. "Look, life wouldn't be worth living if we didn't give each other shit, we just can't in this instance."

"Can I still give you shit in private?"

"Anytime."

He glanced at her, gauging the temperature. "But you never get mad in private, and it's just so damn cute when your cheeks turn all rosy and you get murder in your eyes."

"You *really* don't want to slip up, Al, because I might have a compromising photo of you carrying a unicorn umbrella."

"No!"

"Oh, yes."

He raised his hand for a high five. "Well-played, Mags."

She kept her smug smile undercover and gestured out the window at the man coming down the steep flagstone drive. "Aaron Solange's on the job."

Crawford unclipped his seat belt. "We better meet him halfway, he had triple bypass last year. Probably in better shape now than he was for most of his life, but why push it?"

They'd worked with the detective on occasions when murder brought them to this tony part of the world, which seemed to be often lately. He was an intelligent man with a hawkish nose and penetrating, khaki eyes. And apparently, a recently renovated heart.

He greeted them with an earnest smile. "Good to see you two again. We should meet under better circumstances for a change."

"Wouldn't mind that. How's the ticker?" Crawford asked.

"Beating as smooth as a Buddy Rich groove, thanks. Nothing like a near-death experience to get your mind right. I drink less, eat better. It's boring." He waved toward the ersatz French chateau looming over the crest of the hill. "I couldn't find a single sign of robbery. No sign of an intruder at all, except for the footprints in the foyer. They were fresh, but smeared. No distinct markings left."

"Did you happen to see a pair of boots?"

Solange shook his head.

She looked at Al. "So there was an intruder inside when Jackson was there. She's damn lucky. Aaron, was there any sign of a break-in or tampering with the alarm system?"

"None. No cameras, either. Come on up, I'll give you a full rundown on the way."

Crime Scene was packing up when they entered. Nolan didn't recognize any of them, but they all looked very young and hip. A lot of people were looking young and hip to her these days. Since she was still in her early thirties, it amused her more than depressed her. Ten years from now, she might feel differently, but she hoped not. Cynthia Jackson didn't get it, but rage against age was a battle eventually doomed to failure, and a shameful waste of energy better spent elsewhere.

She approached the nearest tech, a woman with a pierced nose and lavender hair who was crouched over an aluminum case, carefully arranging the tools of her trade so it was ready for the next trip to somebody else's tragedy. "Excuse me, did you cover outside?"

She looked over her shoulder, then stood at full attention. "Just the house, Detective Nolan."

"I'm sorry, have we worked together?"

"No, but I've heard a lot about you from Ross."

"All good things, I'm sure."

She smiled. "All good things. I'm Jenna, by the way. Tell me what you need."

"I'd like you to check the fence line, in case whoever left the footprints came in that way."

"We'll get right on it, Detective Nolan."

Crawford approached, stuffing his phone in his jacket pocket. "Just talked to ADT. Messane disarmed and immediately rearmed the system at quarter to one last night, which synchs with the burner call he received. It was disarmed again at quarter to nine this morning. The intruder *did* know the code."

Chapter Nineteen

MESSANE'S HOME WAS AS OBNOXIOUSLY FROTHY as his office was spartan, which probably explained his penchant for asceticism in the workplace. He clearly hadn't been responsible for the décor, and it must have driven him mad. Nolan wondered why he hadn't redecorated after the divorce.

The main level of the house had a vast, open floor plan, reminiscent of the great European manor houses and meant to impress. She recognized some of the art on the walls, and they weren't cheap prints. Every flat surface was cluttered with objets d'art that looked old and valuable. A high-tech sound system array was concealed behind an elaborate baroque screen to avoid anachronism in the carefully curated fantasy environment of court life before the French Revolution.

Crawford poked at a thick wad of hundred-dollar bills sitting on a side table. "What kind of a thief walks by all this cash? All this stuff?"

"Not the Ty Mattison kind." She started opening drawers on a sideboard in the dining room. Sterling silver flatware gleamed in a nest of soft, green felt. Easy to fence, pawn, or take to a precious metals dealer.

"You won't see a thing out of place or obviously missing," Solange said, leading them up a broad staircase to the master bedroom. "That chest on the dresser has a dozen watches in it. Patek Philippe, Franck Muller, Rolex, you name it."

Nolan marveled at the yellow and blue curtains encumbering the space. She wanted to meet the designer who'd thought they were a good idea so she could slap them silly. She opened the door of a walk-in closet. All suits, arranged by color and season, each hanging equidistant to the next with excruciating precision. It made his office look chaotic.

She followed Al into a master bath that felt as large as her entire rental house in the San Fernando Valley. They both started rummaging through cabinets and drawers. If drugs had been a secret problem in his life, this was a likely place to keep them. She found blood pressure medication, acid reflux medication, and erectile dysfunction medication. ED had to suck if you were a sex addict.

"I'm just seeing over-the-counter stuff over here, Mags."

"Everything's legit over here so far, too." She moved to the next cabinet. Low-dosage aspirin, Tylenol, multivitamins, a box of antihistamines with two pills missing from a blister pack. And behind that, a bottle of oxycodone. She uncapped it and examined the contents. "Oxy here, Al. Prescribed three years ago, a few pills left." She tossed him the bottle. "Look at the doctor."

"Kang, huh? So, the surgeries his wife mentioned were cosmetic. I thought he looked a little tight."

"Anybody who lets oxys expire doesn't have a drug problem. Check that off the list."

The guest bedrooms were undisturbed and devoid of anything useful, but at the end of the long hall was Messane's home office, easy to identify because it was an exact duplicate of his Peppy Pets one, right down to the characterless rug. But there was one flagrant anomaly: three large, exquisitely painted oil portraits of cats hanging above the desk. She stared into the beautiful celadon eyes of a pale orange tabby; the brindled eyes of a calico; and the stunning emerald eyes of a huge, sleek black cat that looked more puma than domestic shorthair.

Crawford whistled. "We're looking at true love right there. Probably the only true love he ever knew."

Nolan stepped closer and read the gold plaques fastened to the frames: SUGAR, CINNAMON, OLLIE. Messane hadn't been able to bond with people, but he most certainly had with his pets. "These must be the cats he lost from tainted food."

"Quite a shrine. There are even little kitty urns."

Nolan's throat tightened. Jackson was wrong, Peppy Pets had been more than just business to him. Messane had a different, softer dimension after all. "No computer, that's strange."

"I'm sure there was one here a few hours ago." He opened the door to a large closet filled with cold-weather gear. "Looks like he was a skier, too. Must have been a bitch trying to keep up with his wife." He started shuffling the parkas, ski bibs, and sweaters. Tucked in a far corner was a small chest. "How are your lock-picking skills?"

* * *

Solange was waiting for them at the bottom of the stairs and his expression brightened when he saw the laptop under Crawford's arm. "That's a good score, where did you find it?"

"In a locked chest stashed at the back of his office closet."

"Must be some good stuff on it."

"That's what we're hoping. What about the garage, Aaron?"

"Neat as the house, with oriental rugs on the floor, if you can believe that. A Tesla Roadster in the second bay. Aside from the Beemer at your crime scene, there are no other cars registered in his name."

One more valuable thing the intruder didn't take, even though they probably had the keys. As they passed the kitchen, she noticed another anachronism: a rustic wooden door tucked in an alcove beneath a secondary stairwell. Ornamental ironwork wrought with grapevines covered a small, round window. "Wine cellar?"

Solange nodded. "Yeah. Hell if I could see if any bottles were taken, there have to be five thousand in there at least."

Houses in LA didn't have full basements because of earthquakes, but some had small cellars like these. It was down a short flight of stairs, putting it below ground level. Natural climate control. The walls were rough stone and it smelled pleasantly sour and earthy, like wine-soaked mushrooms. The smell transported Nolan back to her trip to Napa last fall. The wineries and the scenery had been spectacular, the boyfriend less so. Actually, he'd been a cheating asshole, she just hadn't known it at the time.

Racks of bottles lined all four walls from floor to ceiling. Some sparkled in the low light of the sconces, some had a dull patina of dust. Dust was bad anywhere but a wine cellar, according to the asshole boyfriend. *It gives a collection old-world credence.*

What a crock of shit. Nolan had made a snide remark about old-world dust versus bad housekeeping, but she couldn't remember his reaction. Messane seemed like the type who would import dust to sprinkle on his bottles.

There was a granite island with a sink in the middle of the room; a diverse array of stemware, each with its own purpose, hanging from lattice above. Dozens of wooden wine crates stamped with French names were stacked in a corner.

Crawford sighed wistfully. "Damn, I'm thirsty. I would have cleaned this room out, no matter what else I was looking for. I'm not an oenophile, but I know a good thing when I see it."

"I'm impressed you know what oenophile means."

"I'm not a total Neanderthal, Mags."

She snickered, then turned on her penlight and started coursing the small, dim room. Without the aid of her mini-Mag, she might not have noticed the square of dust-free floor next to the wine crates.

"Look. There was something here recently. Smaller than a wine crate."

Crawford sidled up next to her. "Messane could have just been rearranging."

"I think our intruder found what they were looking for, and we have to figure out what it was." She turned to Solange. "Would you set up a canvass, Aaron?"

"Will do. There's not really any line-of-sight from the adjacent properties with all the privacy fences and foliage, but residents and staff come and go at all hours in this neighborhood, and they pay attention to their surroundings. They would notice somebody walking around with a box."

While the Beverly Hills detective gathered uniforms for the task, Nolan and Crawford crossed the expansive, soggy lawn to the north side of the fence, where Jenna and her team were working.

"You're crouched over something, I take that as a positive," Nolan said.

Jenna leaned back, exposing a patch of flattened, muddy grass. "Looks like somebody slipped, see the skid mark? Unfortunately, there's nothing we can cast, it's pretty much dirt soup. There are also two deeper depressions here, but they're indeterminate."

"This is the only place you found that was disturbed?"

"Yeah, we covered the whole fence line."

"Then we have a point of ingress and egress." She gazed at a stand of myrtles and lemon trees on the other side of the fence. Techs were doing the grid-search zombie walk, eyes to the ground. "Anything out there?"

"They found a faint trail, but it dead ends at the street."

Crawford shoved his hands in his pockets to warm them up. "This fence is pretty high, Mags. And it's steel. Slippery, and no good place for a foothold."

"They managed it somehow. Maybe they brought a ladder."

Jenna looked up again. "That would explain the mystery depres-sions. They really wanted in bad. Weird there was no theft."

"Actually, we think there was, in the wine cellar. Would you check that out, too?"

"You got it."

Chapter Twenty

THE LAST TIME SAM HAD SEEN Rome Bechtold was at one of his mother's many fundraisers a few months ago. A very different man was sitting across from him now, understandably unglued. Before today, he'd had no comprehension of the evil lurking just beyond his sheltered world; how close it was to seeping through the delicate membrane of privilege. His poor dog was equally distraught, whining pathetically and pulling out tufts of hair. Classic transference.

"Rome, I know your life just shattered into a million pieces, but you need to calm down and focus. This is a dangerous situation, and you're on somebody else's timeline now. Every minute counts—"

"Addison and I have been through this house a dozen times," he rambled, stroking the dog mechanically. "Every inch of it. There's no trace of her, Sam. Not a trace, and no clues. I can't understand . . . well, it's for money, but why won't they call back? Can you help me find Nicole? If we know where she is, we could make a plan and go in and—"

He wasn't just crumbling, he was delusional. Sam dug deep for forbearance. "You have to go to the police. They have the experience and resources to deal with this. You and I don't."

"They'll kill her!"

"Kidnappers always say that, they all read from the same bad script, but they'll never know. They're stupid criminals, not international spies. Trust me, you'll never get Nicole back alive without the police." Sam watched his fear-blanched face turn gray. It was the reaction he was looking for. He needed to get through to him.

"I can't lose her."

"You won't. I'm going to call some friends."

He wiped his eyes and looked around the kitchen mindlessly. "I don't even live here anymore, did you know that? We're separated, she said we needed some time apart. If I'd still been here—"

"It wouldn't have changed a thing, and it may have turned out worse." Sam heard the frustration in his voice, and moderated his tone.

He lowered his head and nodded. "I know. I'm sorry I dragged you into this, I just didn't know what else to do."

"It's okay. Everything is going to be okay." He tensed when he heard a car door slam, then felt the hot surge of adrenaline suffuse his body and sharpen his mind. He knew it was an overreaction—they were in a city, in a neighborhood, and car doors closed all the time, a million times a day. But war had taught him to always anticipate mortal danger no matter how safe you felt. It was a hard way to live, but it only took one moment of laxity to change the future forever.

He withdrew his Colt Python from its belt holster.

"My God, what's wrong, Sam?"

"Hopefully nothing, but go to the back of the house and stay there. Don't move until I tell you."

"Oh, Jesus, they're coming—"

"Go!" Sam sank to a crouch and crabbed toward the door, deafened by the pounding of his heart.

* * *

Nicole Bechtold was counting seconds. She'd forgotten the tally a long time ago, but her internal metronome was the only thing preventing her from falling off the precipice of sanity. Hysteria wouldn't help her situation. She had to stay calm. Pay attention. Find hope.

Where do you find hope when you're bound and gagged and blindfolded?

Lyrics from her youth entered her mind; the mantra that anger was an energy. Yes, get angry. Fight. And she did, with a silent scream of rage and despair, once again struggling against her tethers as if they would somehow magically loosen this time. The pain was almost unbearable because the skin of her wrists was already raw and bleeding, but she had to do something. It was a psychological battle at this point.

She froze and held her breath when she heard a door creak open; heard heavy footfalls thumping toward her. Tears escaped the blindfold and dripped down her cheeks.

A rough hand that smelled of cigarette smoke pulled down her gag, and she released a great gust of air, as if she'd been holding her breath for hours instead of seconds. "What do you want?" she sobbed in a weak, broken voice that had finally been freed.

He didn't speak—neither of her two captors had spoken since they'd taken her. She didn't even know what they looked like, because the bastards had appeared out of nowhere in her own goddamned backyard and put a hood over her head. If she lived through this, she was going to move far, far away, to a place with no people. And buy a hundred guns and a hundred guard dogs.

"My husband will give you whatever you want, just let me go. Please." She recoiled when she felt the rim of a plastic bottle against her lips, but her burning thirst eventually prevailed, and she gulped greedily, not particularly caring if it was laced with poison or drugs.

A few minutes later, she regretted it. Time deformed and drifted, and her head became impossibly heavy, lolling on the stalk of her neck like a seed-laden sunflower in the fields of her family's farm in Iowa. Oh, God, she was going to die here, in this horrible, unknown place, with these horrible, unknown people. For what? Money?

As her consciousness receded, she thought she finally heard a voice, muffled and flat. "Have a nice sleep, Nicole."

* * *

Sam gaped out the front door window as Maggie and Al came up the walk, but his astonishment was quickly replaced by dread as his thoughts cleared. Homicide cops had one job. He opened the door, and they both stopped abruptly, as flabbergasted as he was.

Maggie recovered first. "Sam. What are you doing here?"

He stepped out and closed the door behind him. "It's Nicole, isn't it?"

"Who's Nicole?"

"She's not dead?"

"We have no idea what you're talking about," Crawford said. "Is this the Bechtold residence?"

Sam let out a shaky sigh. "Yes. Rome and Nicole Bechtold are old family friends, and she was kidnapped this morning."

He watched his two friends share a disbelieving glance. "Did he call it in?"

"No. He's a disaster. He just asked me to come over, and told me a few minutes ago. I was about to call, then I heard your car doors slam and got nervous. Why are *you* here?"

"To question Rome about the murder of his ex-business partner."

"Jesus." Sam braced his arms on the porch railing of the beautiful Craftsman house that would never feel like home to the Bechtolds anymore, whatever happened. "Come in."

Chapter Twenty-One

SAM WAS RIGHT. ROME BECHTOLD WAS a disaster, and with good reason—the photo of his bound wife was soul-destroying. Nolan was frustrated that he'd wasted so much precious time, but she understood. There were no how-to manuals for dealing with something as outrageous as this, and he clearly didn't have the personality for crisis management. The cute, fat dog on his lap seemed to be his sole comfort. He was giving the fur a workout, like a frightened child worrying a stuffed animal.

Her eyes once again coursed the house that was as understated as Messane's was gaudy. Opposite ends of the spectrum, two very different personalities. Love of animals seemed to be their only common ground. "Mr. Bechtold, Robbery Special Section and a response team are on the way. It's going to feel overwhelming, but trust them and do whatever they say. They're trained for this, and they'll find your wife and bring her home safely."

His eyes shifted downward, tracking the free fall of his life. "But she was kidnapped. What does robbery have to do with it?"

"They handle kidnappings. It's extortion."

"But . . . if you're not involved, why are you here?"

Nolan took a breath before she dropped the next bomb on the ruins of his life. "Bruce Messane."

"Bruce? Is he in trouble?"

She found it interesting that Messane's ex-wife and ex-partner both assumed he was in trouble. And he was, just in a very different way than they'd imagined. "He was murdered last night."

Bechtold gasped and clutched his dog, eliciting a squeak. "What?"

"I'm very sorry."

"No. No. This all can't be real." A tear slipped down his cheek.

"I'm afraid it is, Mr. Bechtold. We're hoping you can answer some questions for us now while we wait for Robbery to arrive. It's important to our investigation, and it might be important for your wife as well."

"How could it be important for Nicole?"

"He was murdered and she was kidnapped in less than twenty-four hours. We have to consider the possibility that these two crimes are connected."

"We had nothing to do with Bruce after I left Peppy Pets. That was two years ago."

"We spoke with Cynthia Jackson this morning, and she seemed to think you were on good terms."

"We were cordial."

From his shift in expression and demeanor, Nolan realized that the childhood friends hadn't been on such good terms after all, they'd just put on happy faces for the benefit of company bonhomie. Knowing Messane's profligate lifestyle, her thoughts automatically veered to the most fundamental of grievances between men. "You mentioned you and your wife are separated. Did something to do with Mr. Messane precipitate that?"

His eyes drifted to a point in the distance. "She said we'd grown apart."

She exchanged a glance with Al. He nodded briefly, and stepped in. "You didn't answer the question, Mr. Bechtold."

What little composure he had disintegrated. Tears splatted on his dog's back. "It was a long time ago. Years ago."

"What was?"

"They had an affair. But Nicole and I worked through it."

It was Nolan's turn again, but she didn't feel like the good cop, she felt like crap. But this schlubby, devastated man sitting across from her might be capable of a crime of passion, so she couldn't indulge her pity. "Is that why you left the company?"

"I left because Peppy Pets was killing me. Literally."

"How so?"

"I was working eighty hours a week, every week of the year. I had a heart attack. Peptic ulcers. Growing Peppy Pets into a juggernaut wasn't my dream, it was Bruce's. I'm a small-town vet who grew up on a farm in Iowa and married my high school sweetheart. I just wanted to help animals."

Nolan felt worse. "I'm sorry to have to bring this up, but is it possible the two of them rekindled something recently? Something that may have put them both in harm's way?"

"No," he said decisively. "Nicole hated him, said he was a predator. They took my wife for the money, it's no secret I have a lot of it. I don't know why Bruce was killed, but he lived on the edge."

"Can you elaborate?"

"He had a weakness for women. He was a charismatic train wreck." He wagged his head sadly. "She never would have been involved with him again."

Nolan wasn't convinced, and she wasn't sure Rome Bechtold was, either, but it was time to move on. They'd have visitors soon, and there was more ground to cover before he was completely consumed. "We understand his shares in Peppy Pets revert to you."

His eyes widened in surprise. "Nobody outside my attorney and a few people in the company know that."

"Anything to do with Mr. Messane's personal and professional life is our business now."

"Then Cynthia must have explained that it was part of the buyout deal."

"Yes. You've just come into a substantial windfall."

He gave them a crestfallen look. "It wasn't about money, it was a contingency meant to preserve the integrity of the company in case something happened to him after I divested. I'll be giving it all to charity."

"How did you feel about him selling to Wilder Foods?" Crawford asked. "Company integrity would have probably gone out the window if the deal had gone through."

"Oh, no, not at all. A company like Wilder doesn't buy a formula for success and pivot away from the core concept. That's business suicide."

"What is the core concept?"

"Food good enough for a human to eat. No fillers and premium organic ingredients. We call it whole care for four-legged family members." He stroked the dog's head thoughtfully. "I was happy about the deal. Happy for Peppy Pets, and for Bruce. This may sound strange, but I forgave him, just like I forgave Nicole. I'm a better man for it."

"I have to ask: where were you this morning from midnight on?"

He sighed wearily. "Sleeping. I went to bed at ten and got up at six like always. And no, I don't have any witnesses. Except for Addy, and he can't vouch for me."

"Your alarm system could. I assume you have one at your rental."

"Yes, but it hasn't been functioning properly since I moved in. I've been waiting over a week to get a technician out to replace the master battery."

Nolan saw a broken, betrayed, distraught man pushed to the limit of his endurance, but she didn't see a killer, and she was sure his alarm story would check out with the company. "How long ago was the affair?"

"Four years ago."

"And you were able to keep working together?"

"We made our peace. Life comes with baggage and it keeps accumulating. If you don't let it go, it will crush you. I didn't kill Bruce, Detectives. I loved him in spite of everything, and we did good things together. A percentage of all the profits went to animal welfare charities. That was *my* dream, and without Bruce's business acumen, the company wouldn't have been able to afford to do that. I'm grateful to him."

"But the company was in trouble."

"COVID hurt every business, top to bottom, but we pulled through, thanks to Bruce. I just wanted out."

*　*　*

Once RSS arrived, Nolan, Crawford, and Sam stepped out onto the porch.

"What happens now?" Sam asked.

"A lot of things. Very simply, they'll debrief him, start a comprehensive investigation, set up command posts; try to trace the first call, get recording equipment set up for the next. Then it's all about waiting for contact. Kidnappings are fluid and things can change from one minute to the next, but these people are the best."

"You two don't think Rome had anything to do with the murder, do you?"

Crawford shrugged. "An affair could send a certain type over the edge, but crimes of passion don't bubble up four years after the fact, and money isn't an issue. Not feeling it. Mags?"

"I'm not, either."

"Do you have any leads?"

"There's a lot of noise in this case, but nothing is coming together yet." Nolan looked up at the cloud deck shredding in the raw wind. The sun was thinking about making a full-fledged appearance. A scrub jay was cheeping in a liquidambar tree, sharing the good news. "Are you sticking around for a while, Sam?"

"I think he could use the support."

"Your family has known him for a long time?" Crawford asked.

"Since I was a kid, and he's never been anything but a kind, generous man. Real salt of the earth, still an Iowa farm boy at heart. I've never seen him past first gear."

Nolan sensed an underlying ease in Sam that hadn't always been there, like he was trying to keep it in first gear, too. He and Melody were a couple now, and things were obviously going well on that front. She was curious to know if he was taking any other steps forward. "Have you given any more thought to SWAT, Sam?"

He lifted his brows. "Funny you should ask that. I just interviewed with Captain Margolis this morning."

"What do you think?"

"I like him, I like the vibe, and he offered me the position."

Crawford clapped him on the shoulder. "That's great, Sam. Really great."

"Thanks. He told me to take some time to think about it, sit in on some sessions and observe an op."

"Good advice."

"Thanks for your recommendations. Remy's, too."

"That was a no-brainer. We have to get back to the workhouse, but know Rome is in good hands. Let us know if we can do anything."

Chapter Twenty-Two

THE PLANE WAS SILENT EXCEPT FOR the clattering of multiple keyboards and the sound was lulling Montserrat to sleep. The thought horrified her, so she ordered another coffee. As ridiculous as it was, she didn't ever want to be unconscious around Wilder, even if it was in the fuselage of a plane with four other people. While her coffee cooled, she pulled up her personal email. As usual, it was empty. She had no life outside of work, but it didn't seem unhealthy to her. It was all she had ever known in her adult life.

Wilder slammed the lid on his laptop and cleared his throat, commencing an important interruption. "Ms. De Leon, I've just been in touch with legal in our Barcelona office. The general counsel position there is yours for the taking. The sitting counsel is an American, and we need a native in that position. I've been saying that all along, but we haven't been able to find anyone with your qualifications—not even close."

He was relentless. He also looked pathetic, like a child offering a parent a crayon drawing, hoping it wouldn't be disregarded. She smiled sweetly. "Mr. Wilder, that is certainly a kind offer."

"Nothing kind about it, it would be good for business. And good for you, closer to home."

"I will take it into consideration."

"Yes, well, do that," he blustered.

Lee Chen, head of public relations at Rothschild Smythe, hurried up the aisle toward them, his lank face flushed. "Mr. Wilder, I have some news. Bad news, I'm afraid."

"What is it?"

"Bruce Messane is dead. Murdered."

"Son of a bitch!" he shouted, slamming down his glass and sending a wash of vintage Pol Roger across his side table. "This deal is as dead as he is. Goddammit."

Montserrat wasn't surprised by his callous reaction. Someone had dared interfere with his fun and games by having the nerve to get killed.

"But there may be a positive spin to this, sir," Chen said nervously.

He glowered at him. "I don't see how."

"*This* particular deal is dead, but we could make a second offer and negotiate for a much better price. It's essentially a distressed asset now, and the board was quite eager for this to come to fruition. Messane was the holdout for the hundred million. His heir or heirs might not be so acquisitive. With no emotional investment in the company, any price would seem like pennies from heaven, and I doubt you'd encounter resistance from the remaining principals."

Wilder gnawed on his bloated lip, and Montserrat imagined cosmetic filler bursting from the wound his teeth would open if he continued to self-cannibalize.

"That's an interesting thought, Mr. Chen. I admire your vision. What do you think, Ms. De Leon?"

She shook her head. "I strongly advise against it. There is the possibility of some very negative press if you were to pursue this route. It's exactly the kind of thing the media would turn into a scandal because they need scandals to stay alive. All the better if the villain is a big, evil corporation. They would call you a vulture. They might even go as far as to call you a murderer."

"Murderer?!" he thundered. "A human life for a better deal?"

"I believe they would love to imply that in a way that wouldn't qualify as libel. The harm to the company image could be quite significant."

Wilder's face reddened with simmering fury as he stroked his fat chin. "Yes, the craven bastards would probably do exactly that. The business rags have been gunning for me for years. As tempting as the prospect is, Wilder Foods can't be embroiled in this unpleasantness. There are plenty of other companies out there to buy." He drained the scant remainder in his flute and threw it on the plush blue carpet. "Fuck the champagne, Katya, bring me scotch now!"

Chapter Twenty-Three

BACK IN THE SEDAN, CRAWFORD DANGLED a baggie full of cookies. "Corinne's specialty. Dark chocolate and macadamia, want one?"

"Hell, yes, I want at least one." Nolan hadn't eaten anything since the dreadful lemon yogurt, and she needed the sugar rush.

Crawford chewed thoughtfully, crumbs raining down the front of his windbreaker. "What's your take on Bechtold?"

"He didn't kill Messane, and he didn't kidnap his wife. But two violent acts against the founders of Peppy Pets? It's way too coincidental for my blood."

"I'm with Bechtold—his wife was kidnapped for money. Messane got offed by a lover or the lover's husband. Two solid motives for two separate crimes."

She let the dark chocolate chips melt on her tongue, wishing she had a cold glass of milk to complete the childhood, after-school vibe. "The timing stinks."

"Nothing to connect them. Unless you have a theory that links the two."

"Not yet."

He leaned back in the passenger seat and laced his fingers over his stomach. "Okay, how about this: disgruntled former employee has a beef from back when they were both running the show. The guy finally snaps, maybe because he hears about the big deal he missed out on. He sees just remuneration in dusting Messane and taking Bechtold's wife for ransom."

"Disgruntled employees are impulsive rage killers. They don't think, they don't plan, they just snap and barge into the workplace with their guns blazing. And they're certainly not capable of organizing a kidnapping."

"The homicide belongs to us, the kidnapping belongs to RSS, so let's not waste brain cells trying to connect them. If there is a link, they'll find it."

She pressed her temples, trying to still her kaleidoscopic thoughts. "Doesn't it bother you? The timing, the coincidence?"

"No. I'm a man, I have a one-track mind."

"It's driving me nuts."

He sighed. "Corinne and I were having a disagreement about a year ago, and she told me about a study," he said in a somber voice that presaged he would be revealing a profound truth. "There's this bridge that connects the two sides of the brain, and they discovered women have a big bridge so they can worry about a million things at once. Men have a tiny one."

"That explains a lot," she gibed. "What were you fighting about?"

"It wasn't a fight, exactly, I just wouldn't listen to her suggestions when I was trying to put together an IKEA cabinet without reading the instructions. In retrospect, I should have."

"It didn't turn out well?"

"I thought it was normal that there were a few leftover screws, like extras, right? Wrong. The fucking thing collapsed in the middle of the night and broke her great-grandmother's Lladró collection. Believe me, I paid for that."

"I sense a parable coming."

"The parable is focus on Messane. All signs point to an affair gone bad. The missing box in the wine cellar fits."

"How?"

"They were looking for evidence of the relationship to keep themselves off the suspect list. With Messane's pathology, he probably kept a stash of compromising photos and videos, and where better to hide it than a wine cellar tucked underneath the stairs?"

"I'd be looking for a computer. That's the first place I'd assume had incriminating photos or video, and if they found a box in a wine cellar, they sure as hell could have found that computer."

Crawford challenged her with a triumphant grin. "You think that's checkmate, don't you? But here's your checkmate: they never made it upstairs because Cynthia Jackson surprised them and they bolted. Game, set, and match."

"That's tennis, not chess."

"Whatever."

"Is that study real?"

"I don't know. Ask Corinne."

Chapter Twenty-Four

THEY SPENT THE REST OF THE drive to the Glass House in companionable silence, digesting and regurgitating facts in the privacy of their own minds. Nolan was surprised to find that Al's reasoning had been somewhat grounding. Her thoughts were no longer careening wildly between multiple points of conjecture. Of course, she would never admit this to him.

As she pulled into the parking ramp, her phone blatted Ike's ringtone. "We just got here," she answered.

"I hope you're bringing a personal computer, because Messane's office rig is all boring corporate gobbledygook."

"We are. You didn't find anything at all?"

"No juicy emails, no juicy Google searches, all work, no play. He was a serious businessman, and good one, too. Peppy Pets was in financial trouble a couple years back, and now profits are up forty-two percent."

"That's a fast turnaround."

"The time frame pricked up my ears, too, but everything looked clean and tight to me, and there are so many lawyers involved in this deal with Wilder, no way Messane was involved with any backdoor monkey business that got him killed. He eliminated a few divisions that were bleeding money, cut costs on packaging, and switched to a cheaper manufacturer. Basic austerity stuff."

"Any word on his phone?"

"Sorry. It's either dead or destroyed."

Crawford grunted. "Par for the course on this case. See you in a few."

"I'll score for you, don't worry your pretty little head, Al."

"Love you, too." He hung up. "Ike has another computer to work with, and we have a shitload of phone records to go through. There's gotta be a silver bullet in there somewhere."

* * *

Nolan hated phone records. Especially the records of people who made and received fifty or more calls and texts a day. She'd been at it for the better part of an hour, and all the rows of numbers were starting to look like a magnified petri dish of amoeba. One thing was clear: for a sex addict, Bruce Messane didn't seem to have much of a social life. Most of his phone activity was to and from colleagues, starting early in the morning and persisting into the evening. The rest were either mundane, day-to-day calls anyone would make, or burner calls. She chalked those up to lovers. And it made sense that if his lovers used burners, he would, too.

Crawford leaned back in his chair and rubbed his eyes. "Where are you at, Mags?"

"I'm back two months. You?"

"Finishing month three. I'll take four, you take five."

Nolan refocused on the blur in front of her, looking for anomalies, a pattern, numbers she hadn't seen before. Perseverance was the most vital skill in this job of seemingly interminable slogs.

She was eventually rewarded. Her discovery wasn't particularly illuminating, but it was a new addition to the growing mosaic; a scrap of cloth for the unattractive collage. "Al, I just found several calls to Nicole Bechtold five months ago. Nothing after that."

Crawford flicked off his reading glasses. "Long calls or short calls?"

"All short."

"Either he was harassing her, or she wasn't done with him and they were setting up meets."

"The burner calls pick up around the same time frame they stopped communicating. Maybe some of them were from her. Separating is pretty much a precursor to divorce, and in a lot of cases, it's because there's someone else in the wings."

"Why would she use that kind of spy craft to conceal an affair from a guy she's not living with and is probably going to divorce anyhow?"

"They're not divorced yet. Things could get bad for her if Rome found out. If they had a prenup, that might be a condition of the payout."

"So you think Nicole Bechtold is paranoid and conniving. And how is this relevant?"

She sighed. "I suppose it's not."

He screwed his fists into his eye sockets. "I'm going blind. And those cookies made me realize I'm starving."

Nolan's stomach responded in kind with an impolite growl. No one could live on cookies alone, no matter how good they were. "Take a break, take a walk before it rains again, and pick up some Chinese at Jade Gardens while you're at it. I'll take number forty-six."

Twenty minutes later, Crawford returned with a fragrant, grease-stained bag. "They're processing Ty Mattison now at County Central. Found him holding four shiny BMW wheels. Eat up, we've got places to go and felons to see."

Chapter Twenty-Five

TY MATTISON WAS SLOUCHED IN A metal chair in an interview room, glowering down at his cuffed hands. Nolan was always amazed by the sullen indignance of criminals, like they were ordinary citizens who'd just gotten a bogus speeding ticket. He was a handsome kid with striking amber eyes, and looked younger than his twenty-three years; not as brittle as the typical gangster who'd done prison time. She wondered if he'd ever had dreams of becoming something else before the streets chewed him up.

"I already talked to a detective," he mumbled churlishly. "I ain't got nothing more to say."

"I really think you want to talk to us, Mr. Mattison. We're homicide detectives, and your fingerprints were all over a BMW with a dead man behind the wheel. It doesn't look good for you."

He lurched back in alarm. "I didn't merk him! I want a lawyer."

"Evidence is evidence, and you're our only suspect. And with your record and this parole violation, I don't think a lawyer's going to do you much good."

"But you could always take your chances," Crawford commented blithely. "Or you could convince us you're telling the truth. Otherwise plan on an extra ten to fifteen on your sentence."

"This is profiling!"

"You can't profile fingerprints. Tell us what happened."

He just stared at the wall, his mouth set in a stubborn slash.

"Okay, then, let me tell you how we see it. How a judge will see it. How a jury will see it. A multiple felon was trolling for a mark and found a great one. You approach him, he doesn't cooperate, so you shoot him and rob him. Classic carjacking."

"That's not how it went down, man! I just took the wheels, he was dead, he wasn't gonna be needing them."

"He was already dead when you got there?"

Nolan caught his eyes before they flicked away furtively.

"Uh-huh."

He was a horseshit liar. "We don't care about the wheels, all we care about is solving our homicide. If you really didn't kill him, then start talking. And if you're protecting someone, they won't return the favor, so do yourself one."

He shook his head dispiritedly. "You're not gonna believe the truth, no way you're gonna believe it."

"Try us. Nothing to lose."

"Okay, okay. I'm in my cousin's van, he ain't got nothing to do with this, he didn't know I took it. Just riding, you know? A little freedom, didn't have any for a long time."

"Yeah, right," Crawford grumbled. "Stop with the bullshit, you're not very good at it. We know you weren't looking for freedom. What I don't get is why you jumped the fence into rival territory. Death wish?"

He scowled. "Hell, no, I was just looking for opportunities. I got no money and mouths to feed. I do a job outside my turf, nobody's gonna come looking for me."

"Unless you leave your fingerprints all over the scene of the crime. Maybe you should watch more cop shows." He rolled his hand impatiently. "Start when you saw the car. What time was this?"

"Maybe one thirty, I don't know, man, I don't wear a watch."

"Paint us a pretty picture of what happened next."

"Fuck, man, look, I come across this parked Beemer, engine running, somebody behind the wheel. A ride like that, it's gotta be some boss Culver City Boy and I ain't messin' with that. If they notice me, I'm dead, understand? So I pull over, cut the lights, lay low. It's dark, it's pissing rain, I can't see shit, but whoever was in the car wasn't dead, they're looking around like they're expecting someone. Then a few minutes later a truck pulls up next to him and blocks my view."

"What kind?"

"Big, black Escalade. Dark windows. I figure they're gonna do their business and I can finally glide. Then a flash-bang and the Escalade peels away."

"I don't suppose you got a plate number."

Mattison found that amusing. "Shit, no, last thing on my mind, I was just trying to stay alive."

"Anything distinguishing about it?" Nolan asked. "Bells and whistles that could help us ID it?"

"Nothing special that I noticed."

"Did anybody get out of the vehicle?"

"Naw, it was a drive-by, it happened in a heartbeat. And I'm sitting there frozen like a fucking Popsicle. Didn't move for a long time. Felt like it, anyhow."

Nolan glanced at Al. The story seemed too detailed to be a spontaneous fabrication, and Ty Mattison was no genius raconteur, but you couldn't jump to conclusions. "Then you took the wheels."

"I was *thinking* about it, then she showed up. Like a fucking ghost, walking toward the car. Pauses, walks up to the window, and next thing, she starts laughing. Sick shit. Then she opens the door, cleans him out, and strolls away like she's out walking the dog."

"What did she look like?"

"Told you, I couldn't see shit. She was white, that's all I know."

"Clothing?"

He tipped his head, considering. "She was wearing a long black coat and tall boots. A watch cap, like. She wasn't street, though, I know that much. Didn't walk the walk."

"Meaning?"

"She was class. Don't know what the fuck she was doing there, or why she fleeced a dead guy, but she was enjoying herself."

Chapter Twenty-Six

NOLAN WAS ON HOLD WITH ROSS as she and Crawford left the jail and walked out into a much more favorable climate. It was still crisp, but the wind had stilled and the sun was close to full-beam now, glancing cheerfully off the shiny leaves of a plane tree. The only indication of the earlier deluge were palms weeping rainwater, spotting the sidewalk in Rorschach patterns. No need for an ark anymore. The meteorologists would shift their focus to the impending apocalypse in Big Bear.

"Hi, Maggie."

"Ross, we have a witness who saw Messane being robbed by a woman after he was dead. Did you find any prints on the door handle?"

"Just Messane's."

"You're sure?"

"Of course, I'm sure. It was cold last night, she was probably wearing gloves."

"Damn it."

"We're still working on the trace inside the car and the prints they pulled from his house, but nothing promising, sorry to say. Weil pulled the bullet from Messane's skull—a twenty-two—and I ran it through ballistics, but no match on any registry. I'll let you know if anything good pops on the rest."

"Thanks. Chat soon." She looked at Al. "Dead end."

"That interview with Mattison was bizarre as hell, Mags. A drive-by and a 'class' woman walking around the 'hood in the middle of the night, laughing at a dead man and stealing his stuff. No way Mattison spun that yarn on the spot."

"She wasn't the shooter. And the shooter knew Messane would be there, so that phone call was a setup."

"Well, we can't trace an untraceable call, and we can't put out a BOLO on a woman in black or a car with no plate number, so this isn't going to get us anywhere."

"It's Gonzales's beat, his neighborhood. Poppy's, too. If anybody's seen the car or the woman, it would be them. Poppy wasn't being forthright, and I don't blame him."

"It's worth a shot." He excavated his phone and Gonzales's card from his windbreaker, then scrolled through his messages. "Fantastic. Weil called."

"Put it on speaker."

Amazingly, the overextended coroner answered. It was rarer than snow in San Diego, because he always had his hands in somebody's body. "Hey, Doc, what do you know? Maggie's on with me."

"Good afternoon to you both."

Nolan heard the rustling of papers, the officious clearing of his throat, then he got straight to the point like he always did. There wasn't a trace of his previously garrulous self.

"I retrieved a single bullet from Mr. Messane's brain."

"Ross told us. A twenty-two."

"Correct. I estimate time of death to be between one and three in the morning, but do remember, it was quite cold, so decomposition would have been slightly retarded. The initial toxicology is clean, and the condition of his organs is consistent with a man his age. No indication that he abused substances. And no signs of sexual activity before his death. In fact, there was nothing unusual at all, except for the scarring. I've never seen anything like it."

"What kind of scarring?" Nolan asked.

"An extensive network of vertical and horizontal hypertrophic scars on his back. Hypertrophic scars don't extend beyond the boundary of the original wound, and these are quite significant, so the wounds were, too."

"Can you tell what from?"

"These weren't precise wounds, as you might see from a blade. He was beaten with something that tore and slashed the skin deeply. According to his medical records, he never sought treatment, which is outrageous. Without medical intervention, it's a miracle he didn't die from the injuries. Shock, blood loss, and infection would have been the primary dangers."

Nolan braced herself against the trunk of a palm, trying to make sense of massive scarring on the back of a business executive. "Do you know how old the scars are?"

Weil sighed heavily into the phone. "Hypertrophic scars thicken up to six months before gradually improving, and these were still quite pronounced, so I would say within that time frame. But it's difficult to say for certain."

"Can you tell if there was earlier scarring?"

"No indication."

"So, this was a one-off incident."

"It appears to be, yes. I've seen horrendous photos of the backs of whipped slaves, and this looks very much like that."

Nolan had seen those photos, too, and they'd made her physically ill with fury. Her job sometimes did the same, but there was still goodness hiding in corners of the world like shy dust bunnies, so she focused on that to stay sane. "Thank you, Doctor, we appreciate you getting to him so quickly."

"You're welcome. Good luck, Detectives."

Crawford hung up. "Why wouldn't Messane report his beating or get medical attention? That's damn strange."

"He didn't want anybody to know about it."

"He could have been a masochist. Somebody went too far."

"His injuries were life threatening and that's not part of the game. Whoever beat him that violently would have no qualms about killing him, but I don't see a woman behind it."

Crawford sucked his cheeks, something he always did when his mind was in overdrive. "Which tips the scale in the direction of an angry husband. But why beat him, then kill him six months later? He could have gotten the job done the first time without all the blood."

Nolan pushed away from the palm tree. "Different perpetrators. Messane could have pissed off a lot of people. But why would he protect whoever beat him?"

"They must have had something on him. Guy like him probably has a lot of dark, embarrassing secrets."

Chapter Twenty-Seven

SAM WAS AMAZED BY THE COMPLEXITY of a kidnapping response—it had to be one of the most intricate of all police procedures. The amount of personnel involved was staggering—the house was like a beehive, every individual focused on a specific task; the sum of their individual efforts coalescing seamlessly to serve a common purpose. But it was a lot of activity, a lot of high tension, and after the debriefing, Rome was exhausted and overwhelmed. Sam had taken him to the sunroom off the kitchen for some privacy and a break from the turmoil.

While he picked listlessly at a chicken salad, feeding most of it to his dog, Sam stepped away and listened to his voicemail: Melody checking in before band practice to see if everything was okay; four messages from Vivian, increasingly anxious and cross that he hadn't called her back yet; and one from Captain Margolis, which he listened to twice. There was a joint op with Narc and DEA tonight in Anaheim, if he'd like to observe.

He had a lot to look forward to these days, but this stirred a very different type of anticipation, primal and energizing. It was time for this; time to advance his life, as incremental as the steps may be.

Rome was looking at him curiously. "Good news?"

"I think so. About a possible job. How are you holding up?"

"Trying my best. I'm not sure where I'd be right now if you hadn't come over. Thank you for staying . . . for your kindness . . . for everything, Sam, but you should go. I've taken up half of your day."

"I'm glad I could help. This is all going to work out, Rome. Believe it."

His dull eyes sparked with emotion. "I remember when I first met you, Sam. You were seven, and you brought me a bird that had stunned itself on our living room window. You asked if I could fix it, because your parents told you my job was to help animals. Do you remember?"

Sam's memory rolled back to that day at a big house with strange people he knew his parents liked a lot. He'd been exploring the yard, looking for pirate's booty when he'd found the bird. Its eyes were glazed, the beak opening and closing pathetically. "I haven't thought about that in years, but I remember it vividly. You sat with me until the bird recovered and flew away. I thought you were magic."

"You were a special boy, Sam, caring about every living thing. And you haven't changed. You did something for me today that I can never repay."

The maudlin reverie made him uncomfortable, considering he'd killed a lot of people in Afghanistan. But he understood where Rome was at, because he'd been there many times himself. Memories could be horrible things, or very safe and happy things that could lift you out of hell. Everyone had moments in their lives where they sought succor by traveling back to a better place. "You don't owe me anything."

"Will you tell Vivian for me?"

"Of course. She's worried, and I know she'd drop everything to do whatever she can to help." Even dinner with the Carlisles, just back from Aruba.

The sunroom door opened and Detective Maya Lucerno walked in. She was short and comfortably built, with compassionate brown eyes and a calming, gentle manner. Somebody you could talk to, somebody you could trust. With all the head-shrinking Sam had received over the past two years, he was certain she had a background in psychology.

"I'm glad to see you eating, Mr. Bechtold."

He tried for a smile. "It tastes like sawdust, but Addison seems to like it."

"Is there something else I can get you?"

"My wife, but I know you're working very hard on that, and I'm grateful. Did any of the neighbors see anything?"

She shook her head. "No, I'm sorry. But know this investigation is our number one priority, so please stay positive, it's important that you do. Mr. Easton, a quick word?"

Sam followed her out French doors to the pool deck where camellias were in full bloom. Lucerno still projected warmth, but she was a cop now, not a psychologist. "The decision's been made to set up the field command post in Mr. Bechtold's rental home and let the investigators continue working here."

"And you wait for contact."

"Everything that follows hinges on the next call. Presumably the ransom demand and further instructions for the exchange. But things can turn on a dime, and no two kidnappings are the same except that they're all unpredictable. I assure you we're ready for whatever action the situation requires."

Sam wondered how you could prepare for something so volatile and unknowable. At least in war, you could anticipate the enemy's next move from all the operational intelligence gathered before a campaign. But RSS didn't know the enemy. And they didn't know where the battle would take place. They were all holding their breath. "You have his trust, so I'm going to take myself out of the equation and let you do your work. He's in good hands, and he knows it."

"Thank you. And you're correct, the fewer distractions, the better."

Rome stepped out with Addison in his arms, a leash in his hand. "I have to take him for a walk. Poor old boy is upset by all the commotion, he doesn't know what's happening. Just like his owner."

"Go ahead, Mr. Bechtold, but just around the block, we're going to relocate to your home soon. You know what to say if you get a call. Keep them on the line as long as possible. We'll be monitoring everything from here and headquarters, and hopefully, we can trace it."

"I'll stay close."

"Should I go with him?" Sam asked after he'd left.

"No. Routine is important, any semblance of normalcy is important. He won't have much of that for a while."

Chapter Twenty-Eight

WHEN ADDY STOPPED AT HIS FAVORITE urinal—a pruned rosemary hedge a block away, Rome sagged to the curb. His legs couldn't hold his weight anymore. His mind couldn't hold his fear anymore. And no matter what the detectives thought, this had nothing to do with Bruce.

He gazed across the street at a house that used to be a glorious Spanish revival built in the 1920s, once owned by a legendary actress of the Golden Age of Hollywood. When she'd died, the new owners had razed the architectural treasure and rebuilt a contemporary monstrosity. It was a giant boil on the face of the neighborhood. People didn't respect history anymore. They didn't respect each other anymore, either, and he and Nicole were suffering the consequences of a society in devolution.

After completing his ablutions, Addy climbed onto his master's lap with concern and empathy—a trait all great furry friends shared—and licked his face. With the single lash of his velvety pink tongue, Rome's miserable upside-down, inside-out world righted itself just a little. He stopped feeling sorry for himself, and felt renewed vitality for the fight ahead. "We'll get Mama back."

The dog rumbled a whine, then yipped once enthusiastically.

"That's right, boy, let's go." He struggled to his feet and felt the sharp, damnable pain in his right knee again, reminding him he'd been doing too much too soon in an attempt to win his wife back. And now she was gone, and he might never see her again. He gritted his teeth and started limping toward home, trying not to think of bad outcomes. Detective Lucerno had been adamant about keeping a positive attitude.

Halfway to the house, a Mercedes sedan slowed beside them, then stopped. An attractive young woman with long platinum hair and big sunglasses lowered the passenger's window. "Are you alright, sir?"

"Nice of you to stop, but it's just a bum knee."

"Do you need a lift somewhere?"

"Thank you, but I'm just around the block."

She leaned across the seat and looked down at Addison. "What a charming dog. An old gent, but good bloodlines, I can tell. I have a corgi, too, descended from Dipper."

Rome smiled genuinely for the first time in what seemed like years. "Addy is a Jasmine descendant."

She smiled and it was as bright as the sunniest Southern California day. "We both have royal dogs, isn't that something! Are you sure you and Addy don't want a ride? It looks like both of you could use a break."

Rome vacillated. This nice, concerned, pretty woman almost gave him hope for the human race. "It's no trouble?"

"A block out of my way? I think I'll survive the two-minute inconvenience. Hop in."

He smiled gratefully and trundled into the car with Addy and snugged him on his lap. "Thank you very much. I'm just up on Mesa."

Rome felt a stone serpent coiling in his stomach when she accelerated in the opposite direction. Which was ridiculous, she probably didn't know Santa Monica, she looked more Beverly Hills. There were plenty of 90210 residents that wouldn't deign to leave the city limits. But fear and paranoia were the only two emotions he could access right now. When this was all over, how long would it take to banish them? Would he ever? "Mesa is the other way."

She tapped the steering wheel irritably. "You really shouldn't have called the police, it's been quite an inconvenience."

The trepidation turned into shocky, full-blown panic. His heart was pounding dangerously, and he wondered if now was the time it would give out once and for all. He was so desperate, so distracted, so *stupid,* he'd gotten into a car with a kidnapper.

Sweat erupted on his forehead when she pulled over and stopped; his bladder almost released when she aimed a small handgun at his chest. "I'm sure I won't need to use this because you want to see your wife again."

Until now, Rome had never known true terror, and it was suffocating. Paralyzing. His mouth moved soundlessly around a jumble of unformed questions he knew wouldn't be answered, even if he'd been able to ask them. His head bobbed up and down in a frantic nod. Addy squirmed in his lap and started to whine.

"Give me your phone. Thank you."

Rome watched his lifeline soar into the yard of a bungalow with a white picket fence. "How . . . how much . . . money do you want?" he finally stuttered.

Her laughter was like the whine of a dentist's drill. "That's the fun part about all of this! We don't want money."

Fun? This woman was deranged. "Then what do you want?"

"We'll talk about that later."

"You're going to kill us both, aren't you?"

"Oh, don't worry, that's not the plan at all. It's much better if we keep you both alive. Unless you don't cooperate, then you should worry."

"I'll cooperate!"

"Your wife is the insurance policy that you do, and of course, to drive home the point that we can destroy your lives whenever we want to if you don't keep your mouths shut. We'll find you wherever you are, and you'll never see us coming."

"I already told you people I'd give you anything you want." Rome was shaking so hard, his teeth were chattering. This couldn't be his life, it was too surreal. Too horrific. *Never get in a car with a stranger, especially if they have a gun. Fight, even if you get shot. Chances are better you survive a bullet than an abduction . . .*

But he couldn't fight, because if he did, Nicole would die, whatever happened to him. He knew that with all his weakened, damaged heart.

Addy's distress was escalating, because he knew this was a bad woman, too. He was helpless to do anything but comfort his dog, and by extension, himself, so he leaned over and murmured into his fur. Then he felt a sharp prick in his neck.

"Can't have you see where we're going, now, can we? Have a nice nap, I'm sure you could use the sleep. Stress is exhausting," she said breezily.

Chapter Twenty-Nine

MIKE GONZALES WALKED TOWARD POPPY'S, THINKING about the old man's recollections of the neighborhood, back when kids played baseball late into the night without fear. The gangs had already planted deep roots here before he'd been born, so it was impossible to imagine. As if to remind him of the precipitous decline, a jacked-up Chevy crawled by, woofers thudding beneath the melodious tenor voice of a corrido singer. Most of the ballads these days romanticized gang life. It made him sick.

He found him in the back, sanding a lime-green Barracuda that had seen better days. "Is that a 1970?"

Poppy smiled and flipped up his safety glasses. "It's a 'seventy-one, I found it in a barn in Fallbrook. It's not much to look at now, but it will be a beauty when I'm finished with it."

"I'm sure."

His demeanor turned somber. "No more trouble, I hope."

"Just a couple more questions if you don't mind."

His doleful brown eyes coursed the shop nervously. "I don't have any answers, Miguel."

Poppy was more jittery than he had been earlier, which made Gonzales jittery, too. He'd probably been visited by someone who wanted to know what he'd told the cops. Straight-up intimidation. That infuriated him even more than the corridos that glorified killers. "I still have to ask. It's my job, and I'm trying to help the detectives."

He nodded reluctantly. "Come to the office."

Gonzales followed him, eyes on the move, hand hovering near his sidearm. It still felt like an awkward appendage sometimes, even after three years on the job, but now the weight was supremely reassuring.

Poppy pulled two Cokes out of a cooler by his desk and sank into his creaky old chair. "Maria won't let me keep this in the house, she says it rots your guts."

"She might be right, but your secret is safe with me."

He took a long pull, then gestured to a framed dollar bill on the wall. "My first sale was a Coke, to a little boy. His name was Miguel, too. I used to keep sodas in a big chest cooler out front, I sold them for a quarter. A little extra money when I was just getting started." He chuckled at the memory. "He came whenever he had spare change, and sat right where you're sitting and asked me about cars. He never ran out of questions. I hired him to sweep out the garage when he was eleven. I told him he'd have a permanent place here when he got older. Good, smart boy. Hard worker."

"Is he still around?"

"He was killed by a stray bullet two months after I hired him. That was the beginning of the end here."

"I'm sorry."

"I am, too. I still pray for him. Ask your questions, Miguel."

Gonzales took a sip of his Coke, but the story of his namesake made it bitter on his tongue. "You notice cars. The detectives have a witness who saw the man in the BMW shot by someone in a black Escalade."

"Escalades aren't so popular around here."

"Have you seen one recently?"

"No."

The air was stagnant, laden with fumes and tension. "I know you're getting squeezed, Poppy. But if the detectives can solve this, that's one more killer off your streets. Our streets."

"I haven't seen an Escalade around." He patted his heart. "My word. But I will keep an eye out."

"You notice people, too."

"I have to notice everything around me."

"The witness also saw a woman at the scene shortly after the shooting. Classy, not street, he said. Somebody that would stand out here."

Poppy's face stilled. "Not a buchona?"

"Not a buchona. Why? Have you seen her?"

"No. But there is a new corrido. It talks about a woman like that. A brave, beautiful heroine who destroys all her enemies without mercy. The angel of death." He spat on the floor like he was expelling poison.

"You meant that literally earlier?"

"It's just a song, Miguel."

Gonzales thought about the tradition of the corrido. All across the globe, since the dawn of human history, bards and minstrels offered narrative in poetry and song that discussed current events, populated with warped, glamorized versions of real people. It was an ancient form of social media, all but obliterated by modernization long ago, yet it endured in Hispanic culture. He didn't doubt some version of this angel of death was real, but a song wasn't going to help the detectives.

"Tell me how I can help you, Poppy."

He straightened in his chair and gestured expansively around his tiny kingdom, pride giving steel to his spine. "I've decided to help myself. This place has been my whole life, but there is a time to stand your ground, and a time to surrender. Family is what matters, so I'm selling the shop. Maria and I are moving to Albuquerque to be close to the children and grandchildren. Life is short, and around here, it can be shorter."

Another supporting timber of the neighborhood felled, further clearing the path for chaos. Depression settled heavily on his chest like the lead apron they put on you for X-rays. "I'm sad for you, but happy for you, too. Good luck, Poppy."

"Thank you, Miguel. Be safe."

Gonzales hit the floor when a salvo of gunshots tore the air around him. The front window imploded and a jagged shard of glass impaled his left cheek. The pain was white-hot, and he felt blood dripping down his neck. His sidearm was no longer a comfort, because it was useless against the stealth attack of a drive-by. But at least he was still alive. He called it in on his shoulder unit as he crawled across the treacherous, sparkling minefield toward Poppy.

The old man hadn't been so lucky—blood was gushing from his leg. Bright red arterial blood. He wouldn't ever transform the Barracuda into a beauty. He wouldn't be going to Albuquerque. He wouldn't be going anywhere except the morgue, and hopefully heaven. But these days, he had his doubts about God and heaven. The only thing he knew for sure was that hell was real, and it was right here on earth.

He held him in his arms, and stanched the wound with his jacket, knowing it was futile. "It's going to be okay, Poppy, just stay still."

His eyes rolled up to meet his, but the life in them was already fading. "Maria . . ."

"Stay strong for her, my friend, help is on the way."

Gonzales felt tears stinging the gash on his face as the light in Poppy's eyes finally went out.

Chapter Thirty

REMY WAS LOITERING NEAR HER DESK when Nolan entered the Homicide pen. She had an amplified awareness of the glances cast their way, but they were indifferent, and none of them lingered. How arrogant to think anybody cared what she and Remy did outside the office. And even if they knew, they wouldn't rat them out; they were both well-liked and respected. She had to get a grip on her paranoia.

"Fancy meeting you here, Detective Nolan. I was just passing through."

"Uh-huh. I know a stalker when I see one."

He gestured helplessly. "You caught me red-handed. Ike told me a little about your case. Intriguing."

She sagged into her chair and jiggled her mouse to wake up her computer. "It's getting more bizarre by the minute. We went to interview Messane's ex-partner and his wife was kidnapped this morning."

"I heard about the kidnapping. Does somebody have it out for Peppy Pets?"

"It crossed our mind, but we can't connect the kidnapping and the murder."

"But nobody likes a coincidence."

Nolan shrugged distractedly, her mind right back to flailing around a disorganized flow chart of possibilities. "I like it less than Al."

"Is the ex-partner a suspect?"

"For a drive-by in the 'hood? Hardly. He's about as meek and mild as a person can get. Sam Easton confirmed that."

A deep frown creased his forehead. "What does Sam have to do with it?"

"When we arrived at Bechtold's house to interview him, Sam was there, talking him off a cliff. He's an old family friend."

"That *is* bizarre."

"It's also a genuine coincidence."

"They do exist."

"Any luck tracking down the rainbows on your end?"

Remy smiled snidely. "According to my CI, they're being distributed by the angel of death. . . . Why the funny look?"

"We have a witness who said the angel of death is here, too. Figuratively, at least."

"Justin passed along the disturbing news that a new incarnation of Los Zetas is back. They certainly qualify."

"Be careful, Remy."

He raised a brow curiously. "What happened to Detective Beaudreau and absolute propriety?"

Nolan felt a hot flush creeping up her neck. "It recently occurred to me that I'm being a little neurotic, but I'm over it."

"I'm glad to hear that. Want to make out now and end all the speculation?"

Her laughter came fast and unexpectedly. "You are a rogue."

"I suppose I am. I was just on my way to Benji's Java Hut. Join me."

"I really shouldn't—"

"Oh, but you should. Fifteen minutes away from the office will clear your head and prepare you for the arduous mental tasks ahead. No work talk, just silly talk."

"You're capable of silly talk?"

"When the occasion demands it. If Benji's doesn't appeal to you, perhaps you'd prefer something stronger?"

Remy was tugging on the invisible tether between them that was gaining tensile strength every day. He knew damn well she couldn't refuse, because she didn't want to. "Let's leave drinking on the job to Ike."

Benji's was blessedly quiet, and Nolan did feel her mind relaxing as Remy delivered two coffees and a clamshell of cut fruit with the grace of a career waiter.

"Caffeine and natural sugar to fortify you for the marathon ahead, madam."

She inhaled the aroma issuing from her cardboard cup. "Smells . . . festive."

"Chocolate peppermint, our finest vintage. 'Tis the season for overwrought potables."

She repressed a giggle and sipped cautiously. "It's actually delicious." She watched him slouch into his chair with a faint smile. Anybody else would have looked slovenly in the posture, but he looked like a contented cat.

"So, what's on your list for Santa, Maggie?"

She thought about that for a moment, and a childhood memory bloomed in her mind. "A pair of fuzzy bunny slippers."

"I'm glad you're embracing the spirit of silly talk." He speared a piece of cantaloupe and held it to her mouth. "But, seriously."

The cantaloupe was sweet and juicy, and it occurred to her that everything tasted better when Remy was around. "I am serious. They were a Christmas gift from my parents, and I still think of Ernie and Bert this time of year. They were my version of a security blanket, I guess. We moved around so much, always a new school to navigate. Sometimes, they were my only friends."

His expression softened. "A *Sesame Street* aficionado, I see. What happened to Ernie and Bert?"

She coasted back to a more innocent time, before her life had become consumed by the darkest, most depraved depths of human nature. She'd felt safe back then, because there were never any monsters to worry about. "I wore them into shreds, and Daddy said it was time for a proper burial to honor fallen loved ones. They were put to rest with military honors in our backyard. One of his colleagues even came over to play 'Taps' on the bugle. Max was the honor guard." She glanced away, wondering why she'd even told that ridiculous story.

He covered her hand with his. "You're lucky to have such an extraordinary family."

The sudden sting of tears in her eyes astounded and embarrassed her. "I am. God, I feel like an idiot, getting emotional over my stupid slippers."

"You're emotional because of what the funeral meant to you. And what it still means. It was never about the slippers, and they were never stupid."

She looked upward, hoping her eyes would reabsorb the tears before they fell. "What about you? Did you have a security blanket?"

He reclaimed his hand and dispelled the weightiness of the moment. "A literal one. Pale blue, cashmere, of course."

"Of course."

"It got me through Louis's death."

A reminder that she and Remy had both lost brothers, and had more in common than not. "Did it receive a proper burial?"

"No, I still have it. It's the only thing I'm sentimental about."

The air was getting thick again and Nolan exhibited displacement behavior by sipping her coffee noisily. "I think we both violated the silly talk policy."

"Things come out when we want them to. Should I tell a joke?"

It was absurd, imagining Remy Beaudreau telling a joke, and she started laughing. "Please, no."

When they got back to the office, Crawford was clutching his phone with a red, furious face. He saw them and slammed it on his desk.

"Mags, Poppy was killed. Gonzales was talking to him, and his place got shot up. Goddammit, I feel like nuking this whole city right now."

Anger and despair vied for dominance as she glanced at Remy. "He was the witness I was telling you about. A sweet old man who built his dream and held tight even when the gangs moved in."

"Too many stories like that," he mumbled somberly.

"Is Gonzales okay, Al?"

"Yeah, just a nasty gash to the cheek and a broken heart. Before it happened, Poppy told him he didn't know the Escalade or the woman. But he said there's a new corrido about a woman they call the angel of death. The songs usually have some basis in truth, aside from the fact that the narrative is ass-backwards and the heroes are all serial killers."

"Even if Mattison saw this angel of death, she isn't our shooter. We need to find that Escalade, Al. Start on all the Culver City Caltrans footage from last night, maybe we can catch a plate number. I'll see if Ike has anything for us from Messane's personal computer."

Chapter Thirty-One

NOLAN WAS HORRIFIED TO SEE THE mug of licorice on Ike's desk empty. "You're going to slip into an irreversible sugar coma if you don't stop eating that crap by the pound. We can't live without you, so try some carrot sticks."

He looked up from his computer with a crooked smile. "Keeps me off the Jack."

"You quit drinking?"

"I quit drinking at work. At least for now." He handed her a file stuffed with paper. "I killed a ton of trees and printed out the emails I thought deserved a look from the past year. All raunchy cybersex with various partners, they'll make you blush. The rest are garden variety—correspondence with his daughter, airline and dinner reservation confirmations, stuff like that."

"Did one of his raunchy pen pals threaten his life?"

"I didn't read every one, not even half of them, but it seems like he was a popular guy. He really had it hot and heavy with somebody calling herself Mimi. Very intense for a while, then they stopped communicating back in June. She sounds batshit crazy, so maybe Messane broke it off with her and she seethed for six months before she snapped. I tried to trace her through the IP address, but it's cloaked behind a VPN. Everybody's using virtual private networks these days, it's a pain in my ass."

"This is really good, Ike, thanks."

He pushed away from his desk and rubbed his eyes. "His personal computer is infected with spyware. Somebody had eyes on him."

"That's not unusual. People are always getting duped into downloading malware files from a spoofed address. It's happened to my parents a few times."

"For sure, it's even happened to me, but I can't find anything in his email logs that tracks with a download. I think it was installed manually via flash drive, by somebody with access to his laptop."

Nolan thought about all the lovers he'd probably had, including batshit Mimi. Plenty of opportunities for a postcoital sneak to infect his computer and gain access to his life and his money. "Any indication he was swindled or had his identity stolen?"

"Not that I could tell, but looking into it, his personal finances distracted me. Big red flags there."

"You waited to tell me this?"

He waggled his brows. "I always save the best for last. Messane was on the verge of bankruptcy two years ago. Cashed out his investments, leveraged his property to stop the hemorrhaging, but his bad luck didn't last long. Out of the blue, he's got three LLCs and some offshore accounts, and the money starts flowing in like milk and honey in the promised land. He went from broke to millions in the black just like that. Beach house in Malibu, a big cigarette boat docked in Naples, Florida called *Pet Me*. Clever. Bet he scored some babes off that."

Nolan rolled her eyes. "What a sleaze."

"He was a sleaze who made a lot of unaccounted cash, and spent it just as fast. He wasn't just a sex addict, he was a money addict, and money kills. I can't tell you where it came from or how he was laundering it, but he had to be. Call the SEC and the IRS, they'll be happy to pick apart your corpse free of charge. Well, not for free, we're all paying their salaries."

Nolan felt some teeth on her mental flywheel catch. "His windfall was about the same time frame Peppy Pets was posting losses according to the CFO. Embezzling?"

"That was my thought."

She sat down and rubbed her temples against an incipient headache as the mire of this case got thicker. "But he made the company profitable again, enough that Wilder Foods was willing to pay a hundred million for it. How could he do that if he was draining it?"

"Cooked books come to mind."

* * *

When Nolan got back to the pen, she found Al scowling over Caltrans footage. "Any Escalades?"

"Not yet. And Solange called—their canvass didn't yield a damn thing. Please tell me Ike had something for us."

She tossed the folder of emails Ike had given her on his desk. "Lots of blue emails, and one chain in particular needs a closer look. Look at the top page, I pulled it out of the sewer for you."

"You're so considerate, thanks a bunch." Crawford started reading; after a minute, he looked up in disbelief. "Are you kidding me? This Mimi freak is talking about doing things to him I never even heard of and wished I hadn't. And he was into it." He slammed the cover on the folder and swatted it aside like a venomous insect.

"Those sick puppies stopped corresponding six months ago, around the time of his beating."

"Then she's a good candidate."

"Here's another kicker that doesn't have anything to do with kinky sex: it looks like Messane was embezzling from the company, and the books were cooked to make it look good for the Wilder deal. He had financial problems and then he didn't, just like that."

He flicked off his reading glasses. "Cynthia Jackson. Chief financial officer, lover, maybe co-conspirator for a piece of the action. I like it."

"I called her, she's on her way in."

"But co-conspirator or not, I think it's safe to say she wouldn't kill off her payday. And she hasn't lied to us about anything." He leaned back in his chair and regarded the crack in the ceiling that was metastasizing down the wall, a reminder of the last two tremors that had unsettled the Glass House. "My bet is on this Mimi, or her angry husband or lover. But money makes people psycho, so who knows? I have a feeling we're just scratching the surface." He gestured to the crack. "Are they ever going to patch that thing? It keeps getting bigger, like it's going to swallow us up one day."

Los Angeles had a voracious maw, and it swallowed up a lot of things and people every day. "The budget sucks this year, they're probably waiting for the next earthquake to do more damage before they fix it. Keep looking at footage while I handle Jackson."

Crawford nodded and jumped back on his computer. "On it."

Chapter Thirty-Two

MONTSERRAT POURED A GLASS OF TEMPRANILLO from her family's Iberian Peninsula vineyard, celebrating a rare afternoon off. She hadn't even felt guilty when she'd called in sick after Wilder and the wasted trip to Los Angeles. A person could only take so much.

She gazed out the window of her pied-à-terre. Snow had started to fall, dusting the streets and Central Park below her. She hated snow. It was definitely time to leave New York. Her family was dysfunctional by any standard, but missing home had become a dull ache that never ebbed.

As the wine began to unfurl her knotted shoulders, she indulged the kind of maudlin nostalgia only a light buzz could summon. Playing hide-and-seek with her little sister Magdalena among the gnarled vines; begging Armand, the winemaker, to let them steal sips from the wine thief he employed to sample the contents of the big, oak barrels; horseback rides with Papa; picking bursting, ripe tomatoes with Mama for pan con tomate. It had been an idyllic upbringing on the dry, hot slopes of Rioja Alta until Mama had been killed in a car accident. The family unwound painfully during those terrible years—Papa became violent and bitter, Magdalena reckless and defiant. As for herself, she'd withdrawn almost completely, escaping into a solitary world of books and studies to please her father.

You're the smart one, Montserrat, and the family needs a new generation of lawyers. I'll find a use for your sister, but it won't be in law. She has no brains, none at all.

That wasn't true. Magdalena had plenty of brains, she just didn't have any restraint or common sense. Things would have been different for her if Mama hadn't died so young; if Papa hadn't turned into a sullen ogre. Her greatest fear was that she would burn out like a supernova and die young, too.

Her personal phone jarred her out of the reverie, which was just as well, because her thoughts were taking a dark turn. She checked the ID—her memories had somehow conjured her sister. They didn't speak often, and the exchanges were always prickly. Sibling rivalry never fully abated, and Magdalena couldn't let go of a perfectly good grudge. "You must have heard my thoughts," she answered. "I was thinking of us playing in the vineyard and trying to badger Armand into getting us tipsy."

"You're such a sentimentalist."

"I'm thinking of moving back."

"To Rioja?" she asked incredulously. "It's so boring, you'd die there after New York."

"Madrid, actually. Uncle offered me a partnership in the firm."

"Papa would be *thrilled*. The golden daughter, finally returning home!"

She bristled at the bitterness lacing Magdalena's voice. "Why can't we have a normal conversation?"

She bleated a strange, manic laugh that made Montserrat wonder if she was using coke again. "This is a normal conversation for us. But I didn't call to fight, I called to see how work's going."

"The Wilder deal fell through." She refilled her wineglass, weary of the conversation that had barely begun.

"Well, that's just a *shame*," she said sarcastically.

"How is your charity work going? You are still working, right?" A cheap return shot. Magdalena brought out the worst in everyone.

That seemed to amuse her. Or satisfy her. "All roses. But managing people is so tiresome, I'm thinking of a change. Something less human resources and more upper-level management."

Her sister was far too scattered for more responsibility, but Montserrat kept the opinion to herself. "I thought you liked your job."

"I'm good at it, but I get bored easily. I could do so much more." She veered off topic. "Jaime and I are going to Cabo tonight for a few days on the beach. He sends his fondest regards."

One of her many ill-advised affairs. "Be careful with him. I don't trust him."

"I'm all grown up now, big sister. I can take care of myself. Thanks for the free legal help, by the way. Papa was right, it's important to have lawyers in the family. And we *are* family, no matter what."

For better or worse. "Yes, we are, and Papa's not doing well. You should think about a visit."

"It's just his kidneys, he can get new ones."

"Magdalena! He gave us everything, and you're joking about this?"

"He gave *you* everything. But that's all water under the bridge."

"Clearly, it's not."

"I really should go, big sister, I have houseguests. I'll come to New York when I'm finished with Jaime. We'll have dinner. Maybe a slumber party."

"I look forward to it."

"You were always a horrible liar."

The needling was senseless and endless and exhausting. "Why do you always have to push buttons?"

"It's good sport. I don't always like you, Monty, but I do love you. That will never change."

Montserrat sighed, wondering if her sister was capable of caring about anybody but herself. "I love you, too. I'll see you soon in New York. Dinner and a slumber party."

Chapter Thirty-Three

MAYA LUCERNO STARED DOWN AT THE discarded phone with the recently installed GPS tracker. It was a black mistake blemishing the green yard of a charming Santa Monica bungalow not far from Nicole Bechtold's house. Glinting in the sun with accusation. Bechtold was gone and there was no way they were going to find him, because this phone was their only tether to the kidnappers. Her fault.

This is all your fault, Maya, so stop crying, take your punishment, and keep your nose out of adult business. How many times do I have to tell you?

Detective Brandon Robb, a recent transfer from San Diego PD Robbery approached her, dispelling one of her many ugly childhood memories. His eyes were concealed behind mirrored sunglasses, making him look like a seventies TV cop. "Homeowners aren't here."

"Figures. It's a work day."

He regarded the phone with a baffled expression. "Why the hell would they take him? They're never going to get their money now. All his accounts are flagged, and they have to know that."

"They want something else. Maybe from us. But if they threw out the phone . . . God, I really fucked up."

"No, you didn't."

She remembered telling Sam Easton how unpredictable kidnappings were. How she'd promised they were ready for any eventuality. How she'd dismissed his offer to go with Bechtold on his walk. She was the broken cog in the wheel that had derailed everything. Stupid, stupid, stupid. "This is on me. If they both die, that's on me, too."

"Don't go there, Maya," he warned. "This isn't a third-world hot zone. Nobody could have anticipated this, so save the guilt for later, because we need to scramble. A fat man with a dog was taken in broad daylight. Somebody saw something. Maybe traffic cameras did, too."

Brandon was pragmatic and focused, which she appreciated. He was right, she had to put the mea culpa aside for now. There would be plenty of time for self-flagellation when this was all over. Right now, she had to salvage some redemption. It might not save her job, but it would save her. "Yeah."

"Are you okay?"

Her reflection in his glasses informed her that she looked as bad as she felt. No, she wasn't okay. Far from it. "I'm going to start knocking on doors."

Robb glanced at the small cluster of gathering rubberneckers. "Go. I'll get a canvass together and get this phone dusted for prints."

"Thanks, Brandon." She followed his gaze and saw a willowy brunette in expensive workout clothes standing at the end of her driveway, which was directly across the street. It was a promising place to start, and she moved swiftly to intercept her.

"I'm Detective Lucerno, LAPD Robbery Special Section, ma'am."

Her eyes widened as she fiddled anxiously with the diamond tennis bracelet on her wrist. "Were the Novaks robbed?"

"Your name?"

"Mallory Lydon. Were they robbed?" she pressed.

"No, a man was abducted near here."

Her manicured hand flew to her mouth. The diamonds flashed in the sun. "That's awful. In this neighborhood?"

A natural reaction. How could anything bad happen on the west side, where people accessorized their yoga wear with diamonds? "Have you seen a heavyset man walking a dog?"

"No, sorry."

"Anything that seemed unusual or suspicious?"

Her frozen, Botoxed brow made a gallant effort to furrow as she considered. "I was getting the mail, and saw a silver Mercedes park in front of the Novaks' house. That's not unusual, but then the driver opened her window and threw something over the roof, right into their yard, then drove away. I was furious, people are so rude. I was about to go pick up the litter, but then a police car came and I knew something was wrong."

Lucerno felt the first glimmer of hope since she'd screwed up so royally, because now she had a witness. "A woman?"

"Yes, with long, platinum blond hair."

"Did you see the license plate?"

"It took off so fast, but I'm pretty sure I saw 4D7."

"Was there a passenger?"

"I couldn't tell, the windows were smoked. Very dark."

"What type of Mercedes?"

Mallory Lydon blinked her lush, fake lashes at the barrage of questions. It wasn't the standard cocktail banter. "A sedan."

"Could you tell what model?"

"No. I'm not a car person at all."

"It was silver, you said?"

"Yes."

"I need you to talk me through this again so I can write down every detail about what you saw. There are two lives in the balance and you could help us save them both."

"Please, come inside."

Chapter Thirty-Four

WHILE CRAWFORD TOOK A CALL FROM Ross at the crime lab, Nolan ushered Cynthia Jackson into an interview room. The stress of the day had scuffed off all her careful polish, and she looked hollow-eyed and afraid. Police interview rooms did that to anyone, even the innocent, so it wasn't a good indicator of culpability.

"Thank you for coming in, Ms. Jackson. As you can imagine, we're very busy and you saved us the trip." As if she'd had a choice. But a little graciousness relaxed people. "Can I get you something to drink?"

"No, thank you. Are you making progress?"

"Some," she replied noncommittally. "I'm recording this interview, just so you know."

"I expected that. How can I help you?"

Nolan had thought carefully about what strategy to employ. She'd decided on shock and awe. Get right to the point while Jackson was vulnerable. That's when people panicked and made mistakes. "Mr. Messane's personal computer yielded quite a bit of information on his personal finances. We believe he was embezzling a lot of money from the company." The shock and awe was successful.

She gawked at her in disbelief. "That's outrageous! I'm the chief financial officer, I would have known."

A potentially damning statement, but Nolan would come back to that. "He was near insolvency two years ago, and suddenly, he's got a beach house in Malibu and a fancy boat in Florida. Shell corporations and offshore accounts with millions in them."

Jackson gaped at her. "What?"

"Did you know he was broke?"

"He mentioned having some liquidity issues, but I had no idea he was in that kind of trouble."

"Where do you think he got that money?"

"I have no idea, but he had a lot of investments."

"From what we can tell, he drained all of those to stay above water." Jackson looked genuinely stunned, and Nolan let her sit on it while she made a show of looking at the paperwork in front of her. "Perhaps you cooked the books for a cut. And to make the company look good for a sale you would profit from."

"No!" she shrieked. "I would never do that!"

"If you did, the Security and Exchange Commission will find out. Honesty might help get you some lenience."

Tears started rolling down her cheeks. "I did *not* cook the books."

Nolan almost felt sorry for the woman. *Almost.* "Peppy Pets and Mr. Messane went through a significant reversal of fortune about the same time, which coincides with him setting up LLCs and opening offshore accounts. Something you wouldn't normally do for investment income, correct?"

She lowered her eyes and shook her head.

"But it is something you would do to conceal illegal activity."

"Yes. But if Bruce was embezzling, the company wouldn't have turned around."

"That's exactly what we were puzzling over, it doesn't make sense.

Unless you consider the possibility that the company didn't actually have a stellar comeback, it just looks that way. He would need to cover the fact that he was gutting it, which takes us back to the books."

She lifted her chin, defiant through the tears. "Peppy Pets made a turnaround because Bruce was a visionary businessman. He launched three new product lines that were overnight successes. He changed manufacturers and distributors to cut costs. Slashed divisions that weren't pulling their weight."

Nolan pushed a box of tissues toward her. "You know all of this is highly suspicious. Maybe Mr. Messane had outside help and was deceiving you, too."

"Trust me, he wasn't embezzling."

"How can you be sure?"

"Bruce bragged to everyone about the house and the boat. He'd just recently told me about his financial problems, so it rang big alarm bells. It's my job to be suspicious and thorough, so I spent days going through the books. I'm a forensic accountant, I know what to look for."

And what to do, Nolan thought cynically. Time to circle back. "So, you're saying he couldn't possibly have embezzled without you knowing about it."

"That's exactly what I'm saying. And if I were lying, I wouldn't implicate myself like that. I did not cook the books, and he was not embezzling. Besides, it would be impossible for that to slip past Wilder. The scrutiny in a deal like this is as intense as any SEC investigation. But you can be damn sure I'm going to start another audit as soon as I leave here."

Nolan was inclined to believe her. Al would have his own take on the interview. "Do you know anyone connected with Mr. Messane who drives a black Escalade?"

"Bruce was almost pathologically private. I never knew anyone connected to him outside work, and none of us drive one."

"Somebody in a black Escalade killed him. We have a witness."

Jackson slumped in her chair as she felt adrenaline drain from her body like someone had pulled a plug. You only had so much of it, so your body couldn't maintain the high for long. It was as if it had been propping her up. "I'm sure you found out about Bruce's personal life during your investigation."

"We did."

"He had dark sexual proclivities, and multiple partners. When he was bored with you, you were gum on the bottom of his shoe. I knew who and what he was, and I was okay with the arrangement, but that's where I'd look."

"Did he ever mention anyone named Mimi?"

She sniffed ruefully. "No. He bragged about his conquests, I think it turned him on, but he never used names."

Nolan thought about his beating. "When did your intimate relationship end?"

"Around six or seven months ago. It was early summer."

"When you were with Mr. Messane, did he have scars on his back?"

"Scars? God, no, he was the vainest person I've ever known. He would have had skin grafts if that's what it took to get rid of a flaw." Jackson frowned. "That's an odd question."

"It's an odd case, to put it mildly. Was he into S and M?"

"Not at all. His thing was role-playing."

Nolan didn't want to hear the creepy details. "One last thing. Rome Bechtold's wife was kidnapped this morning."

Jackson's jaw sagged in disbelief. "Oh my God. Do you think it has something to do with Bruce's murder?"

"We're looking into that. Can you think of something that might tie them together? Something to do with Peppy Pets?"

She shook her head, mystified. "Rome hasn't been a part of the company for years, but you already know that. That poor man. Nicole was his world."

The interview had run its course, and Nolan stood. "Thank you for your time, Ms. Jackson. Please let me know if you think of anything that could help us. And keep us apprised of your audit."

"Absolutely." She rummaged in her handbag and held out her card. "This is my private mobile. Call me anytime if you have more questions. Bruce had his issues, but he didn't deserve what he got."

Chapter Thirty-Five

CRAWFORD LOOKED UP HOPEFULLY WHEN NOLAN got back to her desk. "Did you crack her like a nut and get a confession?"

"You can listen for yourself, but she convinced me that Messane wasn't embezzling and the books weren't cooked. She's doing another audit to make sure. What did Ross have to say?"

"He confirmed there were no signs of anyone besides Messane in the car. Most of the prints in the house were his; the ones that didn't belong to him came up donuts on the registries. All trace is inconclusive. And I finished going through the traffic footage. No Escalade. You'd think Caltrans would put up cameras in the shittiest parts of town. It would make our job a hell of a lot easier."

Nolan rummaged in her desk for a roll of Tums. Jade Gardens' number forty-six was raising hell in her GI tract. "Do you have any good news?"

"Interesting news. His computer wasn't the only thing that was bugged—the police garage found a GPS tracker on the Beemer's undercarriage. The tool of choice for jealous lovers. Cheaper than a PI and just as effective."

"Can they track it back to the owner?"

"They probably could if the serial number wasn't scratched off."

Nolan's brief flirtation with optimism ended and her language suffered for it. "Son of a bitch."

"Don't worry, it's not the end of the road. I did some thinking while you were putting the screws to Jackson. We dismissed the mystery woman because she wasn't the shooter, but she could be the scorned lover. She could even be Mimi. Whoever, she systematically stalked him, confirmed his infidelity, but didn't want to do the wet work herself."

"You're talking accomplice?"

"Yeah, Mr. Escalade. She hired him, then went to the scene to make sure it was mission accomplished. That's why she was laughing."

"Makes a lot more sense than a posh woman stumbling onto the scene in the middle of the night in one of the worst neighborhoods in LA. I like it, Al, but it still doesn't bring us any closer to a suspect."

"If I'm right, she knew his patterns and properties. She took his keys and everything else, so it stands to reason that she was the one in his house this morning. But she didn't find everything she was looking for in Holmby Hills, so she hits his beach house to cover all the bases."

Nolan raised her brows. "Good old Locard and his exchange principle."

"You got it. And the more places a person is, the more likely they are to leave something behind."

"I'll call Malibu and have them look for signs of B and E or trespassing."

"Already did."

* * *

On the drive home, Sam prioritized his mother in the queue of callbacks to preserve familial amity. They had a great relationship, but failure to respond in a prompt manner was a serious violation. There had been a time not so long ago when silence could mean tragedy. That fear would linger forever in her mind.

Vivian Easton was forged from titanium, and handled even the worst news with grace, but Nicole's kidnapping nearly rendered her speechless. How many people knew somebody who was a victim of this rare crime? If you took parent-child abductions out of the equation, he figured it was less than 1 percent of the population.

When she found her voice again, she peppered him with questions he couldn't answer, then chided him again for not calling sooner. And of course, she had a plan of action that entailed moral support in the form of food and wine. She didn't understand the kidnapping response any better than he had.

"Mom, we have to let the police do their jobs. We'll be there for Rome on the other side of this, but right now, he belongs to them. It's the only way he'll get Nicole back."

"Oh. Yes, of course. It's just so shocking, I guess I'm not thinking clearly. I shouldn't call him then?"

"No. No distractions. But it was important to him that you knew. Just hang tight, this will be over soon." One way or another, which he didn't mention.

"I'm so upset, Sam."

"I know. I am, too."

She sighed. "You'll let me know as soon as you hear anything?"

"I'm observing a SWAT operation tonight, but I promise I'll call with any news as soon as I can. And don't tell the Carlisles anything, Rome needs privacy right now."

"Oh, I'm canceling dinner. I can't listen to Arnold windbag about Aruba and his new film when two of my best friends are suffering so much."

Sam coughed to cover a chuckle. Arnold Carlisle *was* a pretentious windbag, and his mother had her priorities straight. "Everything's going to work out."

"You be careful tonight, Sam."

"I'll be safely stashed in a command vehicle, don't worry."

"I always worry about you. And I love you."

"Love you, too, Mom."

Melody was the next call, although lately, she was always first in his mind. She answered breathlessly.

"Sam, I was worried. You're not getting yourself into trouble again, are you?"

"When have I ever gotten into trouble?"

"Death Valley comes to mind."

"Nothing like that. Why are you panting?"

"I just carried my guitar and amp up three flights of stairs. The elevator is out in the practice space again. That's why we can afford it."

"Not to sound sexist, but don't any of your male bandmates have a sense of chivalry?"

"I carry my own gear. What's going on with your friend?"

Sam relayed Rome's story for the second time in five minutes. Somehow it sounded worse on the retelling. He ended on what he considered a positive note, telling her about his evening plans with Metro.

"Please be careful, Sam."

"I'll tell you what I just told Vivian: I'll be safely stashed in a command vehicle."

"Stay there."

"I will. Do you have plans on December thirteenth?"

"I have no idea, why?"

"Mom asked if you would come to her holiday party at the country club. It's going to be a nightmare, but she wants to meet you. And I want you to meet her."

"How could I resist an invitation to a holiday party nightmare?"

"Pretty easily, but I'd love it if you could come."

"I'll be there. What do you wear to a country club?"

"Leather and spikes. It's all the rage with Pasadena's idle rich."

She guffawed. "You're ridiculous."

"Will I see you tonight?"

"After practice."

There was an awkward pause in the conversation. They were closing in on the time when they would sign off with "I love you," but they weren't quite there yet. With their difficult histories, it was taking a while for the language to catch up to the feeling. "Great. I have beer and leftovers from Taco Loco."

"You're a class act, Sam Easton. I was getting so sick of foie gras." She snickered and hung up.

Beer and leftovers from a food truck? He really needed to up his game. As he let himself into the house, Maya Lucerno called. Her news affirmed his conviction that no matter how bad things were, they could always get worse.

*   *   *

Nolan ended the call from Sam and looked at her partner with a glazed expression.

"What? I've never seen you look dumbstruck before."

"Sam just heard from Maya Lucerno. Bechtold took his dog for a walk around the block, and he got abducted."

"You have *got* to be shitting me. Why the hell would they abduct the ransom-payer? It doesn't make any sense at all. In fact, it's pretty goddamned ominous, you ask me."

"RSS has never seen anything like it. Who are they playing? The cops? Bechtold?"

Crawford shook his head, baffled. "Taking him was a risky move, but I don't see an endgame. Do they have any leads?"

"A bleached blond woman was seen throwing his phone out of a silver Mercedes sedan. The windows were smoked, so the witness didn't know if there was a passenger, but they assume he was in the car. They're working off a partial plate number."

"This is getting really weird."

"Sam thought so, too, that's why he called."

Chapter Thirty-Six

ROME RESURFACED FROM HIS DRUGGED FOG; it dissipated slowly, like the scales of a disturbing dream falling away. But this nightmare wasn't going away with consciousness.

There was a searing pain in his temples. His mouth was dry and foul, and he was seeing in triplicate. But he was aware enough to know that he was lying on a leather sofa in a dimly lit room. His thoughts were scattered wisps he couldn't seem to gather, but as they gradually reformed, he remembered the woman. The evil, evil woman who'd pulled a gun on him and stabbed him in the neck with a syringe of God knew what.

"Addy?" his voice was a low croak. No click of nails on the floor, just the sound of his heart shattering as he envisioned all the horrible things that might have happened to him. What might have happened to Nicole.

He blinked away the devastating images before they incapacitated him. He needed to ground himself in the here and now and focus on his situation, his surroundings. If he ever got out of here, details would matter, so he started by assessing his prison cell.

The room, windowless and sparsely furnished, was a puzzlement. There was an empty bookshelf and a basic table with two chairs. No décor, blank white walls. A large monitor with nothing connected to it. An interior door opened onto a tiny bathroom with a stool and sink. This spartan space wasn't meant to be lived in, it was strictly utilitarian.

He pushed himself up slowly and tested rubbery legs to make sure he wouldn't topple over. He used the toilet, splashed his face, and gulped water from the faucet. His consequent exploration yielded nothing he could use as a weapon, no clues as to where he was. The exterior door—the only way out—was an industrial-looking thing made of steel, with brackets for barricade bars. He realized this was a safe room.

He pounded on the door in desperation. "Hello? Hello?" The sound of his voice and fists on the steel were muted. The room was probably clad in concrete. An upsurge of nausea swept over him, and he sank back down to the sofa, clawing at the leather as if he could scratch his way out.

Minutes later, there was an electronic beeping and the door swung open. An enormous man with a baseball cap pushed low over dark glasses tromped in on heavy boots. Rome quailed when he saw the big gun holstered on his hip, but he simply tossed a bottle of water on the sofa.

"Where is my wife? My dog? I want to see them," he ventured meekly, not what he'd intended.

The man shrugged indifferently, and shut the door behind him with a resounding thunk.

He felt numb inside and out. The terror had been too intense to sustain, and now he was impossibly exhausted; totally defeated. There was nothing he could do. There was no getting out of here, no chance of fighting people with guns. He was trapped; at their mercy. He didn't even know what they wanted, or if they would kill them both no matter what he gave them.

He laid down and tried to empty his mind to make room for

optimistic thoughts and visions, like in his meditation classes. They were going to get out of this, and he and Nicole would reconcile. If they really had grown apart, this horrific shared experience would certainly close that gap and stitch them back together.

But all the positive thoughts he marshaled were scattered by images of violence, and his heart started galloping. "God, please don't let me die in this room alone," he whispered.

* * *

In a plush, high-tech control room, an array of large screens cycled through security footage that covered every angle of the property. Twenty-four cameras in all. A few years ago, Sal's jaw would have dropped right off his face at the remarkable sight, but now he was used to it. He'd been in many rooms like this.

He was enjoying his time in the cockpit as he monitored the north and west side feeds. He felt valued. Trusted. And hopeful. One day, he might own a house with a command center; it wasn't out of reach now. Madam had hinted at that when she'd recruited him for this important job.

Slash was sitting across from him, monitoring the south and east feeds while he guzzled another giant bottle of Mountain Dew. Didn't he know that shit was poison? That your body gave back what you put into it? No, he wouldn't. He didn't have anything between his ears but air.

Things had been quiet, as he'd hoped they would be. Boring, actually, but boring was good in his line of work. And it was pleasant here, almost soothing, all things considered. But there was still that burr, lodging deeper into his brain as time passed, telling him it was a bad idea to be here.

Slash executed a lazy spin in his chair to face him, eyes shaded by his Raiders cap. "How much longer, you think?"

"Soon. We need to get out of here."

"Yeah? I never want to leave." He pushed his vast bulk out of his chair. "Cover my screens while I take a leak."

"All you do is piss Mountain Dew."

He gave Sal a crooked smile and patted the bowie knife strapped to his thigh. "You know I do more than piss."

He watched him lumber away; a man with the body of an ox, the mind of a child, the heart of a killer. A deadly moron who enjoyed his work. A sick fuck, uniquely suited to his position. Useful, but a liability because he lacked impulse control. His life span would be short.

Sal returned his attention to his feed, double-checking each view before rolling his chair over to Slash's station to check his. He froze when he pulled up camera seven. A cop car had just parked on the street in front of the house.

Chapter Thirty-Seven

OFFICER RAY CHAUNCEY WAS HAVING A bad day in Malibu so far, a plum assignment that sometimes had rot in it. First, the drunk, stoned surfer sleeping beneath the beachside overhang of somebody's deck had puked partially digested fish tacos all over him. Then there was the stray, snarling dog, scarfing up food from the outdoor tables at touristy Sunsets Café, terrifying diners. The fucking thing had bitten right through the muscle of his calf before running off to terrorize another part of the beach. He'd spent an hour in the ER getting it cleaned and stitched, and it hurt like a son of a bitch. The rabies vaccine hadn't felt much better—the nurse had slammed the needle into his arm like she was fending off an attacker.

And now this ominous request from Homicide to check for B and E at the vacant house of a dead man. What if the house wasn't vacant? That always scared him, even here in Lotus Land.

"Looks okay from the front," his patrol partner Jim Lewiston commented, trying the door. "It's locked, no signs of tampering. Let's circle around, check all the windows and doors."

As they approached the beach side of the house, Jim let out a low whistle. "Man, this is a sweet place. Hell of a thing—you make it to the top, and some asshole cuts you off."

Chauncey was starting to feel queasy with pain and anxiety. "Won't be so sweet if we find another dead body. That would really ice the shit cake of my day."

"If Homicide was looking for that, they'd be here instead of us."

His partner had a point, but Chauncey was still strung tighter than a drumhead as they made a pass around the circumference of the house, then another. His tension finally loosened its grip. Nothing unusual here, they'd checked twice, time to get out of here. As they walked to the squad, the third bad thing happened to him: he stepped in a fresh pile of dog crap.

"Goddammit!"

His partner was almost blue in the face, trying not to laugh. "Guess your buddy caught your scent and laid that trap for you. Pissed off the wrong dog, Ray. Get cleaned up, I'm going to take another walk and pretend I live here."

While his partner cursed and scraped his shoes, Lewiston walked down to the beach and gazed at the ocean. It had been stirred to a deep blue by the morning's storm. There were a handful of surfers skimming the shallow waves, a few joggers, but they were too focused on themselves to pay any attention to him. Welcome to LA.

Whenever he was anywhere near the water, he wondered if he would be living in Malibu instead of patrolling it if he'd really pursued acting; really given it all he had. He knew he had talent, but his backup plan had taken precedence when there was suddenly a baby on the way. Life was a long series of forks in the road, with no signs directing you.

An elderly man, dressed like seventies Hollywood and baked by the sun to a crispy burnt sienna, interrupted his dreams of what might have been. He toddled from his big house next door to the property line, puffing on a cigarillo. "Something wrong, Officer . . ." He squinted at his name plate. "Officer Lewis?"

Close enough. "We're just following up on a call about a possible break-in at your neighbor's house, but it looks okay. Did you see anything unusual today?"

"Hell no, it's been quiet as a crypt, just the way we like it here. And Bruce is hardly ever here, so I keep an eye out." He released a phlegmy chuckle. "The only excitement today was when his assistant stopped by this morning. She comes occasionally." His smile was lascivious, and an unnatural, blazing white. "She's a looker, that one, very sexy. Her name is Mimi."

Lewiston was no detective, but you didn't have to be to know that there was something wrong with an assistant coming to the house of her dead boss. "Your name, sir?"

"Reggie Blattner."

That surprised him. "As in the car dealerships?"

The old man nodded proudly and spoke in a cheesy radio announcer voice that anybody from LA would recognize instantly. "It's Blattner Blow-Out Days! Rock-bottom prices, every vehicle must go to make room for the new models!"

He smiled. "*You* did all those voice-overs?"

"I wasn't going to pay somebody else to do them, it would have been a waste of money. That's the key to success, save a dollar where you can."

"Good advice."

Blattner gestured to Ray. "What's wrong with your partner?"

"Stepped in some dog doo-doo."

"Ah. I did see a fat corgi doing his business there earlier. One of the neighbor's dogs got loose, I suppose."

"Are you going to be home for the rest of the day, sir? My colleagues will want to follow up with you."

He waved his cigarillo amiably. "Most definitely. It's almost happy hour, and I never drink and drive."

Chapter Thirty-Eight

NICOLE WAS NO LONGER BLINDFOLDED, GAGGED, or tied to a chair, but that was almost worse than what she'd endured before. In the movies, if the kidnappers revealed themselves to you, you were as good as dead. And she'd been allowed to see the ragged faces of the men that smelled of sweat and cigarettes.

She paced the tiny room to keep her blood circulating. She counted her steps, nineteen from wall to wall. It was empty except for the evil metal chair she'd been bound to for hours. A storage area, perhaps, or a closet. She prayed it wouldn't be her tomb.

She flinched when she heard footsteps, then the creak of the door, because maybe they were coming to kill her now. *If you close your eyes, the monster can't see you . . .*

"You've been a good sport, Mrs. Bechtold."

Nicole's eyes flew open. A woman in black stood before her with a mocking smile. Her hair was concealed beneath a cap, eyes covered with sunglasses. Her bearing was unmistakably authoritative. It was clear that she was running the show, and now she'd seen the boss. They couldn't possibly let her live now. "Please, please, I want to go home." She started weeping; weeping for her life.

"Just as soon as we relocate and take care of some business. Your husband doesn't listen very well. Does he listen to you? Wrists, please."

Nicole thought her heart might take flight straight out of her chest. "What did you do to Rome?"

She tightened the zip ties. "It's what he did to me. He's here, by the way, so you'll have a little reunion soon."

"*What?*" Her savior, now as helpless as she was.

"He called the police when he was told not to, otherwise he would still be at home, and you would be on your way. He's made things more difficult than they had to be, and I'm very angry about that." She flashed a sadistic smile. "You looked so pathetically hopeful when I mentioned the cops. Don't be. The two who were just snooping around here are gone."

"The police were here?" she whispered.

"Yes, which is why we have to leave. Another inconvenience, all because of your husband. Now, keep your mouth shut and follow orders. You're going to behave, right? I don't have to drug you again?"

Nicole shook her head, and tears splashed down her face, collecting in the hollows of her collarbones.

"Good girl."

* * *

Nolan was weaving through traffic on the way to Malibu, earning several impolite gestures from fellow drivers, and sharp sighs of anxiety from Al.

"Slow down, Mags. Mimi is long gone."

She banged her hand on the steering wheel. "She was there, and we weren't. Dammit!"

"We didn't even know about the beach house or Mimi this morning, so stop with the twenty-twenty hindsight. This is how things come together in every case, dribs and drabs, you know that. We move forward with what we have."

"I'm still pissed."

He pinched his eyes shut and braced his hand on the dashboard when Nolan executed a particularly reckless move. "Don't let your temper kill us before we can solve this case."

She eased a little on the accelerator to mollify him, but her foot was twitchy; it really wanted to punch it back to the floor. Which was stupid. Mimi *was* long gone, and if she'd left any evidence behind, it was waiting for them. Reggie Blattner was waiting for them, too. Gaining five or ten minutes wasn't going to make a difference. "Sorry."

"Get us there alive and all will be forgiven."

Chapter Thirty-Nine

WHEN CYNTHIA RETURNED TO THE OFFICE, the executive floor was swarming with panicked employees in full damage control. There were press releases to approve, an interim CEO to elect, board members who needed reassurance that Peppy Pets wasn't in a free fall. And it could very well be, especially if Bruce had been involved in some sort of chicanery she hadn't caught. Her calm, steady world of prosperity was in complete chaos. She'd bet everything on the Wilder deal, and now she was facing personal ruin.

There's a difference between wanting to die and not wanting to live, Cyndi.

The words of her tragic, chronically depressed mother had always confounded and haunted her. But those ravings of a broken mind resonated with her now as she faced an uncertain future that had been unthinkable just hours before.

As she settled at her desk, Tim stalked into her office, his second violation of her privacy today. She didn't have the energy to admonish him. She didn't have the energy to deal with any of this.

He was looking bad, like he'd just been savaged in a rugby scrum. His blond hair stuck out at odd angles, his suit looked slept in, and his face was a livid red. "Sit down before you have a heart attack, Tim."

He shut the door and sagged onto her sofa, dragging his fingers through his hair. "Did the cops find out who killed Bruce?"

"No. And now Rome's been kidnapped."

His scarlet face blanched in the space of a second. "What the fuck is going on?"

"I don't know, and I don't think they do, either. They asked me if Bruce was embezzling."

"That's outrageous!"

"That's exactly what I told them. But apparently, he came into a lot of unexplained money two years ago. Funneled through LLCs to offshore accounts. Do you know anything about that?"

"Christ, no! I mean, I hardly knew the guy, even though I've been here almost as long as you have."

"Did you ever work on Bruce's personal legals?"

"Of course not. I'm corporate, he had those wankers at Rothschild Smythe on retainer for personal matters."

"So they would have set up the LLCs?"

He shrugged. "Not if he was doing something shady. Are the cops serious about pursuing this angle?"

The question aroused her suspicion. Today she'd learned that people you thought you knew could be complete strangers guarding dark secrets. But a conspiracy between Bruce and Tim, right under her nose? It was ridiculous.

Was it?

"They're very serious. The SEC was mentioned, which is why I'm going to start tearing apart the books today. If I missed something, I have to find out what and let them know. If I screwed up and we get red-flagged . . ." She dropped her head in her hands. "We could all be in serious trouble."

"You didn't miss anything. And Wilder's people didn't, either."

"I still have to look," she snapped.

"Yeah. Yeah, you do. Can I help with anything?"

The paranoid thoughts of conspiracy and collusion invaded her mind again. "Be my proxy at the board meeting, because I'm going home. Vote how you want, I don't care."

He jumped off the sofa and gaped at her. "You *can't* go home! We reconvene in less than an hour, and we have decisions to make!"

She stood and started filling her briefcase with files. "I can't focus on the audit in the middle of this circus. If that son of a bitch really was dirty, I'm the first one who goes to prison, and I'm not going to let that happen."

Chapter Forty

AFTER FILING HIS REPORT WITH THE captain, Remy decided to take a late lunch at the Bel-Air instead of dinner without Maggie. Dining here alone with several martinis had always been the one thing of stability and permanence in his life in LA, but now it seemed lonely. Lunch, on the other hand, didn't require a companion to be enjoyable.

As he stepped through the doors and into his sanctuary, the relentless hauntings of his job vanished. The Bel-Air was shielded by an impenetrable wall of luxury and security. Nothing bad ever happened here. Well, that wasn't exactly true—a few months ago, a poisoned man had been found dead in the property's storied Swan Lake, but that had been a foreign assassination. Somehow, that was less offensive than the homicides that happened beyond this fantasy world every day, to average people with average lives.

He'd intimated to Maggie that he was considering changing departments, but she didn't know he was getting closer to leaving LAPD entirely. The job was slowly corroding him from the inside, like poison that didn't kill you right away. So was Los Angeles. It had a shrill, dangerous hum that hadn't existed five years ago, and it scared him. The voice telling him to get out was growing more strident.

But there was a quandary. She would never uproot her life and move to New Orleans with him, and he didn't know if he could live without her. He was a man in limbo, watching a spinning roulette wheel with no hope of placing a winning bet.

He was greeted warmly by every employee as he passed through the lobby to the lounge. It was his home away from home, which was conveniently just blocks away. Micah was working the bar today, and gave him a broad, movie star smile as he took a seat among the smattering of other afternoon patrons. The young man had just landed a minor role on a popular streaming series and he hadn't stopped showing his teeth since. Remy didn't know if he was talented, but if you had heartthrob looks like his, perhaps that was a secondary job requirement.

"The usual, Detective?"

"Please, Micah. When do you start shooting?"

"Next month."

"How many lines did they give you?"

"Just four, but that's better than one."

"It's a fine start."

"It will be if they don't edit me out. It happens all the time. But either way, it's a great break, and I really hit it off with the director."

Remy watched the handsome tender mix his martini with the concentration of a man defusing a bomb. If he was as devoted to stagecraft as he was mixology, he would go far.

He slid the cocktail across the polished bar. "Will Detective Nolan be joining you for lunch today?"

"Unfortunately, no. What do you recommend today?"

"Definitely the diver scallops."

"Diver scallops it is, but no rush. I'd like to savor your superior skills first. Excellent martini, as always."

"Thank you. Are you working a case?"

"I just closed one. Dr. Kang."

"He was *murdered*?"

"As it turns out, no. He died from a fentanyl overdose."

"Depressing. But it figures."

"How so?"

"He still came here, even after he lost everything. And he was always hinting about pills, how he had some if anybody was interested. You'd be amazed by how many big shots come in, have a couple cocktails, and start asking for drugs. Like we're all scumbags running a side-deal out the back door."

"I'm not surprised at all." He watched him start mixing another martini. You never had to ask a good bartender to keep the drinks coming.

"You know we don't kiss-and-tell here, but Kang crossed a big red line, so I told the manager, and he banned him from the premises last month."

Remy popped a cocktail onion in his mouth. "I found a lot of pills in his apartment, and figured he was dealing. I see he was aiming for high-end clients, even though he probably could have done better from his studio in Chinatown. Did he ever come in with anybody?"

"He was usually alone, but he did meet up with somebody occasionally, looked like a businessman. Kind of stiff, always in great suits, never walked in wearing anything that cost less than five grand." His mouth quirked in a smile as he assessed Remy's. "You're a Brioni guy."

"You know your suits."

He shrugged a little gloomily. "When I moved here from Florida two years ago, I saw people first. Now the first thing I notice is what they're wearing. There should be rehab for *that* in this town."

Remy's esteem for Micah expanded beyond his easy banter and talent for perfect martinis. "I agree. I suppose you're wondering if I'm a dirty cop, dressing in Brioni and dining here almost every night."

"Not a chance. You seem like you come from old money."

"Bartenders are the most observant and insightful people. I assume you have an opinion about the relationship between Dr. Kang and his occasional companion."

Micah nodded. "They seemed like friends. I figured him for one of Kang's clients. He looked perpetually surprised like people do when they've gone under the knife one too many times."

"Do you know who the man was?"

He flashed his movie star smile again. "You're still working the case."

"Just tying up loose ends."

"I know his name, because he always paid the bill. It's Bruce Messane."

Chapter Forty-One

MALIBU HAD ALWAYS SEEMED SLEEPY TO Nolan, at least if you were viewing the front of the homes from the Pacific Coast Highway. All the action was out back: on decks, patios, on the beach. Messane's was a sleek, modernist structure in keeping with his minimalist sensibility—certainly a rebellion against the faux chateau.

It sat on premium land, north of the "cheap seat" properties worth less than ten million. It was set back from the PCH and nicely sheltered from prying eyes with strategically placed trees and plantings. It wasn't gated—surprisingly, a lot of the real estate in Malibu wasn't, as if the zip code possessed talismanic powers which repelled all malefactors. And maybe it did. The crime rate was extremely low.

She and Al approached cautiously and flanked the front door, guns drawn. They didn't anticipate fireworks, but you had to be prepared for anything. Clearing a building was one of the most dangerous, harrowing duties of the job, and there was no such thing as an abundance of caution.

She pounded on the door. "LAPD, open up!"

Nothing.

She repeated the command, waited, then tried the handle. Her arms broke out in gooseflesh as the door opened. "Lewiston said this was locked. That was less than an hour ago."

Crawford looked inside warily. "Somebody was here between then and now."

"Or somebody was inside when patrol was checking it out, and they didn't bother to lock up on the way out."

"Stay sharp, Mags."

Her pulse pounded in her ears, and every nerve was stripped raw as she stepped inside, paused, and listened. "Let's do it."

They veered off in different directions, always staying within sight of each other as they went room to room. All their senses were honed to painful clarity by the slipstream of adrenaline that was carrying them both. Nolan's heart had climbed up her throat, and with every step, every breath, it hammered harder, threatening to suffocate her.

Her vitals finally settled when it was evident the house and garage were empty. But more than one person had been here recently, and they'd vacated in a hurry.

They were standing in a media room that was dedicated to security. The computers were all on, showing a mosaic of feeds from outdoor cameras. Empty bottles of Mountain Dew and cigarette butts filled one small trash can. In a storage area, zip ties and rope had been left behind. The home's panic room had been occupied, too—the sink was still wet.

Crawford holstered his gun and rocked back on his heels. "Jesus, we are really down the rabbit hole now. The Bechtolds were here, Mimi is probably a killer and for sure a kidnapper, and even Lewis Carroll didn't smoke enough opium for this to make sense."

"They knew Messane wasn't going to be walking in on them."

"Stupid move. You keep hostages in a trailer in the desert or a shitty motel outside the city limits, not in the beach house of a dead man who's *connected* to the hostages. They had to know we'd get here eventually."

"Stupid, or they really are playing some kind of a game."

"Whatever, it almost got them burned."

"Damn that it didn't."

He walked over to the console and stared at the security feeds. "It still could. They miscalculated and got surprised. There's a ton of evidence here, a lot of mistakes waiting to be discovered." He gestured to the monitors. "Archival footage might be our golden ticket. It covers the driveway from three different angles, which would show them coming and going. Could get a plate number, or a match on facial recognition."

"I don't want to touch those keyboards, even with gloves, until Ross can lift prints. If there are any."

He clucked his tongue. "Weird that this place is like Fort Knox, but his big house didn't even have security cameras."

"I didn't see anything here that justified this kind of protection."

"Probably because Mimi took it. I'll call Ross and Lucerno, you go track down the Cadillac King of California."

Chapter Forty-Two

REGGIE BLATTNER LOOKED MORE LIKE A wizened Austin Powers than a car dealership tycoon. He answered the door with a crystal lowball filled with clear liquor in one hand, a slim brown cigarette in the other. He was steady on his feet and his eyes were sharp, but judging by the alcohol fumes emanating from him, Nolan figured he was partially pickled. She introduced herself and his dyed brows lifted as he blatantly scanned her body with appreciation. Pig.

"A homicide detective, and a stunning one at that! I certainly hope there isn't a dead body in the neighborhood."

His keen expression told her otherwise. She felt instant dislike for the man and his offensive, wandering eyes. In fact, she wanted to strangle him with his ridiculous paisley cravat and watch those eyes bulge out of his skull. It should have troubled her that she occasionally fantasized about killing people while she was investigating murder, but there wasn't a homicide cop who didn't. Actually, there probably weren't many people in the world who didn't on occasion. "I need to ask you some questions, Mr. Blattner."

"Of course. Please, come out to the deck. The Golden Hour is approaching, and there's no reason you can't enjoy it while you ask your questions. I suppose you wouldn't be interested in a cocktail."

She was very interested in a cocktail, but not here, not with him. "Thank you, no."

"A good host always asks, even if he knows what the answer will be." He led her through a magnificent great room decorated in beachy-expensive, although the furnishings looked like they'd been waiting patiently for decades to be retired. Like the man, his house was entombed in the amber of a bygone era, but with the view from the deck, who would spend time inside?

The Golden Hour was indeed approaching, and the light was softer and warmer. The sun was tracing its way down to the sea. The beach was empty except for a few joggers and a cluster of seagulls fighting over scraps in the foam-ruffled surf.

"My little piece of paradise." He leveled a shrewd glance, no longer the buzzed happy-hour pervert. "I tried to call Bruce after I spoke with Officer Lewis."

"Lewiston."

He ignored the correction. "I wasn't able to reach him, and nobody answered the office phones. Highly unusual, given Malibu PD's visit, and especially yours. I don't take it as a good sign."

"You're friends with Mr. Messane?"

"I think Bruce is too busy for real friends, but we are certainly friendly. We have drinks out here whenever he's in town, which isn't often—he's a workaholic, something I used to be. Now I'm just an alcoholic." He wheezed out a chuckle.

"But you expected your calls to be answered."

He rattled the ice cubes in his glass. "Bruce always answers his phone. Is he . . . did something happen to him?"

"He was murdered."

He laid his cigarillo in a crystal ashtray, visibly shaken. "Oh, God. That's shocking news. Horrible news. He was killed here?"

"No. Did he ever mention any troubles to you?"

"Bruce never discussed personal issues with me. I really didn't know anything about him outside of business. We had that in common and it was our primary topic of conversation."

"Did he seem out of sorts the last few times you saw him?"

"On the contrary, he was thrilled with the pending sale of Peppy Pets. Who wouldn't be?"

"Tell me about Mimi. What time did you see her today?"

"It was sometime this morning, when it was raining hard. She was letting herself in the front door."

"Did you speak with her?"

Blattner dragged his fingers through his shock of flat black hair, as artificial as his eyebrows. "I've never spoken to her. Bruce mentioned her name when I asked him who the beautiful visitor was. I assumed she was his girlfriend, but he told me she was his assistant."

Assistant in quotes. On the way here, Cynthia Jackson had confirmed that his real assistant was a grandmother of six.

"Did he say anything else about her?"

"No. He seemed uncomfortable discussing her. An illicit affair, perhaps. That's a shameful weakness of many successful men."

"Spoken from experience?"

He looked regretful. "That's why I have four ex-wives. I imagine that's why Bruce was divorced, too."

"Do you know her last name?"

"Mimi is all I know."

"You told Officer Lewiston she came here on occasion."

"Yes."

"Do you know what she drives?"

"I know what everybody drives, it's my stock and trade. A silver Mercedes S 500. Excellent car, but very overpriced in my opinion. Just like Bruce's BMW. I encouraged him to buy a Cadillac, the engineering is far superior in my opinion. I offered him a very good deal, but the younger generations all want German or Italian. A Cadillac used to be an American status symbol," he said morosely. "No more."

The mention of Cadillacs scratched at her thoughts. "My father drives an Escalade. He loves it."

His smile was genuine. "I'm so happy to hear that. I love mine, too, I call her Black Betty. But I don't drive it much, it's impractical for errands around Malibu. For the most part, she sits in my garage, but I do take her out on her paces every few days to keep her running smoothly."

To Culver City to kill a neighbor? It seemed preposterous, but he knew Bruce and he drove a black Escalade, and that was enough to keep the thought on life support. "Did you ever see the license plate?"

"No. I only notice cars and pretty women."

"Do you have security cameras that might also cover Mr. Messane's property?"

"I am old, and old-school, Detective. I don't even have a cheap doorbell camera. What I do have is an impressive collection of weapons from antiquity to present, including a Heilongjiang hand cannon, dating back to the thirteenth century. It's something of a passion of mine. And a morbid fascination—our species has never stopped looking for better ways to kill each other. I doubt we ever will."

Nolan had pegged him as purely fatuous, but apparently, he possessed more depth than the average drunken lech. "I agree."

"I knew you would. The point of that braggart's exposition on my collection—thank you for tolerating it, by the way—is that I'm well-protected and don't need cameras. I sleep lightly, with a modern firearm at the ready. The hand cannon wouldn't be practical these days."

She didn't know what a Heilongjiang hand cannon was, but it sounded like something that might be very effective on the streets of the twenty-first century. At the very least, a surprise. "Back to Mimi. Please describe her."

He turned his attention to the sinking sun and his drink. "Extraordinary blond hair. Not real, of course, but it looked good on her. She's slender, and always wore black."

"Did Mr. Messane ever have any other visitors?"

Blattner relit his abandoned cigarillo and puffed a few times to restart it. "Bruce did not socialize, at least not here. Aside from Mimi, the only other vehicle I've ever seen was an electrician's van this morning. I assume that's why she was here, to let them in."

Nolan tensed. "What did the van look like?"

"White, with blue lettering. A company name, but I can't recall—"

"Please think very hard, Mr. Blattner, it's important."

His face pruned up. He drew on his cigarillo and expelled a balloon of white smoke that briefly obscured his face. "I'm pretty sure there was a G in the name. And a logo with lightning bolts around a . . . yes, that's it, a globe. Global Electric. Never heard of them, the people around here usually use Hohner Electric."

Booze aside, his memory seemed very much intact. "Thank you for your time, Mr. Blattner, you've been very helpful."

"I'm glad to hear that. I know you won't tell me about an ongoing investigation, but please find out who killed him and make sure they rot in prison. I was very fond of Bruce, and I'll miss him."

"I will, Mr. Blattner."

Chapter Forty-Three

IN CENTRAL PARK, THE AIR WAS cold and filled with tiny ice crystals that couldn't decide if they wanted to become snowflakes. Montserrat was finishing her two-mile jog with a sprint, pushing her aching legs to the point of collapse. The pain was intense, but it helped her forget disturbing things, like her father's failing health and her sister's toxicity.

As she slowed to a cool-down pace, her phone chirruped. She almost stumbled when she saw Papa's name on the caller ID. Sebastian De Leon didn't like to speak on the phone, and certainly never past ten his time. He was an unyielding, rigid man, and his schedule never varied—awake by five, in bed by ten. No wonder he butted heads with his peripatetic, youngest daughter.

"Papa, is everything alright?"

"I should ask you the same, you're gasping for air like a landed fish."

"I just finished a run."

"A waste of heartbeats. Einstein said we're born with a finite amount of them."

His perennial displeasure over the behavior of his offspring, venial as it might be, was as galling as Magdalena's bitterness. The two of them were much more alike than either of them would ever admit.

Her role as the family Switzerland was growing stale. Did she really want to go back to the source of the strife?

In a rare act of defiance, she challenged him. "I think Einstein just hated exercise. It wouldn't hurt you to get some." His rolling laughter made her feel guilty for some reason.

"I suppose you're right, precious girl, but the doctors tell me I'm a sick man."

She knew she was being manipulated, but the knowledge didn't ease her distress. "Papa, I'm worried about you. How are you feeling?"

He grunted. "I feel just fine, but they tell me I shouldn't. They say my kidneys are failing. I'm not that old, how did they wear out? I don't get sufficient answers from them, only orders to get my blood cleaned every few days."

"Have you started dialysis?"

"No. That's the beginning of the end, I'll never get off."

And he wouldn't survive the year without it. Unsolicited advice was always met with hostility, even though he had no trouble dispensing it himself. She would have to craft a clever plan to blandish him into dialysis. Flattery was the only thing he responded to. She sat down on a cold park bench and changed the subject. "What's the weather like there?"

"Better than New York, I'm sure. But you'll find out soon enough. I am arranging a plane for you at Teterboro tonight. I want you back in Spain for a few days."

Montserrat was stunned speechless. This wasn't a request, it was a command, and she couldn't imagine what was behind it. "I can't just drop everything—"

"You can and will. Tell your overlords at that pretentious law firm you work for that you have a family emergency."

"Why, Papa? What's so urgent?"

"We need to discuss your sister's future. She's making a mess of things again, and I don't want you anywhere near her."

She felt a sinister tingling creep down her spine. "I just talked to her a few hours ago, and she said everything was fine. She was in good spirits."

"She's in good spirits because she is not mentally balanced, and clearly not taking her medication. And this Jaime makes things worse, he's a guttersnipe. I won't have him dragging her down to his level, casting a blight on our family. She seems to forget she has noble blood. We must make her remember her responsibilities."

"She told me she was going to Cabo with him tonight. I warned her about him."

"I'm sure you did, but my horses have more sense than she ever did. It's time for another intervention. Long past time."

"Let me talk to her—"

"It's too late for that. The plane will be ready for you in two hours. Don't keep me waiting."

She listened to the dial tone, and wondered what would happen if she ignored his wishes and didn't get on that plane. She would never know, because when Duke Sebastian De Leon told you to do something, you did it.

Chapter Forty-Four

WHEN SAM STEPPED INTO THE METRO briefing room with Captain Margolis, he had a flashback, but for a refreshing change, it didn't recount a grisly episode of war. In this one, he was back in third grade on the first day at a new school after the Army had posted his father to Fort Bragg. The teacher, Mr. Barrett, as broad of girth as he was short on hair, escorted him into the classroom where decorous children with voracious eyes sized him up and made him feel like prey. His stomach roiled around a strawberry Pop Tart and his legs trembled.

Class, this is our new student, Sammy Easton. He's here all the way from California. Make sure you make him feel right at home here in North Carolina, y'hear?

Fortunately, the school was on base, and all the students were Army brats just like him, so there was the preexisting camaraderie of common ground. He also soon realized he had a great advantage because he was the only student from California, a decidedly exotic land in their minds. Everybody wanted to know if his neighbors were movie stars, if they were friends of his, if Disneyland was as cool as everybody said. He was also tall, strong, and fast for his age, and apparently cute, according to the girls who whispered excitedly behind his back. If they could only see him now.

The welcome from the assigned squad from D Platoon was equally warm, and like third grade, he felt instantly accepted as a peer, not shunned as an interloper. Part of it was the culture that existed not just in the military, but in law enforcement—they were all driven by the same sense of duty. As a potential consultant, he wasn't a competitor. And he suspected in some small part that his notoriety as native-son-returned-war-hero engendered positive feelings. Sam had always been vocal about his embarrassment over the lofty, unwarranted media proclamations—he'd just been doing his job. These people all understood that, and undoubtedly appreciated his attempts to demur the accolades.

The names were a blur as Margolis made introductions, but he remembered Kathy Gossard, the single woman in this squad. She reminded him of Maggie—beautiful, but clearly tough as hell. He didn't know where she sat in the pecking order, but it was evident she had the respect of her colleagues. SWAT had come a long way.

When Margolis came to a colossus with sandy hair who went by the handle Chain Saw, Sam almost dropped. "Kenny Durden?"

His stern face split in a smile he'd been struggling to suppress, and nearly pumped his arm off. "I couldn't believe it when I saw your name on the agenda. I was waiting to see if you recognized me, Sammy."

"You look exactly the same, only a hell of a lot bigger and meaner. God, it's good to see you, man. What's with Chain Saw?"

"Some folks in the Eighty-Second Airborne said I snored like one—all liars, I don't snore—and the name stuck."

Snickers from the crowd.

"You were Eighty-Second?"

"Just like Pops." He turned to the group. "Sam and I were in third grade together at Bragg. Best buds and holy terrors until the Army reassigned his family."

Smiles and cheers. The mood was buoyant and a little manic, like it was before a battle op briefing, which this essentially was. Light before the dark—it was a critical part of preparation because it burned off your nervous energy and kept you sane. For the most part.

But when colleagues from the DEA and LAPD Gang-Narc arrived, everyone sobered as the gravity of the situation perfused the room. In an instant, they all wore game faces, ready for orders, ready for the mission. That was the only thing that mattered in this singular moment in time, and it had to be that way if you wanted to survive.

Sam was back home, and it felt good. Surprisingly, it felt even better that he would be observing, not participating, and he considered that great personal progress. It was the first time since he'd returned from Afghanistan that chasing the dragon of an adrenaline high didn't consume his thoughts or drive his actions.

After Margolis closed the briefing, he pulled him aside as the squad went to the armory for tactical gear and weapons.

"How are you feeling, Sam?"

"Good, sir. And I'm impressed. I might be a waste of taxpayer dollars."

Margolis broke character and almost smiled. "Nonsense. Any man or woman with your experience is always welcomed and needed. So, you and Chain Saw. Were you really holy terrors in third grade?"

"Yes sir, but Kenny was always the instigator. My role was to talk us out of trouble."

Margolis found a full smile. "Sounds about right. Go on, get your gear on. Since you're not officially on the roster yet, we can't give you a weapon."

"I didn't expect that."

"When you're set up, meet me at mobile command."

"Yes, sir."

Sam was almost to the armory when the tattooed man from LAPD Gang-Narc caught up with him and offered his hand.

"Justin Taggert. I'm friends with Remy. Al and Maggie, too. Happy to have you on board."

"Thanks. I'm happy to be here. Sounds like this could be a big bust."

"We're hoping. But you never know how good your intel is when the informant is under duress."

"I know all about that."

"I figured. I'll take you for a walk-through when the dust settles. SWAT does all the heavy lifting, but LAPD and the DEA will handle the scene after they're finished. It's good to see the whole procedure from beginning to end."

"Thanks. I like the full picture."

"I suppose you didn't get much of that in war."

Sam shook his head. "We just shot things up and got the hell out."

Taggert laughed. "That's pretty much what SWAT does. But don't tell anyone I said that."

Chapter Forty-Five

NOLAN FOUND MAYA LUCERNO WORKING ON a laptop in her sedan, legs out the door like she was ready to run. And maybe she was—Rome Bechtold's abduction had happened on her watch, and she would carry that guilt for the rest of her life. Every cop who'd been around long enough understood the agony of could-have should-have syndrome.

Her sad eyes lifted. "I never thought the worst day of my life would feel so bad. And it's nothing compared to what the Bechtolds are going through."

She was caught off guard by Lucerno's candor. "You'll make it a good day when you find them, so keep your eyes on the prize. I'm sure you know the media is already on fire with this."

"My phone has been blowing up with calls from reporters. They love kidnappings. It's so sick, but they might actually help us out for a change by getting their faces out there."

"Did Al take you through the house and brief you on our end?"

"Yes. He also sent me a copy of your reports so far, and I returned the favor. We all have a lot of information to share, let's hope it connects some dots." She gestured to Messane's house. "I can't understand why they would risk keeping the Bechtolds here."

Nolan shrugged. "We've been mulling over that, too. It may be a simple case of opportunity. We're sure Mimi had something to do with his murder, so she knew he wouldn't be an obstacle, and Malibu is a good place to lay low. She's also familiar with the property."

"She underestimated you. Pure arrogance."

"By all accounts, she's crazy. Whoever she is."

"Did you get anything on her from Reggie Blattner?"

"No last name or any information, he never met her. But he confirmed she drove a silver Mercedes S 500, which narrows it down a little."

"That's very helpful. You wouldn't believe how many silver Mercedes sedans there are in this town, but with the partial plate and a model, we might get somewhere with it."

"The traffic cams in Santa Monica didn't pull anything?"

She shook her head grimly. "But the traffic cams on PCH might."

"Blattner also mentioned that a Global Electric truck was here this morning. White with blue lettering. He'd never heard of the company, and I haven't, either."

She started clattering on her keyboard. "I'll check it out now."

Nolan looked up at the approaching crime scene van. Ross gave her a wave from the front seat. He hated dead ends, took them personally, so this was his big chance for redemptive glory. Al was right, the kidnappers had scattered like roaches before they could sanitize the scene, so something was bound to pop on one of the criminal databases. High-profile abduction wasn't the purview of amateurs, and odds were everybody involved had a substantial rap sheet. A single fingerprint could move the needle in the right direction.

"Bingo. Global Electric isn't licensed in the state, and they don't show up on any search," Lucerno interrupted her optimistic thoughts. "They don't exist. I'll get a BOLO out and keep working the traffic cam footage. The Pacific Coast Highway is the only way in and out of here, and a van with a logo is going to stand out more than a Mercedes. If we know whether they're heading north or south, we can refine the search."

"My guess is north and inland, away from the city." She stepped away when her phone buzzed in her pocket. "Margaret Nolan."

"It's your paramour, checking in."

She felt predictable warmth suffuse her cheeks. Even surrounded by so much darkness, her hypothalamus was in fine working order. "Hi, Remy."

"How goes it?"

"Just great, if you're a fan of *The Twilight Zone*. Rome Bechtold was kidnapped this afternoon, and he and his wife were being held at Messane's beach house. They're in the wind now, but we just caught a break."

Remy was silent for a long moment. "There's a connection, and it has to be Peppy Pets."

"Looks like it. We're working with Robbery now, so we have more hands on deck."

"If things are tumbling into place, you'll close this sooner than you think."

"Not soon enough to keep our dinner date, unfortunately."

"I had a feeling you'd be occupied for a while, so I went to the Bel-Air for lunch instead, which is why I'm bothering you. Micah was tending, and he told me Dr. Kang and Bruce Messane frequented the bar together on occasion, and Kang was always pushing pills. It may have no bearing on your case, but I thought it was worth a mention."

Nolan cycled back to her initial, and discarded, suspicion that Messane had been drug-seeking in Culver City. "We scoured his life, and drugs don't factor in at all."

"And yet Poppy was killed in a drive-by—clearly gang-related—and Messane was murdered right in front of his shop."

"Messane had other things going on in his life more compelling. We're not dismissing it, but he was a loyal client of Kang's when he was still a plastic surgeon, so a social relationship wouldn't be unusual, even after he spiraled into ignominy."

"Maybe. Micah did say they seemed like friends, and Messane always footed the bill. By the way, I submitted my final report on Kang, so I have free time for moonlighting if you want another pair of hands on the proverbial deck."

The call should have ended, but Nolan didn't want it to. Teasing out a few more beats of conversation seemed preposterously like all the oxygen she would need to get through the night. "Thanks, but enjoy the break. You know it won't last long."

Remy sighed. "Sadly, that's true. Solve your case so I have a dinner date for tomorrow."

"That's what I'm counting on." His long pause was curious—maybe he didn't want to hang up, either.

"Do you have plans for Christmas?" he finally asked.

The question was an abrupt change of subject, and scattered her thoughts. "It's usually just Christmas Eve dinner and gifts with my parents. You?"

"I'm thinking about going to New Orleans. Not necessarily to see my parents, but to spend it with Charlotte and Serena."

Remy's sister had been missing for years before the case in Death Valley a few months ago. He hadn't even known he'd had a niece. Understandable that he'd want to be there for the holiday. "By all means, you should go."

"I will if you come with me."

Nolan's thoughts weren't just scattered now, they were in utter chaos. A holiday with his family? What did that mean? "I wouldn't want to interfere with your first—"

"You wouldn't be interfering, and Charlotte and Serena ask about you all the time. Since you couldn't join me for the last trip, I thought Christmas in the South would be the perfect introduction to my hometown."

"But don't you want—"

"You know what I want."

No, she didn't. She couldn't even fathom what *she* wanted.

"Close your case first, Maggie, then we'll talk."

Chapter Forty-Six

GONZALES WAS SITTING IN AN OLD-FASHIONED velveteen chair next to Maria Rivera, holding her hands while she wept quietly. There was a poignant dignity to her grief that hacked at his heart. In less than a second, her world had been destroyed. She was facing the last decades of life without her partner, and he was complicit—just by being a cop, doing his job, upholding his oath. The anger would come later, but for now, he felt only sorrow and guilt.

She finally looked up at him and released his hands to clasp the rosary in her lap. "Poppy was proud of you, Miguel. For getting out."

He swallowed what felt like a ball of barbed wire. "Whoever did this will die of old age in prison, Maria, you have my word."

Her eyes drifted to the front window framed by crisp white curtains, and he followed her gaze. Carefully tended flower beds skirted the tidy, twilit lawn. This small house in a better part of Culver City was looked after with love and pride.

"I hope you're right, but I'm not so sure justice exists anymore. The people in power, they see the crime and the death, but they don't have money to help us because it's all in their pockets. They're as remorseless as the monsters who pull the triggers."

"I keep thinking that if I hadn't gone back to the garage, maybe—"

"Stop," she interrupted sharply. "This isn't your fault, it's theirs. All of them. If the only people trying to protect us stop doing their jobs, we're all lost. You could have been killed, too, but you did what was right. That takes courage."

Gonzales lowered his head. It was the sign of the times that courage could get a friend killed. "I'm so sorry, Maria."

"I am, too." She reached out with a calloused hand and patted his good cheek. "How many stitches in your pretty face, *mijo*?"

"Twenty-four."

"You'll have a battle scar."

"A big one, the doctor says. I'll call it Poppy."

She gave him a quivering smile that deepened the creases around her mouth. "He's laughing at that right now."

Gonzales returned the smile, hoping it was true. "Will you still go to Albuquerque?"

"Yes. There's nothing here for me now." She took a shuddering breath. "I knew something was wrong. He was nervous, distracted. A few months ago, people started calling him at odd hours. Sometimes he left in the middle of the night and stayed away for a long time."

"He didn't tell me."

"He refused to discuss it with me, too. He always protected everyone he cared about. For all the good it did."

"You have no idea where he was or what he was doing?"

"Oh, I have an idea. He would always come home smelling like the garage. Like paint. Probably those narco pigs forced him to work on their stolen cars."

Gonzales finally felt the anger start to simmer in his blood. Those evil, shit of the earth bastards, forcing slave labor on an old man and terrorizing his family. "Did he ever mention any street handles? Names?"

She frowned and evaded his gaze. "No, he wouldn't dare."

"Maria, if you know anything, please tell me, it could help."

The beads clacked in her hands as she worked them; she made a decision. "He told me there was a new enforcer in the neighborhood, a very bad man, with tattoos all over his body. His face, his neck, arms, everything. 'Turn and run if you ever see him,' he said."

He was frustrated by Poppy's silence, but he understood the fear tactics the gangs employed; he knew what it felt like to have a boot on your throat. He'd lived it. "Did you tell the homicide detectives about this when they interviewed you?"

She shook her head. "I'm telling you. But don't you dare do this alone. A dead hero isn't any good to anybody."

"I'm no hero, Maria."

"You're wrong. Promise me."

"I promise. I'll talk to the gang unit, they'll work it hard." He navigated away from the darkness, hoping to distract her temporarily. "Poppy showed me the Barracuda. He was proud of it."

A tear escaped and slid down her cheek slowly. "He loved that car. It was the one thing he ever did for himself. Miguel, why did they do this? He would never have said anything." She started crying in earnest.

"They're not human, they're terrorists with no regard for life, Maria. It means nothing to them. And if this enforcer is new, then he's looking to establish himself and set an example . . ." He tensed when he saw a white Chevy pickup slow in front of the house; when it pulled into the driveway, he was out of his seat, gun drawn.

"It's my sister and nieces, Miguel," she said calmly. "I'm expecting them. It's okay."

He took a shaky breath and holstered his weapon. Dear Jesus, he'd been ready to shoot them, because everything in this neighborhood seemed threatening to him now. That was fucked up. *He* was fucked up. Sergeant Acosta had told him to take a few days leave, and the advice was sound, but he wasn't going to follow it. "I'll let you go, then, but I'll stop by tomorrow."

"You're welcome here anytime. *Vaya con Dios,* Miguel. Be safe."

It was too late for that. It was too late the day he'd entered the Academy. He kissed both of Maria's cheeks, stepped out into the chilly shadows of early evening, and introduced himself to her family. They were all carrying covered dishes of food that smelled like his mother's house on holidays and made his mouth water. He politely declined an invitation to join them, then plodded back to his car with a sick heart.

Two little boys kicking a soccer ball back and forth in a neighboring yard lifted him a little, but the feeling didn't last long. He'd once been a little boy kicking a soccer ball around with his best friend, Ronny Taggert, when a man had approached them and asked if they'd like to make some money. He'd turned tail and ran, but Ronny had accepted the offer. He was long gone. Kids should never have to run to stay alive.

He wanted nothing more than to get in his car, hop on a freeway—any freeway—and just keep driving. The open road was a good place to forget and reset. But he wasn't a kid anymore, and he wasn't going to run. Instead, he called Ronny's older brother, Justin. He'd made a career out of redressing tragedy in Gang-Narc, and Gonzales felt like it might be a good path for his future.

He answered on the first ring. "Jesus, Mike, I'm so sorry about Poppy, just heard about it. You okay?"

"I'm alive. Listen, I was just talking to Maria. Poppy warned her about a new enforcer in Culver City. . . ."

Chapter Forty-Seven

NOLAN AND CRAWFORD STOOD BY AS Ross dusted the security room and keyboards with his usual precision, fidgeting like anxious parents at their kid's first piano recital. Chatty as he was, he preferred to work in silence, but Nolan couldn't keep her mouth shut. Probably because it kept her mind in the game and off the unsettling coda to her conversation with Remy. "Are you getting anything?"

He didn't look up, just kept dusting and lifting. "Plenty of prints, but I wouldn't get my hopes up. Baby criminals grow up watching cop shows and surfing the internet, so only morons and the desperate don't wear gloves during the commission of a felony these days."

"I don't think we're dealing with either," Crawford muttered.

Ross paused and looked over his shoulder at them. "Neither do I. Everything has been pro up until the cig butts and pop bottles. That's a big screwup. They're loaded with DNA, and you can't wear gloves on your mouth, can you?"

In Nolan's current, semi-delirious frame of mind, the visual of a mouth glove seemed hilarious, but she maintained her composure. "Malibu flushed them out before they could clean up. Hopefully, we'll get a match with the felon registry."

"I'd say there's a decent chance of that." He hesitated, then asked, "Is Gonzales okay? I heard about the drive-by."

"Physically, but he had a hell of a scare, and you know he was close with the family. He might appreciate that drink."

"I know I would," Crawford added. "No harm in making a call."

"Yeah. Maybe." Ross gestured to the computer console. "It's all yours, I'm off to the next room."

Nolan sank into a leather office chair, praying for a big score with the footage. Al stood next to her emitting garlic fumes from his Jade Gardens' number twelve. Was her breath as ghastly?

"You sure you don't want to call in Ike to handle this, Mags?"

"I know enough about video management software to get the job done. And this system is running Blue Iris, I'm familiar with it."

"Taking night classes so you can chuck your illustrious career and become a mall cop?"

"Max was a security specialist in the Army, and he taught me a lot of things I didn't think I'd ever use. But knowledge is never wasted." Proving her point, she found the hidden archive library immediately and opened the folder. There was a list of files arranged by dates, going back two months.

Crawford rubbed his hands together. "This could be it."

With a silent Hail Mary, she clicked on today's file, and mumbled an oath. "It's empty, Al. They scrubbed it."

"Try them all, maybe we can catch a previous visit."

Nolan spent the better part of fifteen minutes doing just that, but the entire archive had been gutted.

"Bastards covered their bases," Crawford groused.

"Yeah, but Ike should be able to recover the files. You have to be a high-level techie to make things disappear forever."

"Bringing Ike three computers in one day has got to be a record."

"He'll love it, he's bored with the first two. But we should pick him up a pound of licorice."

Crawford raised an inquisitive brow.

"He quit drinking at the office. Licorice is his new addiction."

"Hmm. Cirrhosis or diabetes. I wonder if he made the right choice. I mean, they both kill you in the end anyhow, right?"

"You are always a ray of sunshine, Al."

Lucerno poked her head in the room, looking a lot happier than she had earlier. "I'm headed north. Burbank PD just found the Global Electric van abandoned in a Walmart lot. It was stolen in San Jose three months ago. Plates are from a Toyota Corolla, and the logo was just a vinyl decal."

"If they left the decal on, the Bechtolds are probably nowhere near there," Crawford pointed out.

"A feint," she agreed. "But a stupid dump. That Walmart has more security cameras than the White House. We're on it."

"Any traction on the Mercedes?"

"The team is still going through film. What about the footage here?"

"It was scrubbed, but we're hoping our cyber guy can recover it."

Lucerno crossed her fingers. "Good luck to us all."

Crawford grabbed an evidence bag and started unplugging cords from the hard drive. "I'm glad we only have to worry about finding a killer, not saving two lives."

"Finding the killer might save those lives."

"Good point."

"Remy called. He found out Messane and Kang hung out at the Bel-Air occasionally, and Kang was always trying to push pills."

He considered. "He had a prior relationship with Kang, so I'd say they were sympathy gigs. I mean, if my go-to plastic surgeon ever hits the rocks, I wouldn't delete him from my contacts, just in case he gets back in business. I might even buy him overpriced food and drinks at the Bel-Air."

Nolan snorted at the image of Al under the knife for a facelift.

"The bartender did say they seemed friendly, and Messane always paid."

"There you go. Chalk one up to Mr. Peppy Pets for looking after a down-and-out friend."

"That's essentially what I told Remy. He just wanted to let us know."

"I appreciate that." He paused and looked at her curiously. "There's something else, I can tell."

"He invited me to New Orleans for Christmas." Oh my God, had she just blurted that out?

"Well, what did you say?"

"Nothing. Yet."

"Do you want to go?"

"I . . . I don't know. I can't think about it now. I never should have brought it up."

"I'm flattered you did. Look, Mags, I've known Remy a long time, and he likes to play it loose and easy, but that's all bullshit. He's a very serious guy, so talk to him. And don't take the invite lightly."

"What's that supposed to mean?"

"Everything he does has a purpose. Sounds like he wants to move the dial, so you should figure out whether you want the same thing before you make a decision."

"It's not a marriage proposal, Al."

He grinned at her. "No, but it might be a step in that direction."

She shot him a nasty look. "Pain in the ass."

"I feel like I've heard that before."

*　*　*

Ross had trained his team well, and he trusted them implicitly. If he hadn't been so confident in their skills and obsessive attention to detail, he never would have excused himself to make a phone call unrelated to work. As he walked a few steps from the house to the beach, he was saddened by the spectacular view, a contrary reaction for most people. But all he could think of was that this had been taken from its owner prematurely by some amoral shithead. Bruce Messane should have had a full lifetime to enjoy it. And Poppy should have been able to live out his.

Not in this world. You see wasted life every day. You're burning out.

Mike Gonzalez's phone went directly to voicemail, as he expected it would. He almost hung up—what did you say to someone you didn't know who'd just been through all kinds of hell?

"Mike, this is Roscoe Miles. I'm so sorry about Poppy. About everything. I hope you're okay. Call anytime. I mean, if you want to grab that drink or just talk . . ." Jesus, he was making a mess of things. He pondered how to close, then remembered his nana's old-world axiom: *Least said, soonest mended.*

"Take care, Mike."

Chapter Forty-Eight

CYNTHIA WAS ON HER SECOND POT of coffee, and her body was humming unpleasantly in caffeine overdrive. She flipped her reading glasses on her head and rubbed her eyes, but even closed, there were tangles of numbers swimming behind her lids, as if they'd been burned into her retinas. A budding headache was sending exploratory tendrils through her brain, and her stomach was protesting, reminding her that she hadn't eaten all day.

She took Excedrin with the dregs of her coffee and went to the kitchen to scrounge for some kind of sustenance. Unfortunately, she had the refrigerator of an important, busy executive: shriveled grapes, a leftover slice of pizza, and a container of gochujang. Why did she think she would ever have the time or will to make kimchi from scratch, like she'd seen on a cooking show?

She threw out the grapes, bolted the pizza, then spied a bottle of viognier hiding behind a liter of San Pellegrino. Sometimes, when she came to an impasse on a work problem, she would drink wine. It unwound cramping muscles and more often than not, unleashed her imagination. Seeing things from a different perspective was often all it took to get over a hump. Or was that just the excuse of a functional alcoholic? She sure as hell wasn't going to ask her therapist about it, he had enough to worry about during their sessions.

She returned to her office with the bottle and a glass, and continued reviewing her previous audit. After several healthy sips, her headache retreated and her synapses were firing with clarity. Even her vision seemed sharper. A glass later, she was more certain than ever that Bruce hadn't touched a dime of company funds.

But his rags-to-riches story rife with the hallmarks of illicit activity made her nervous. The fact that his turnaround coincided with the company's made her even more nervous, although the source of her anxiety was ambiguous.

She poured a second glass of liquid lucidity, reasoning that if one was good, two was better. Shifting focus, she began to look at the austerity measures that had returned Peppy Pets to profitability. The strategy was a standard formula for any business—if you cut costs across the board while raising the price per unit, times several million units, it added up.

Bruce's negotiation skills had also slashed costs on raw materials, manufacturing, and shipping. Pruning the limbs of two languishing lines of raw pet food had also increased profits. The Senior Slim line he'd introduced was incredibly successful, because many pet owners loved their fur babies into life-threatening obesity. These efforts were responsible for 30 percent of the 42 percent growth Peppy Pets had enjoyed under Bruce's management.

The remaining percentage would be from sales. The balance sheets all reconciled, so she decided to do a deep dive into the reports by cross-referencing them with hundreds of pages of actual invoices. That's when she found the anomaly, so deeply buried, even Wilder Foods hadn't picked up on it, even though they should have: one distributor had been paying grossly inflated prices for a cheaper product, adding millions of dollars to the bottom line.

Cynthia scrambled for her silenced phone beneath a stack of file folders. It was bloated with texts and messages from Tim. Not surprisingly, he answered immediately.

"Cynthia, goddammit, you need to—"

"Golden West Animal Supply. What do you know about them?"

"You're worried about a former distributor *now*?"

"Former?"

"They canceled their contract six months ago."

"Did Bruce mention why?"

"I was his lawyer, not his confidant. He asked me to draft the paper, so I did."

"Was there anything unusual about the termination?"

"It was standard. What are you on about? Have you been drinking?"

She took another gulp of wine. "Bruce wasn't embezzling from Peppy Pets."

"I told you that."

"I think he was pumping money into the company via Golden West."

"*What?*"

"Pull their contract and the letter of termination and get them to me now." She hung up before he could respond, and stared at her monitor. "What were you up to, you asshole?"

Chapter Forty-Nine

IKE WAS DAMN NEAR GIDDY WHEN Nolan delivered Messane's third computer drive, along with a pound of licorice. She wasn't sure which special gift thrilled him more. "You take it easy on that stuff, Ike, I'm serious."

"I'll titrate down, Doctor. You hear anything from Ross yet?"

"I don't expect to for a while. They pulled a lot of evidence from the beach house, it'll take time to process. How long before you know if you can retrieve the scrubbed footage?"

He gnawed his Red Vines rope with ardor. "If they just deleted it, then it's a cakewalk. But if they were smarter than that, it's a different story. Get me some coffee, and I'll have an answer for you either way by the time you get back."

"Deal."

Ike deserved better than office-brewed swill, so she walked the three blocks to Benji's and got him his caffeinated potion of choice: a large black with almond syrup and oat milk froth. Yuck. She noticed an end-of-day sale on scones, and bought a dozen blueberry-ginger to spread goodwill and joy in Homicide. Al was indeed very joyful when he saw the bakery bag.

"Cinnamon rolls? Donuts?"

"Dried-out blueberry scones. They were half off."

"You should consider a job in marketing." He plunged a hand into the bag, examined his acquisition critically, then ate half of it in one bite. "Not too bad."

"You might consider a job in marketing yourself."

He smirked. "Nice to know we have other career options. Lucerno just called. The Burbank Walmart footage is a loser. It caught the Global Electric van pulling into the lot, but they parked it where there wasn't camera coverage. No sightings of the Merc, either. They probably ditched it when Malibu showed up. Fucking thing could be in a garage anywhere."

"Let's head to Ikeville, he never lets us down. Bring the scones."

He was wild-eyed and crazy-haired when they returned to his office, his face inches away from his monitor, his fingers hammering the keyboard. He didn't even register their presence in the room until Crawford cleared his throat.

"You're in that weird fugue state again, buddy."

He blinked and looked up, as if he'd just been wakened from a strange dream. "Oh. Yeah. Guess I was." He sniffed the air and his bleary eyes slid to Nolan's. "You walked down to Benji's?"

She smiled and handed it over. "Only the best for you."

"You're a doll, Maggie. Scones, too?"

"Less sugar. Is your fugue state a good sign?" She watched desiccated crumbs scatter on his desk as he broke one in half. He didn't comment, but he didn't eat it, either.

"Yeah. They just deleted the files, it was a snap to recover." He gestured them over to his desk. "Gather 'round the campfire and take a look at today's footage. The Global Electric truck arrives at eight thirty a.m., but pulls into the garage—nobody got out, so they had a remote."

"They weren't worried about getting drenched in the monsoon, they were bringing Nicole in out of sight."

Ike nodded and toggled forward. "The Merc shows up two hours later. I enhanced the image and got a plate number, but it came back as stolen, just like the van's." He paused on an image of a blond woman getting out of the car. "That's your Mimi, but she knows where the cameras are and pops her umbrella before they could catch her face. Five minutes later, someone pulls the van back out, probably to make all the action look legit. One guy gets out, but he knows where the cameras are, too, because he uses the van for cover and goes in again through the garage."

Nolan caught the briefest glimpse of a big man wearing a baseball cap. "It all fits with the timeline we have from Jackson and Blattner. And it places the kidnappers there beyond a doubt."

"Yeah, but we still don't have anything that will help us find them. No offense, Ike, this is great work, but were there any better shots when they were leaving, something you could kick into facial recognition?"

"Nah, they were just as cagey when they left. I mean, there's some more car shuffling going on, and by the time the Malibu boys in blue showed, Mimi was gone and the van was back in the garage. Not really worth showing you now, you've got better things to do, but it's going to flesh out your timeline, and it's really solid stuff for building your case."

Nolan knew Ike was holding out on the big reveal, as he often did. But Al didn't have a clue, and she was going to enjoy watching it ride out. "Don't look so dejected, Al. This is great news."

"Yeah. It is. Thanks, Ike."

Ike rolled his head back and looked up at the ceiling, which was as close to God as you could get in the Glass House. "You are so tired, you don't even know I'm fucking with you. Didn't I tell you I'd show you some love?"

Crawford narrowed his eyes. "Spill it. I'm wearing a gun."

"And so am I, friend, but mine's bigger." Ike snorted and rubbed his hands together with relish. "Let's go back a few weeks, when

Mimi didn't have a reason to be so careful." He jumped through screens until he retrieved a full-frontal shot. "I put out a BOLO on her, and I'm running it through recognition software right now."

Crawford reached over for a fist-bump. "Love received and reciprocated. You're the man."

Nolan stared at the grainy image of a stunningly beautiful woman. Not a face you'd associate with kidnapping and murder—more like one you'd see in a magazine, or on the sundeck of a yacht floating somewhere off the French Riviera. "How long will that take, Ike?"

"Depends on a lot of things, like how many photos of her are on the web, but criminals are just as vain as everybody else. People's obsession with internet exposure these days makes it easier for the program to yield faster results, especially with the latest update on the Monkeewrench software. Have a seat and chill for a few minutes, we'll see if anything pops, it's been running for a while."

Nolan collapsed in a chair, feeling the day in her bones. She grabbed a scone while Al got on his phone. It was tasty, and she made a mental note to get some fresh ones in the morning. "Who are you calling?"

"My beloved wife. She needs to know that she's going to be a bachelorette tonight. . . . Hey, honey! Yeah, it's good, we're getting somewhere, but don't hold dinner . . ."

Her thoughts drifted. No matter what was going on with a case, Corinne always made him smile with all his teeth and facial muscles. She responded to Remy the same way, which propelled her imagination to a possible future together. His not-so-subtle intimation of a career move plus an invite to Christmas with the family meant he was serious about pursuing one, Al was absolutely right about that. Was she ready for that next leap of faith that might end well, or horribly, like all her other relationships? Theirs had been fast, passionate, and magical, but if it burned out suddenly, hearts would be broken . . .

Broken hearts always heal.

The words of her mother after her last disastrous entanglement with a cop. But Emily Nolan's heart hadn't healed after her son's death, and it never would, even though she'd finally reached a new plateau of acceptance. Which really had nothing to do with a romantic relationship, there wasn't even the slightest analog between the loss of . . .

Her overwrought reverie was interrupted by an obnoxious bleating from Ike's computer.

"That's a hit on facial recognition, kids. Damn, this is better than Christmas morning."

Christmas. It just kept haunting her.

Chapter Fifty

ROME'S BODY AND MIND WERE NOT holding up well. His muscles throbbed and a searing pain had settled between his eyes, distorting his thoughts. His bloodless hands were numb from the zip ties. But the hood was the worst of the psychological warfare, suffocating him in his own hot, fetid breath.

After a long, miserable ride in the back of a van, they'd led him into a stuffy room that smelled like cheap motel, and pushed him onto a flimsy mattress. He had no idea how long he'd been lying on the rank bedspread like a beached whale, unmoving and uncaring, waiting for the harpoon to finish him off. The thought of seeing Nicole was the only thing that kept him from succumbing to complete despair, but that single tether to hope was fraying, too.

They already killed her.

For the first time since he'd been taken, he started to cry. Without Nicole, he didn't care what happened. Death would be a welcome release. He didn't even flinch when he heard a key in the door lock; almost hoped it was one of the men with the guns coming to shoot him in the head.

But he didn't smell cigarettes, he smelled familiar perfume. It was the evil woman, pulling off his hood and cutting the zip ties. His first glimpse of the room confirmed his suspicion that he was in a motel. A disgusting, filthy, decrepit one. The single window was covered with a torn bedsheet, and the only feeble light came from a shadeless lamp. Her eyes glittered like a cat's in the gloom. She moved like a cat, too, sinuously and with intent.

The platinum hair was gone, replaced by a black cap; the frivolous designer dress of her Beverly Hills persona had been replaced with black leather jeans and jacket. Objectively, she was beautiful, but the cruelty in her visage obliterated any impression of loveliness. She repulsed and terrified him, so he looked away.

"Don't be so shy, Rome, I don't bite. Unless provoked." She giggled. "I'd like to say I'm sorry I put you through all this, but I'm not, because it's your fault, bringing the cops into this. Still, I'm a forgiving sort."

He looked up warily. "Is Nicole still alive?"

"Of course she is. So is your dog. He's such a good boy, but a little neurotic. Animals take on the characteristics of their owners, as you surely know. You need to relax."

Rome felt the overwhelming urge to strike out and hurt her. It was the only time in his life he'd ever considered an act of violence against a woman, and in spite of the situation, it horrified him. "Tell me what you want and let us go."

"That's the plan." She looked toward the door and snapped, "Bring her in."

The door opened and he saw his beautiful, *living* wife being led into the room by the two men, her face tearstained and vacant. But when she saw him, her eyes sparked back to life. In them, Rome saw hope; saw love; and nothing that had happened before this moment mattered anymore. "Nicole," he choked.

She started sobbing, then ran to him. Nobody stopped her.

He held her tight and murmured into her hair. "Thank God, thank God. Everything is going to be okay, sweetheart, I promise."

"I hate to break up this touching reunion, but we have some business to attend to before I send you on your way." The woman gestured to a canting table in the corner, where a sheaf of papers lay atop a leather portfolio. "Sit down, both of you."

Nicole held fast to her husband. "You're not going to kill us?"

Her smile was cold as a winter grave. "I told you I wouldn't. In fact, I really *can't* kill you. If I did, the transaction we're about to complete would come under unwelcome scrutiny, and we can't have that. No, you have to be alive to make this work. And you must cooperate, but I know you will, because we'll be listening and watching. Every second of every day."

Rome blinked in confusion. Criminals demanded cash or a wire transfer to an untraceable account, they didn't create a paper trail. "What kind of transaction?"

"I'm giving you the opportunity to continue your legacy of philanthropy in support of animal welfare organizations. You sign over your recently inherited shares of Peppy Pets to a wonderful but woefully overlooked charity called Animal Rescue International, which will give them a controlling interest in the company. Isn't that wonderful? In exchange, you and your wife and your dog get to live. More than fair, I'd say. And it's not like you need the money."

"How . . . how do you know about the shares?"

She reprimanded him with a scowl. "That's none of your business."

Rome was certain he was dealing with one of the radical factions that placed animals' lives above people's, and had no compunction about using violence as a means to an end. He'd been approached by their likes before, and they refused to accept the fact that human conservation efforts were the only things standing in the way of unfettered cruelty and mass extinction. "But you kidnapped us. Even if I sign it, it will never hold up—"

"You're wrong about that. The documents will be postdated two years, when you made the deal with Bruce. They will be notarized and electronically filed in your legal portfolio like it was always there. There will be records confirming that. Here are the rules: neither of you will breathe a word of this to anyone. The cops will hound you mercilessly for information, but you won't remember anything because you're going to tell them you were drugged. Which you will be. Again. If you are ever approached about the transfer document, you will both confirm it was signed two years ago, and you were happy to do it, because it's such a wonderful charity."

Nicole was cowering against her husband, but she spoke up in a quavering voice. "Then how do we explain the kidnapping? The cops are going to wonder why you took us, then let us go for nothing. They'll be suspicious."

The woman's face suddenly morphed into an ugly mask of fury, and she started pacing in agitation. "You don't explain *anything*, weren't you listening?"

Rome knew instantly that Nicole had hit a sore spot—if you challenged an unbalanced person's fragile delusions—and she was definitely delusional—it infuriated them. He'd been a coward his whole life, but he sensed an opportunity to seed more doubt without fear of repercussion. She couldn't kill them, she'd said it herself. That was the chink in her armor, and if there was ever a time to find courage, to make his wife see that he was a stronger man than the one she'd left, it was now.

"Nicole is right. The police will never believe you kidnapped us and set us free without anything to gain. So that paperwork," he gestured to the stack, "is going to come under scrutiny eventually, no matter what."

She stopped in her tracks and leveled a withering gaze that made his gut writhe. But there was a flicker of uncertainty in her dead eyes. "I appreciate your advice," she sneered with malice, "but I know how to do my job."

He glanced at the brutes with the guns standing by the door. There was uncertainty in their eyes and posture, too.

"Kidnappings are risky," she continued. "And sometimes it's necessary to abort a mission. The cops know this. They'll just be happy to see you alive, and take credit for saving you. Now hear me: any transgression, any mistake, a single *word* to anybody, and you'll end up like your friend Bruce. I gave him everything he wanted, but he got greedy and betrayed me. You don't want to betray me."

Nicole looked up in alarm. "What happened to Bruce?"

She cackled, pulled a gun from her waistband, and pressed it against Nicole's temple. "He was shot in the head. There's a funny story behind that, but I doubt you'd find it amusing. Now pick up that pen, Rome, and sign the papers."

Rome did, watching his signatures smear as drops of sweat dripped from his face. "What are you going to do with us once I sign these?"

She turned the gun on him. "Not one more word."

*　*　*

The desert night was cold, but Sal's pores were streaming nervous sweat as he and Slash loaded the bodies into the back of a pickup truck. The dog and the woman had been no problem, but he staggered when they lifted the fat guy. Jesus, he had to weigh at least three hundred pounds.

This was the part of the job that could go very wrong, but he kept his mind on the money that would be coming his way very soon. He looked over his shoulder, then quickly returned his attention to his unpleasant task. Madam was watching them from the doorway of the abandoned motel, and she didn't look happy.

"Don't drop him, you idiot."

"Just lost my balance for a minute. We got him."

"You remember exactly where to dump them?"

"Yes, ma'am. Madam."

"Don't you dare fuck this up."

Sal swallowed hard as they shook a tarp over the bodies and closed the cover of the bed. "We won't."

"I'm counting on it. Call me when you're finished, and I'll meet you at the usual place to close our deal." She smiled. "I think you've both earned a bonus. It's been an awfully long day."

Chapter Fifty-One

CYNTHIA FINISHED THE BOTTLE OF VIOGNIER, and brewed a third pot of coffee before she plunged herself into the Golden West paper. It didn't take long to confirm her suspicions. In their contract, the agreed price per unit was what every other distributor paid, not the inflated price the invoices reflected. There was no question Bruce had been falsifying documents to hide cash flow from another source. Had he done this solo, or was Golden West complicit?

It was right there in front of her eyes, but it was all so absurd. Surreal. Bruce had been undeniably brilliant in business, but this kind of subterfuge was not only next level, it was highly specialized, and not remotely in his milieu. He couldn't have pulled this off without help. And this, not a dangerous love affair, had gotten him killed, she was now sure of that.

The thought made her shiver as she toggled through the Peppy Pets spreadsheets month by month, checking balances. The extra money had stopped six months ago, when Golden West had pulled out. Who the hell were they?

Her search ended in frustration. She could find nothing outwardly unusual about them—they were an established, midsized distributor based in Texas with a solid track record over the ten years they'd been in business; they serviced many of their competitors. She found no association with any scandal or questionable practices, and the CEO was Elliot Rangel, who'd helmed several established companies before his move to Golden West. Because it wasn't publicly traded, she couldn't access any further information, but they hardly seemed dubious. Which meant nothing—if you were dirty, you obviously went to great lengths to conceal it.

She pushed away from her desk and looked out the double doors that led to the patio and pool. The wind had calmed, the night was moonless, the darkness seemed threatening and impenetrable. She didn't have the capability to go any further with this. But the cops did. They already had access to Bruce's financials, and with their resources and subpoena powers, the information she'd mined tonight might help them. And help her. Cooperation would show she wasn't involved. It might even save the company and her job.

Or it might get you killed, just like Bruce.

She dug through her bag with shaking, panicked hands, and found Detective Nolan's water-stained card at the bottom.

*   *   *

Ike was fully animated, high on his success with facial recognition. He gestured to his monitor, where a column of photos paralleled newspaper headlines and text. "This is Mimi in her early twenties, about ten years ago. Her real name is Magdalena De Leon, Spanish national. Looks like she was an international party girl, screwing up like most rich, spoiled club kids do. Drunk and disorderly, minor possession, public nudity."

Nolan scanned the photos. Most of them were very unflattering shots of her in various states of dissolution—blown pupils, white coke rings around her nose, and a particularly disturbing shot of her standing on a table in a nightclub, drinking champagne from the bottle while men groped her with leering smiles. The corresponding headlines were predictably salacious, the upshot being that one of Europe's wealthiest heiresses had been arrested again. "Anything current on her?"

Ike frowned. "That's the weird thing. The search didn't pull anything after 2015, which makes me wonder what happened ten years ago. She was clearly high-profile, so you'd think there would be something more recent, even if she cleaned up her act."

"Too much money and not enough parenting," Crawford sniped. "I'm not up on European heiresses and their party life, so what's her story?"

Ike switched to another screen of newspapers articles, eyes jittering over the text. "Says here her daddy is Duke Sebastian De Leon of Spain."

"I thought Franco killed all the nobility."

"No, he just appointed his own from a pool of loyalists and family. Spain abolished those titles in 2022, and Sebastian De Leon still holds his, so he's old money, old family."

"It says that?"

Ike scoffed. "Of course not, I just know a lot of stuff. You should watch *Jeopardy!*"

Nolan knew he'd been in treatment at least twice, and when he'd confided in her, he said the only two things that allayed the boredom of sobriety were to read and watch *Jeopardy!* "How did a Euro party girl drop off the face of the earth and reinvent herself in America as something much worse?"

"The family probably wanted their embarrassing black sheep on another continent. Who knows what happened to her in the last ten years?" He continued reading. "She was born in Los Angeles, so she has dual citizenship."

"Plug her into the criminal database, see if she has a rap sheet," Crawford said, helping himself to a piece of licorice.

After a few minutes, Ike shook his head. "Nope, not here. But now that you know who she is, it'll be easier to track her down. At least if she's using her real name."

Nolan blew him a kiss. "Thanks, Ike, you're the greatest, we'll take it from here."

"All in a day's work. I'll keep at it." He smiled. "We're getting closer."

She watched him recede back into his digital kingdom. His personal life might be a wreck, but he had control over zeros and ones.

"A fucked-up heiress sounds right up Messane's sexually deviant alley," Crawford remarked as they headed back to Homicide. "Maybe all his money was coming from her family coffers or her trust fund, and he screwed her. And she screwed him right back with a bullet to the head. Reading those emails, she was obviously into him in the sickest possible way. With her dough, connections, and lack of morals, hiring a hit man would be as easy as getting a manicure. Hell hath no fury like a psycho scorned."

Chapter Fifty-Two

AS NOLAN SITUATED HERSELF AT HER desk, Cynthia Jackson surprised her with a call. She didn't bother with a greeting, just started rambling fast and unintelligibly. The woman was unraveling. "Ms. Jackson, I'm going to put you on speaker so my partner can listen in." She waved Al over to her desk. "Would you please start from the beginning and speak a little more slowly?"

Her quavering voice came through the speaker in short bursts. "Yes, of course, I'm sorry. You were right, Bruce *was* cooking the books, but not to cover embezzlement. He was dumping money into the company by falsifying earnings from a distributor called Golden West Animal Supply. The money stopped coming in when they terminated their contract six months ago. That also happens to be about the time Wilder approached us about an acquisition. I think Bruce wanted to clean up so he could sell."

"That's also about the time Messane was beaten half to death," Crawford mumbled, but she caught it.

"Oh my God . . . the scars . . ."

"Ms. Jackson, do you believe he was laundering money through Peppy Pets?" Nolan asked.

"No, the paper trail in a corporation is too dense. You have to launder through cash businesses. This is something different, but I can't figure it out."

"Do you know anything about Golden West?"

"From what I can tell, they're legit and established, but they're privately held, so they're not required to disclose certain information like a public company is. I know Elliot Rangel is the CEO, and he's well-regarded in the business world. But CEOs aren't usually directly involved in the details of what happens below them."

"Could Mr. Messane have done this without their knowledge?"

"Yes, but he couldn't have done this all on his own, it's extremely complicated. My feeling is Golden West had to have been in on it. We have dozens of distributors, and I can't see him just pulling their name out of a hat." She sighed anxiously. "I can't prove anything but the numbers I see in our books. You have investigative latitude I don't."

Nolan was feeling as jittery as Jackson sounded. It was contagious. "Thank you for letting us know, we'll look into it."

She stifled a sob. "Bruce is dead because of this, I just know it. I'm the CFO, and a former lover of his besides. What if I'm next?"

"We have a solid lead on his killer now, Ms. Jackson, but we'll send a patrol to you right now." She nodded at Al, who jumped on his phone. "They'll check in with you first, and watch your house for the night. Hopefully, things will be resolved by then."

"Thank you. It's probably silly, I'm sorry. I guess it's just the shock."

Nolan was suddenly furious on behalf of Cynthia Jackson and all the other women who'd apologized to her over the years for things that weren't their fault. Women who'd ended up dead. "You have nothing to apologize for. You deserve to feel safe. To be safe."

"Patrol is on the way, Ms. Jackson," Crawford said. "Make sure you're locked up and your security is armed."

"I will."

"Were Mr. Messane's personal legals handled through the company? Knowing more about these LLCs might help us out, it's another piece of the puzzle."

"Our general counsel said Bruce retained Rothschild Smythe for personal matters. But Tim didn't think he would use them for anything illegal; they're a big, international firm."

"Thank you for this information, Ms. Jackson," Nolan said. "You know how to reach us if you think of anything else. Or need anything else."

"I could really use another bottle of wine."

"I'd like a glass right now myself."

She chuckled weakly. "Maybe we can have one together once you figure this all out."

"I'd like that. Take care, Ms. Jackson."

Nolan looked up at Al, who was dragging his hands down his face. "Messane was dirty, and the six-month timeline is pretty damning, so Golden West is a part of this, they have to be. And Mimi is smack-dab in the center of all of it."

"Finding her is number one on the honey-do list. I'll jump into that, you take a look at Golden West. We're getting there, Mags."

* * *

Cynthia dropped her phone, feeling nauseated from stress, exhaustion, coffee, and wine. What a hideous combination. She was also feeling increasingly frightened. Maybe it was unfounded, but caution was free insurance. The patrol was additional insurance, and they would arrive soon to watch over her. Everything was going to be okay, but taking Detective Crawford's words to heart, she rushed to check the patio and front doors and make sure the alarm was set.

When she'd confirmed that everything was secure, she sank into the living room sofa and turned on the fireplace. The silent flicker of flames on a bed of glass pebbles smoothed some of the jagged edges. She could almost pretend it was an ordinary winter night; imagine that she could doze off and sleep dreamlessly, warm and safe.

But a reflection in the glass doors of the fireplace jolted her back into a high panic. She spun around to look out the window, but there was no one in the yard or the driveway. Probably just the reflection of a passing car, she rationalized. Or more likely, the patrol, coming to check in.

It was a reasonable assumption, but she also thought about the gun nestled in the drawer of the end table, just inches away. Ultimately, she decided it was a bad idea to greet a police officer waving her SIG Sauer.

Halfway to the door, she knew something was wrong. Part of it was instinct, manifested in the million needlelike prickles that raced down her arms; part of it was logic—the cops would have rung her doorbell by now. She dropped to the ground and crawled just far enough to peer through the sidelight.

There was a man at the door—a big, ugly man with a pocked face and mean eyes. A man who was wearing a padded flannel shirt and jeans instead of a uniform. Her blood turned to ice, and she scrambled backward, but not fast enough.

He looked down at her in amusement, then gestured to the insulated food carrier he was holding. "Pizza."

She jumped to her feet and started backing away. "Get off my property! I didn't order a pizza!"

Had he been a real deliveryman with the wrong address, he would have turned tail and run from the crazy woman he'd disturbed. Instead, the look of amusement transformed into anger. He dropped the bag and started rattling the door handle.

After a brief second of paralysis, she launched herself at the security pad by the door and slammed her fist against the police call button. The alarm let out a deafening whoop-whoop-whoop as she fled toward her gun and her phone.

Please let me live long enough to go broke, lose everything, and start over.

Chapter Fifty-Three

CRAWFORD WAS HUNCHED OVER HIS COMPUTER, mindlessly shoving crumbling scones into his mouth while he glowered at his monitor. Nolan thought he looked like an angry troll, and wondered if Corinne had ever made a similar observation. Probably.

"Magdalena De Leon is definitely off the grid. No social media accounts, no property or utility records. No nothing."

"She's using another identity."

"Right, but hell if we're going to be able to figure out what it is."

Nolan shrugged. "People are lazy creatures of habit. She might use Mimi and a riff on her real last name. Like Lyon. Lyons. Leone."

"Yeah, maybe, I'll check. Anything on Golden West?"

"Nothing of note. Their distribution center is in Laredo, Texas, and they have several pet food manufacturing plants in Mexico."

"Jackson mentioned it was privately held, so who owns it?"

"The Covina family. As in the grocery store chain. Elliot Rangel is well regarded, like she said. We'll call him in the morning. Keep looking for Mimi and I'll try to get in touch with the De Leon clan."

"They're in for a nasty surprise."

"Given her history, they might not be surprised at all. But they can't fix her problem this time." She switched focus and began the search for a family contact—a seemingly simple task that was turning out to be as frustrating as the rest of this case.

Mimi had done a world-class disappearing act ten years ago, but her prominent relatives weren't much more visible. Current information was scant, but she found a small lifestyle piece in *El Mundo* on Sebastian De Leon. He was still living as of last year, apparently in hermitage at a vineyard villa in Rioja in the years since his wife's death. No mention of his wayward daughter. The Spanish press obviously had more respect for their nobles' privacy than some of their European counterparts. Sebastian's brother, Carlos, had a broader presence online as partner in a law firm in Madrid, but it was the middle of the night there and nobody would be answering phones.

Nolan refined her search parameters, and ten minutes later, she found an article in the *Harvard Law Review* on a rising star alumna. She followed multiple links and eventually slumped back in her chair in relief, taking a deep breath as she stared at the good fortune on her screen. It wasn't a victory yet, but it was a tremendous leap forward. "Al, Mimi has a sister. Montserrat De Leon, a big-shot attorney who works for none other than Rothschild Smythe."

He looked up, his brows reaching for his hairline, which had been gradually receding over the past two years. "That's pretty fucking interesting."

"What's more fucking interesting is that they also represent Wilder Foods. They are the ones who handled the Peppy Pets acquisition."

"Damn. That's almost too good to be true. I think you just found a nest of spiders, so let's figure out where all the creepy-crawlies intersect." He grabbed his desk phone when the Homicide line lit up. "Crawford. Oh, hey, Ross . . . that's great . . . no kidding, a Hessian?"

Nolan frowned. The Hessians were a rabidly psychotic bike gang that made the Hells Angels look like troop of Cub Scouts. They were infamous for everything from drugs to murder, but not exactly sophisticated as far as the criminal species went.

"Right, okay, thanks a million, man. Yeah, will do." He hung up. "Some prints from the Mountain Dew bottles popped, all belonging to Grady 'Slash' Raab. Bad dude."

"'Slash'?"

"He likes his knives, hence the multiple stints in lovely places like Pelican Bay."

"So, he's dumb muscle."

"That's my guess. And if Mimi's running with that kind of company, it doesn't exactly bode well for the Bechtolds. Check him out while I put a BOLO out on him, too."

Nolan pulled Raab up on the criminal database. He was a monster, built like a human tank, with a badly scarred face that had seen more than one shiv. He was smiling for his mug shot, and the partially toothless leer chilled her blood. His record was twice as long as Ty Mattison's and a hundred times uglier. Assault and battery, second-degree murder, manslaughter, drug charges, rape. And those were just the things he'd been caught doing, God only knew what he'd gotten away with. Why hadn't Grady Raab been drowned at birth?

There wasn't a Mimi listed under known associates—no women at all, just a lot of other big, ugly men who should have also been drowned at birth. But his last known address kicked up her pulse: Culver City, less than a mile from Poppy's shop. "Raab may have been our shooter, Al. Find a judge and get a warrant on his place. I'll track down the sister."

Chapter Fifty-Four

MONTSERRAT STARED DOWN INTO THE INKY blackness of the Atlantic far below, just as she'd been staring down at Los Angeles mere hours ago. Too much time hanging in the sky lately, she thought, sipping a glass of champagne in the empty Gulfstream, feeling very alone. Part of it was being in solitary limbo, thirty thousand feet above the Earth; but a larger part was the uncertainty of her father's plans for Magdalena. His mention of intervention and the way he'd said it unnerved her. What did he know that she didn't? Was her sister falling into a black hole of drug abuse and mental illness again?

It was pointless to agonize over it, but she had no control over her anxiety any more than she did the inevitable confrontation that loomed like a roiling black thunderhead. The family was already fractured, but this time, it might fall apart beyond repair.

She didn't know if a warning would make any difference or help matters, but she had to try. She sent a brief text, not expecting a response. Mimi used throwaways far more often than her own phone, which could go neglected for months. Her paranoia was getting worse.

Montserrat tossed her phone on the seat beside her and closed her eyes, hoping the bubbles would help her sleep—she would need every ounce of energy she could bank to deal with her father.

Just as she was drifting off, her phone rang in through the plane's Wi-Fi satellite link. Unknown number. "What the hell is going on, Mimi? Papa called me back to Spain, and he's very upset with you."

"Ms. Montserrat De Leon?"

She jerked up in her seat, wide awake now. "Who is this?"

"Detective Margaret Nolan, LAPD Homicide. I'm speaking to Montserrat De Leon?"

"Yes."

"I need to ask you some questions about your sister, Magdalena."

Montserrat had never felt real panic, real fear, until now. She'd always projected worst-case scenarios about Magdalena eventually doing something so supremely idiotic, it would get her killed, but she'd never really believed it would happen. "Oh my God. Is she . . . she's not . . ."

"She's very much alive, and we need your help finding her. It's critical that we do."

"What is this about?"

"She's a person of interest in a homicide investigation. And a kidnapping."

The astonishment stole her voice for a moment. "You can't be serious."

"I'm very serious. You were obviously expecting her call—we know she goes by Mimi. I need her contact information."

"I'm happy to cooperate, but I don't have it. She's been estranged from the family for ten years—"

"I doubt I have to explain obstruction of justice to a lawyer."

"Detective Nolan, don't insult my intelligence."

"Then don't insult mine."

Montserrat bit her tongue. Now wasn't the time for a pissing match, but it *was* time for a little white lie. "She hasn't owned a phone in years, so I have to wait for her to contact me."

"Suspicious, don't you think?"

"If you're calling me, you already know about her past. Her issues. She's extremely paranoid and struggles with mental illness. I never know where she is. Sometimes I don't hear from her for months. Or more."

"Given the way you answered the phone, I think you've very recently been in touch."

She sighed irritably. "Yes. Magdalena called me earlier today and we spoke briefly. We don't get along, so conversations never go well. I was hoping she'd call me back."

"Can you tell me what you fought about?"

"Our father is very sick, and she won't reach out. I'm on a flight to Spain now to visit him."

"I'm sorry to hear that."

"Thank you."

"You must know something about her. A residence, a job, friends or associates, past or present? Things sisters might talk about on those rare occasions you might be in touch?"

"Detective, I understand criminal investigations, but my sister is a ghost. She could be in Madagascar or Siberia for all I know."

"She's in Los Angeles, I can guarantee that. Who else in your family is in touch with her?"

"No one. She's persona non grata to anyone but me. I can give you the number she called me from last night, but I very much doubt you'll be able to reach her. I wish I could be more helpful."

"Maybe I can help *you*. Your sister was having an affair with Bruce Messane, who was murdered last night. But I imagine you know that already, having been involved with the Peppy Pets acquisition. And his former business partner and his wife have been kidnapped. They might be dead, too. Blood is thicker than water until multiple felonies are on the table."

What did you do this time, Magdalena?

"I had no idea she was romantically involved with Bruce Messane—"

"Very specific, lawyerly phrasing. Perhaps she was involved with him in another way as well?"

Her jaw ached from clenching her teeth. "It's incomprehensible that she would kill him, or have anything to do with a kidnapping."

"But you admitted that you really don't know anything about her."

Montserrat felt her anger building. All cops thought they were so clever. "This conversation is over, Detective Nolan."

"Not until you give me that phone number. Unless you want us to subpoena your phone records and find it ourselves. And who knows? We might find something else interesting while we're looking."

* * *

"She's lying through her teeth," Crawford fumed, punching in the phone number Montserrat De Leon had given them. "I hate lawyers."

"You don't hate prosecutors."

"I hate some, like that smarmy little prick Woodward."

Predictably, Al's mood was degrading with each passing hour of frustration, junk food, and bad coffee. So was hers, but so far, she'd been able to keep her cool. "I agree she's withholding information, but she doesn't know everything. Otherwise, she wouldn't have answered the way she did."

"The problem is, she's not going to say another damn word. Next time we'll be talking to her lawyer." He paused and cheered a little. "But you really threw her a couple of zingers, that was great. If she's really on a flight to visit her sick father, she won't be sleeping through it."

"That would be a weird thing to lie about."

"I think we've established the whole family is weird." His lifted his finger as he listened to the phone at his ear. "It's ringing, Mags, and not going to voicemail. It's still in service."

"If you're thinking about trying to track it, don't. Burner phones are a nightmare. By the time we jump through flaming hoops, it'll be way too late to get a real-time location. And if Mimi is as paranoid as her sister says, it's probably already in a ditch somewhere."

"Ike can find a way to do it faster. He has a lot of tools in his treasure chest."

"Illicit tools. Do you really want to go there?"

He shrugged. "No, but it's not like this is the only thing that's going to crack the case. We have enough on Mimi to roast her alive, we just have to find her."

Digital technology moved at the speed of light, and laws moved at the speed of a glacier. Lots of room for gray areas and Machiavellian justification. "Fine. Just don't call or email him, go to his office."

"I haven't lost all my brain cells yet." The Homicide line rang again. "Maybe Ross has something more for us. Crawford here."

Nolan watched his expression shift, then darken. Not good news.

"What?" she asked when he hung up.

"Attempted break-in at Cynthia Jackson's house. They got a good description from her, but they haven't found him yet."

"Is she okay?"

"Terrified, but fine. She hit the panic button on her security system, and the patrol we sent was almost there. This is bad, Mags. We have *got* to figure this out before more people die."

Chapter Fifty-Five

MAYA LUCERNO WAS STARING OUT THE windshield at a gray froth of gnats seething around the parking lot lights at the Burbank Walmart. It was a chaotic, senseless dance, and one she could relate to. Her whole day had been like that, eroding her emotional strength and allowing the guilt to slip in through the fissures.

Brandon distracted her as he made his way to the car, phone to his ear. He looked good; unfazed, even after this wrenching, endless day. She was only five years his senior, but five years made a difference once you were out of your twenties. She caught a glimpse of herself in the rearview mirror and resisted the foolish urge to put on some lipstick.

He tucked his phone into his jacket pocket, then climbed in. "Ross got a hit from the beach house. A biker named Grady Raab. Maggie and Al put out a BOLO, and they're working on a warrant for his last known address."

She sighed and started the sedan. "Pray to God they find him fast, because time is not on our side."

"It never is." He nudged her arm. "You need something to eat, Maya. I need something to eat. There's a Carl's Jr. a few blocks away. Big Char Chile combo sounds just about right."

Lucerno squirmed as her empty stomach released a shot of acid. "I don't think I could choke down a bowl of oatmeal right now."

"I'll force-feed you if I have to. You need fuel."

She tried unsuccessfully for a smile and decided he was right. Self-deprivation wasn't going to help anything. A plain hamburger probably wouldn't make her puke. As she pulled out of the Walmart lot, her vibrating phone skittered a few inches on the dashboard. A call was something that usually sparked hope and optimism during a case, but her ability to feel positive emotions had disappeared, just like Rome Bechtold. "Lucerno," she answered disconsolately.

As she listened to Officer Angela Tichenor from Foothill Community Police Station in Pacoima, she felt tears streaming down her face; felt Brandon's eyes on her as she eventually hung up.

"What is it, Maya?"

"Pacoima got a call on two bodies by a trail in Hansen Dam Recreation Area."

"Aw, shit. The Bechtolds?"

She nodded and the tears came faster.

"God, I'm so sorry, Maya—"

She shook her head briskly. "They're in ICU at Kaiser Permanente, but they're going to be okay, Brandon. And so is the dog. He's getting checked out at a veterinary hospital." She choked out a semblance of a giddy laugh, and let him take her into his arms. It was awkward, but she didn't care.

"I told you it was going to work out, Maya."

"No, you didn't."

He chuckled into her hair. "I guess I didn't. What else do you know?"

"A night hiker heard a dog yowling—it was Addy. That's how he found them. They were unconscious. Drugged."

"They're alive. This is the happy ending we weren't sure we'd get."

"I can't stop blubbering."

"You've earned the right to blubber."

She pulled away, suddenly embarrassed; by her tears, by so willingly falling into his embrace and liking it. She wiped her eyes with her jacket sleeve, but it was an exercise in futility. "Would you call Maggie and Al and let them know?"

"Of course."

"Can you drive to the hospital, too? I can't see a goddamn thing."

* * *

Rome felt a hand on his arm, heard voices, but it was all a dream, so he ignored the intrusion. He was happy where he was.

"Dr. Bechtold, can you wake up for us?"

Be quiet. Let me sleep.

"Detective Lucerno is here to see you."

His dream began to splinter. Why was that name familiar?

Maya watched his eyelids flutter, then still. She glanced at Dr. Marsten, an older man with thinning blond hair and a round, affable face. "Do you know what they were drugged with?"

"Not yet, but the presentation is consistent with Rohypnol or GHB. He has more body mass, so he's coming out of it faster than his wife, but they're both going to recover. There will be some amnesia, as you probably know. The extent depends on the drug and the dosage."

She knew all about roofies and GHB. Sometimes the blank spots in the memory's matrix were temporary; sometimes they were permanent. It was a waiting game now.

He glanced down at his patient. "It's likely he can hear us, but it might take a while for him to fully regain consciousness."

She remembered standing vigil at her grandmother's bedside five years ago. She'd been unconscious, too, very near death after a long battle with cancer, but the doctor had made certain to explain it was very likely she could hear and understand anything they said. She'd wondered at the time if people actually spoke ill of a relative at their deathbed. Jaded as she was now, she was sure of it. "I'll wait."

"Of course, Detective. He'll appreciate a familiar face when he wakes up. I'll check in again soon."

"Thank you, Doctor."

After he left, she took Rome's hand and squeezed it. "I promise you we're going to find the people who did this."

Chapter Fifty-Six

YOU WILL NEVER FORGET YOUR TRAUMA, Sam, but it's critical that you don't relive it. Do you understand the difference between remembering and re-experiencing?

Not really.

Cognitively, you understand you're no longer in danger, but emotionally, you're living through it over and over again, and your body is reacting to the stress as if it were actually happening. You need to create a mental safe space where you can confront the past objectively. It's a matter of retraining your mind. That will help you heal.

I think I'd rather forget the past, Dr. Frolich.

I understand. But it's not possible.

Sam was holding his breath, like everybody else in the mobile command unit as they watched the monitors and listened to the comm feeds. The SWAT squad was in formation outside the Anaheim warehouse a block away, preparing to breach a side door. DEA and Gang-Narc were situated around the building, covering the two other entrances. The area seemed largely deserted, and no vehicles were parked in the lot, but thermal imaging showed four man-shaped heat signatures inside.

He felt the tension as a crushing physical presence, squeezing the air out of him. The visual and audio transported him to the scene like an avatar, but this wasn't a video game—this was real, and his body was responding for the fight. How stupid to think that taking the position as an observer would allow his adrenal glands to go into hibernation. And quite possibly, stupid to think he was finished chasing the rush. Why else would he take a job that embedded him with a paramilitary unit? Maybe he hadn't made that much progress after all.

This is who you are. Who you always will be. A leopard is still a leopard, even if it's in a cage.

"Showtime, Sam," Margolis said quietly, his eyes never leaving the monitors.

He wiped his sweat-slick hands on his jeans as he watched the shadowy line of officers signal each other, preparing to breach. Kenny Durden was on the front line with three others, their ballistics shields raised. He tried to remember him as a naughty third-grader, not think of him as a man potentially walking into a hive of cartel hornets.

The choreography was balletic and mesmerizing as the door buckled under the ballistic ram and the phalanx moved as one organism into the dark unknown, shouting "Metro SWAT!" Sam's heart squeezed painfully when bursts of automatic gunfire flared red on the screens, the sound filling the command unit; his legs twitched as he fought the instinct to run into the fray. The bouncing body cams were impossible to follow, the chaos relentless.

"David twenty-four, two suspects down!"

Seconds seemed like agonizing hours as the firefight continued, and his mind was rewinding unbidden to the burned-out shell of a building in Kandahar. There had been just enough left of the structure to conceal a ragged group of ISIS fighters armed with US M16s. He squeezed his eyes shut briefly as he tried to banish the memory.

". . . Three down . . ."

". . . North exit, in pursuit . . ."

Remember, don't relive.

"Code Four, we're clear!"

It was Kenny Durden's voice over the comm that finally brought him back to the present. He let out a shuddering sigh, and felt Margolis's eyes on him. If he was waiting for him to crack up, he was going to be disappointed.

"Remind you of the real thing, Sam?"

"It is the real thing, sir. And I'd be damn glad to have any one of them watching my six."

"Think this is for you?"

Sam considered carefully before he answered. "One hundred percent."

"Then welcome aboard. Sit tight until Taggert comes to get you. He'll take you through the scene."

* * *

Sam followed Justin into the warehouse. Emergency response was working on the two men who wouldn't be going to the morgue, at least not right away. The smell of cordite was the overwhelming top note, but beneath it was the metallic scent of blood. It wasn't remotely comforting, but it was familiar.

Justin led him to a bandaged, semiconscious man on a crash cart. His gaunt face, shaved head, neck, and arms were colored with tattoos: snakes, dragons, skulls, the Virgin Mary, and gang tags.

"We've been looking for this scum bunny, he's been making a run on some pretty big territory. They call him the angel of death on the streets, we figure he's an enforcer for Los Zetas. You know about them?"

"Enough that I'm glad he's on a gurney."

Justin gave him an appreciative smile, then addressed the paramedic hooking up an IV bag. "Is he going to make it, Greg?"

"Should. He's shocky, but stable and ready for transport."

"Taking him to Irvine?"

"Yeah, we're ready to load him up."

"If he's stable, I'm searching him first. Kids are dying because of this asshole."

"Be my guest."

While Justin searched him, Sam glanced deeper into the warehouse. Beyond the commotion of multiple personnel taking photos, video, and collecting evidence, he saw broken pallets, rows of empty metal shelving, and not much else.

"Well, lookie here. Got a wallet and a shiny new iPhone. Locked with fingerprint ID. Good thing SWAT didn't shoot them off."

Sam understood gallows humor. In their line of work, you needed it to keep your head on straight.

"Open his phone so we can roll, Justin. He's stable, but not that stable."

"Yeah, yeah . . .'kay . . ."

It took a few tries, but Justin was eventually victorious. "Got it. Take out the trash."

"Who is he?" Sam asked.

Justin flicked a driver's license out of a tooled leather wallet. "Says here Jaime Cabral. Mexican issue, address in Tijuana."

"I didn't realize cartel thugs carried ID."

"Might be a fake, but we'll find out soon enough. I guarantee his prints are on a criminal database somewhere. And his phone is gold. Give me a second to disable the security on it before it reactivates, then we'll finish the tour."

Sam resumed his assessment of the warehouse. "Place looks deserted."

"This part of it does. I'll show you where the action is."

Sam followed him through huge double doors to the loading bay, where a semitrailer was being swarmed by DEA agents. "That's what they were protecting. It has a full cargo of boxes, and the ones they pulled so far are loaded with pills. The same shit that's been flooding the streets. The landlord should have done some site checks, don't you think?"

"I think the landlord knew exactly what was going on here."

"The DEA has their hands on him now. He's not going to have a good night."

"With two survivors and the landlord on hot rocks, you might get somewhere fast."

"Unfortunately, the foot soldiers have no idea who's at the top of the food chain. They just follow orders from another peon one rank above them."

"Sounds a lot like the military."

"By design. That's why the cartels are so successful. We have to take what they know and piece it together with what we know. Sometimes we have to sit on the information for a bigger takedown. But an enforcer is a good catch."

One of the agents waved them over to the trailer. "Every box we've opened so far is pay dirt, Justin. This is a huge bust. If the whole cargo load is pills, we're looking at hundreds of millions in product."

Sam stepped closer, then froze as he stared at the boxes.

Chapter Fifty-Seven

CRAWFORD RETURNED FROM HIS FORAY TO Ike's office with a fistful of licorice. "Want a piece?"

"Absolutely not. Is Ike up for tracing the burner?"

"He's elated, you know he loves a challenge. But he said it was a Hail Mary, no promises." He tipped his head curiously. "You look pretty happy yourself."

Nolan smiled, and it felt good after a frustrating day of frowns. "Brandon Robb called. Pacoima found the Bechtolds in Hansen Dam rec area. They're in the hospital, but they'll be fine."

"Thank God. What happened?"

"Don't know yet. They were drugged and they're still unconscious. Lucerno is there, waiting for them to wake up."

He sank into his chair. "If Mimi is finished with them, she's going to scatter to the wind. She might already be gone."

"She'll try, but her face is on every phone and computer in California law enforcement."

"She could be out of state by now. Shit."

Nolan stood and shrugged on her jacket. "That's why we're going to pay Grady Raab a visit. We don't need a warrant to knock on his door. And if he's home, the idiot might actually let us in."

* * *

Sal helped himself to a tattered corduroy recliner and gulped his Corona while Slash sat on a bare mattress on the floor and drank whiskey from the bottle. The place sure as hell wasn't a beach house in Malibu, but he always had booze, weed, and pills, which trumped ambience any day. "Cheers, man, we did good."

He fired up a second fat joint and passed it over. "Damn right, we're getting a bonus. How much do you think it'll be?"

"We'll find out soon enough."

He wiped a dribble of whiskey from his chin. "What are you gonna do with your money?"

Sal took a long toke and shrugged. "Maybe hit the beach in Mazatlán for a few days. You?"

Slash released a stoner's giggle. "A few days? Man, you don't know how to live. I'm riding my Hog to Vegas and staying drunk and high for a month. I know some great whores there, you should come with me."

No way Sal was going to Vegas with this dumb fuck, not even for a night. "Thanks, I'll think about it."

He gazed at the label of his Four Roses bourbon bottle reflectively. "This was a weird job. Why do you think Madam made the fat guy sign away his money to charity?"

"It's none of our business. Jesus, Slash, how many times have I told you to keep your head down and your mouth shut?"

"I don't say nothing to her. I'm asking *your* opinion."

Sal had to admit it was strange, but money was money, so who cared? "I don't have an opinion. Got anything to eat?"

"Nah, I gave it all to the dog."

"What dog?"

"Some stray. Thing is skin and bones, so I throw food out for it."

Sal was purely amazed. "You got no problem killing people, but you feed stray dogs?"

Slash looked offended. "Dog didn't ask for the life he got. People have free will, and if they need killing, they obviously deserve it."

* * *

"My, what a charming domicile," Crawford commented as Nolan pulled up to a tiny cube on a patch of dead grass littered with assorted trash, a rusting skeleton of a motorcycle, and piles of broken roof tiles that had given up the ghost, probably years ago. The stucco exterior was scabby, like a peeling sunburn, and the front door was sagging on its hinges. "Corinne has shoeboxes that wouldn't fit in that thing."

"I can't believe there are still working streetlights here."

"There's a light on in the house, too. Looks like somebody might be home."

Nolan felt a conflicting surge of anticipation and dread. Grady Raab was a wild card—he had answers, but he was also big and violent. It was impossible to anticipate his reaction. She patted her tach vest. "Let's hope we don't need these. Ready?"

"Yep."

They both got out of the car cautiously, and she probed the darkness with her flashlight as they approached the house, heart thumping. No movement, no threatening shadows that she could see. Dogs barked in the distance; music droned; somewhere a baby started crying. She hated these parts of LA—not just because they were dangerous, especially at night, but because they were just so damned sad. And coming off a visit to Malibu, it was even more depressing. There was vast canyon separating the city's rich and the poor, and the poor often ended up with sociopaths like Grady Raab for neighbors.

As they mounted the broken concrete steps, Nolan saw the door wasn't just sagging, it was partially open. The faint smell of marijuana drifted out into the cool night air. They both unholstered their weapons and took their positions on either side of the door, just as they had at Messane's beach house. The only difference was the fear factor, which was multiplied tenfold by the dark, the neighborhood, and the man who might be inside.

Crawford reached out and rapped on the door. "Grady Raab?"

No answer.

"Grady Raab, it's LAPD, we'd like to speak with you."

"I'll go around to the side in case he makes a run for the alley," she whispered.

He shined his Mag into the opening, then shouted and stumbled backward as a skinny, snarling dog appeared in the doorway, eyes glowing like a demon's in the circle of light. Its muzzle was covered in blood. "Fuck," he gasped. "I have a feeling Raab won't be running anywhere."

* * *

Crawford managed to coax the dog out with a piece of licorice while Nolan called Animal Control. The pathetic creature broke her heart and would probably be euthanized, but at least it wouldn't suffer anymore. Seeing a hurting child or animal was like a gut punch, and made her want to blow the planet into space dust.

With the dog safely distracted, they stepped inside, staying close to the door so they didn't further compromise the crime scene. The sorry mutt had done enough damage. A lamp on a fruit crate illuminated two bodies—Grady Raab on a bare mattress, his companion slumped in a chair, both with large gunshot wounds to the head. An overturned whiskey bottle and a broken Corona bottle had leaked their contents onto the floor, diluting bloody canine footprints.

"Mimi was tying up loose ends," Crawford raged. "And we missed her again. How the hell does this keep happening?"

"I don't think it's beginner's luck. She's been living in the shadows for ten years, probably to cover her ass while she did crime." Nolan skirted carefully around the blood and booze and touched Raab's neck. He was obviously not of this world anymore, but you had to check. "He's still really warm, Al. She might be right under our noses. We've got to move fast."

"Move on what? Like her sister said, she's a ghost."

"She's going to leave town, she has to. If I were her, I'd head straight to LAX and get the hell out as fast as possible. Alert the TSA and I'll see if Ike got anywhere with the burner."

Chapter Fifty-Eight

ROME FELT LIKE HE'D BEEN BLUDGEONED with a sledge-hammer. He moaned and cradled his head as Detective Lucerno held a cup with a straw to his mouth.

"You've been getting IV fluids, but you need to drink, too, Dr. Bechtold. It will help flush out your system."

He took a small sip, but his stomach didn't like it. Not one bit. He looked down at the kidney-shaped pan on his lap, and prayed he wouldn't need it. Unpleasant bodily functions demanded privacy. "Are Nicole and Addy really alright?"

"I promise you they are. Your wife is still coming off the drug, but you'll be able to see her soon. Addy is at a local veterinary hospital, and he's fine, too. And quite the hero—he was by your side howling, and a hiker heard him. That's probably the only reason you were found tonight."

Rome's heart contracted. "Man's best friend."

"Yes, I'd say so. Dr. Bechtold, I know this is an impossible time, but I need you to tell me everything you can remember. Even a small detail might help us. We're getting close, but you could bring us to the finish line."

He let his eyes fall shut. There were two things he recalled clearly:

the gun pressing against Nicole's temple, and the chilling warning not to talk to the police. But he had to tell the detective something, and convince her his day in captivity was mostly lost. "When I was taking Addy for a walk, my knee starting hurting. A woman pulled up in a Mercedes, a silver sedan, and offered us a ride. Then she pulled a gun on me and stabbed a syringe in my neck."

"The woman's name is Magdalena De Leon, aka Mimi, does that mean anything to you?"

"No. Who is she?"

"A former lover of Mr. Messane. We think she was involved in his murder."

"Oh, God."

"What's the next thing you remember?"

"Waking up on a couch in a safe room. I shouted and pounded on the door, and a man with a gun came in, gave me a bottle of water, then left. It's all very hazy, like a bad dream."

"You were held at Mr. Messane's beach house for a while before they moved you, did you realize that?"

Rome was genuinely shocked. "No! Why?"

"Something to do with Peppy Pets, don't you think?"

"I can't imagine what. You know I haven't had anything to do with the company or Bruce for years."

"Do you remember where they moved you? The location is a crime scene and there might be valuable evidence there."

He hesitated. A moment too long, he realized, because her gaze intensified. He'd read somewhere that liars avoided eye contact, so he looked directly at her. "I don't know. Detective, I hardly have any memories of what happened. I don't even know how I got here." That wasn't a lie. After he'd signed the papers, everything went black again.

"The kidnappers didn't take money from you, we checked. Your bank accounts are all untouched. I'm wondering what they wanted, and if they got it."

The cops will hound you mercilessly . . .

"I sorry, I don't know. I was drugged multiple times."

"They threatened you, didn't they? Dr. Bechtold, they can't hurt you now. Police are stationed at the hospital entrance, and we're scouring the city for these people. I need you to be honest with me."

"I'm very tired and in pain. Maybe I'll have a clearer head once I rest for a while."

"Amnesia from the kind of drug you were given doesn't blot out a day's worth of memories, as I'm sure you know. The blackout is only from the time they were administered."

"I told you, I was drugged more than once. My thoughts are completely scrambled."

She sighed impatiently. "I'm sorry to be hard on you, but I don't think your thoughts are so scrambled. Listen, you can help us, and help yourself and your wife by telling me what they wanted. It's the crux of this case, and our success depends on it."

Rome closed his eyes. He wanted to believe Detective Lucerno, wanted to believe that LAPD was smarter than his captors. But the fear was so deep, the impression that vile woman had left so terrifying, he was paralyzed. Then he remembered what Sam had told him about kidnappers all reading from the same bad script. That they weren't invincible, they were just criminals. He made a decision, and hoped it was the right one.

"She threatened to kill us if we said anything."

"About what?"

"She made me sign papers. Papers that transferred my shares of Peppy Pets to a charity called Animal Rescue International. I think she's one of those violent activists. And she mentioned Bruce. She said he got greedy and betrayed her. And that there was a funny story behind his murder."

"Let's start at the beginning."

Chapter Fifty-Nine

IT WAS WAY PAST HAPPY HOUR, and Ike decided it was finally time to reacquaint himself with his neglected friend, Mr. Jack Daniel's. Thanks to his sister, Chance was in good hands, and had gulped down his epilepsy meds with a plate of hamburger. That was a reason to celebrate. Besides, tracing a throwaway was a leviathan task; without a warrant, it was also extremely dangerous. He had to call on brain cells that only seemed to activate with a generous dose of bourbon. Excuses, he knew, but his flirtations with sobriety hadn't made his life any better.

The first sip was ritualistic, deserving of an appropriate vessel, so he excavated a special crystal lowball from his bottom desk drawer and poured slowly. The brown liquid was more seductive than any woman. It went down like fire, and he relished the burn.

As time passed, he became increasingly consumed by the endorphin high from alcohol and illegal cyber-meanderings. At one point, something tickled the back of his mind, disrupting his focus. Moments later, he realized it was the sound of his phone. It took him four rings to find it beneath the piles of paperwork covering his desk. It was Maggie. The brightest spot in his life after his dog. "Hey, doll, what's new?"

"We have two dead bodies in Culver City—one is Grady Raab, a confirmed accomplice of Mimi's. We think she might be on the fly, literally. Al alerted the TSA. Any luck with—"

"Let's call it a project," he interrupted. "My phone is secure, but discretion is the better part of valor."

Nolan cringed. "Right, sorry."

"Working on it, but things are . . . glitchy. I got a location in Burbank, but I'm having trouble getting a time stamp. It might have been from when they dumped the Global Electric van."

"That makes sense, because we're pretty sure she was in Pacoima not too long ago."

"It might be turned off or in airplane mode, and if that's the case, then I'm up against a wall. Wait, how do you know she was in Pacoima?"

"Best news of the day—the Bechtolds are safe."

Ike let out a breath. "Thank God for that. But what's with Pacoima?"

"She drugged them and dumped them in Hansen Dam rec area. . . . Hey, Ike, can you hold the line? This is Lucerno calling with news."

"Sure, no problem." Ike savored another sip in silent toast to the Bechtolds, who'd been damned lucky. Mimi was scary as hell, and he couldn't even imagine how this was all going to end. He hoped not in another death.

"Sorry, Ike. Ready for another curveball?"

"I've come to expect it with this case."

"Mimi made Rome Bechtold sign his shares to Peppy Pets over to Animal Rescue International. That's why she kidnapped them."

Ike forgot his drink and sagged back in his chair. "That's absolutely bizarre. I think my head just exploded."

"They're looking at it, but see what you can find on them. It could be a direct route to our psychopathic heiress."

"You got it." He frowned down into his empty glass, feeling

another furtive stirring in the recesses of his brain. He was quiet for a long time as he tried to capture it.

"I can hear your mind working. Something I said?"

"Psychopathic heiress."

"That's an odd thing to encourage introspection."

Ike nodded absently as his thoughts gelled. "I'm wondering if maybe the Burbank ping *is* real-time, Maggie. Private flights aren't subject to TSA scrutiny. If I was an heiress, I wouldn't fly commercially, especially after I committed multiple felonies."

"Burbank airport. That is absolutely brilliant. Can you give Captain Mendoza an update? Things are hitting warp speed on our end."

❁ ❁ ❁

Nolan jumped out of the car and made tracks toward Al, who was pacing Raab's scrubby lawn, phone pressed to his ear. He generally avoided any unnecessary movement, so he was either trying to warm up, or the person on the other line had something very interesting to say. "Finish your call in the car, we're going to Burbank."

"Justin, hang on a second. What, Mags?"

"I just verbally beat the shit out of the security chief at Burbank airport to get a ground hold on all private flights."

"She's there?"

"It's a hunch Ike had that she would fly private. He got a hit on the burner in Burbank, but couldn't tell if was real-time, so it's worth a shot. There are four flights scheduled to leave within the next couple hours: two are corporate charters, the other two aren't under her name or any semblance of it, but that's no surprise."

Crawford nodded. "Justin, can I call you back in a few? Yeah, I will, right away, thanks." He held out his hand. "Keys. You almost killed us on the way to Malibu, and I'm not dying before I meet Mimi."

She tossed him the keys and got in the passenger's seat, secretly relieved. She'd spent enough time behind the wheel today, and her vision was blurring from lack of everything, from sleep to food. "Fine. What did Justin have to say?"

"SWAT, DEA, and the narc boys are just wrapping up a huge bust in Anaheim. Millions of dollars in rainbows. And they got the angel of death alive. Name's Jaime Cabral, Mexican national, Los Zetas affiliation. The federales confirmed he's a top-tier guy, slippery as hell, they've never been able to nail him."

Nolan's brows lifted. "Jaime Cabral is one of the charters. Going to Cabo."

"Guess he's not going to make it," Crawford said gleefully, pulling away from the curb with a squeal of tires. "Get Justin on speaker, that could be mighty useful to him. He wanted me to get back to him right away anyhow."

"That's great news on the bust, but why did he want us to know about it?"

"He said something about Sam. He's there with SWAT."

Chapter Sixty

THERE WAS A LOT OF NOISE on Justin's end, but his voice was loud and clear. Big body, big voice box. "Hey, Justin, Maggie and Al here. We're on our way to Burbank airport—"

"You and Al decided to throw in the towel and take a vacation?"

Crawford barked out a laugh. "We think our suspect might be headed there. We just wanted to let you know that Jaime Cabral has a charter flying out in a couple hours."

"No shit? This could be a big score, guys like him are never alone."

"You said something about Sam, but we were interrupted by my very excellent partner here."

"Yeah, he caught something nobody else would have, said it might have something to do with your case."

"What's that?"

"All the drugs we confiscated were packed in Peppy Pets boxes."

Neither one of them spoke for what seemed like a very long time. Nolan finally snapped out of her stupor with great urgency. "Did you get a phone off Jaime Cabral?"

"Sure did."

"Would you check his contacts and messages for us? We're looking for a Mimi or Magdalena."

"Sure, but I'll have to sign it out of this mountain of evidence, it might take a few minutes."

"We'll hold, it's important."

"Holy shit." Crawford breathed. "This was about drugs all along, wasn't it? Golden West and their manufacturing plants in Mexico, their distribution center on the border, and what's more innocent than pet food? That's where the funny money came from, I'd bet my pension. But how do you figure Mimi fits into this?"

Nolan thought about how every case was a puzzle—some were easy enough for a toddler to solve; others were those five-thousand-piece nightmares missing half of them, and you didn't even have the box that showed you what it was supposed to look like. But as you started putting together what you had, a picture began to take shape.

"I didn't have a chance to tell you, but Bechtold is awake and talking. She made him sign over his controlling shares to Animal Rescue International, which we both know is going to turn out to be a sham nonprofit. Remember, Cynthia Jackson suspected that Messane pulled the plug to clean things up when Wilder entered the picture six months ago. My guess is, that ended the cartel's gravy train, and it took them a while to concoct a new plan to get back in business."

"And it really pissed them off. That's why he was beaten and why he didn't seek medical treatment." He shook his head. "Kill Messane, get Bechtold to sign over his controlling shares to a fake cartel-operated charity, and the gravy train's back on track. Mags, if we're right about all this, it's pretty fucking genius. But it doesn't give us his shooter." He goosed the accelerator and flew by a semi at a rate of speed that would make Maggie proud.

"My money's on Raab or his friend. Mimi is going to fill in the blanks. Which is why I'm glad you're driving like me."

"I will never drive like you, and don't think that's a compliment."

"Hey, guys," Justin came back on the line. "No Mimi or Magdalena, but there is an *M*. Left a few angry messages recently, all the same: 'Where the fuck are you?' And 'I'm going to Cabo with or without you.' Is she your killer?"

"She's a killer and a kidnapper," Nolan said. "And we're positive she's cartel affiliated."

"Do you have backup?"

"Some squads coming in stealth."

Justin grunted disapprovingly. "I'm sending some DEA your way."

"We appreciate that. The way this thing is rolling out, an alphabet city of feds are going to be crawling all over everything anyhow, and Al and I are happy to share the misery. Is Sam still there?"

"Yep."

"Will you let him know the Bechtolds are okay?"

Chapter Sixty-One

MONTSERRAT HAD MANAGED AN HOUR OF troubled, unproductive sleep near the end of the flight. Anxiety and the smell of coffee had wakened her, and she drank three cups while she picked at a plate of pastry and fruit. The caffeine did nothing for her exhaustion, and her phone's empty inbox only served to inflame her nerves. But when she lifted the window shade and gazed at the pastel sunrise stretching above the rolling hills and mountains of Rioja, a sense of tranquility smothered her apprehension.

This land of her birth was a direct connection to her mother, the woman who had given her the strength to navigate life as a De Leon. She would, she *could,* handle whatever awaited her with composure and grace. Papa often overreacted when it came to Mimi, and she was well-versed in family détente thanks to Mama. It was her purpose now, and she would make certain this trip would be good for everyone.

The descent was sharp and fast to accommodate the short runway, and as they taxied, she saw a limousine waiting by the single hangar of the private airstrip. Being a member of this family had its challenges, but it also had its perks.

The man who got out took her breath away—Papa, in a crisp

white Oxford with a sweater draped over his shoulders, looking like he'd just ridden off the polo field. He was a large, fit man, but he'd dropped a significant amount of weight; still, he looked robust and not at all like his kidneys were badly failing.

She felt the thrill of a little girl soon to reunite with a missed parent, and also the darker, conflicting emotions of an adult who would soon have to deal with difficult issues. Still, the astounding fact that he had come personally to greet her imbued her with warmth. Had he ever met her plane before? If he had, she didn't remember.

As she climbed down the stairs, she gulped the crisp air that smelled like home and felt the weightless warmth of the Spanish sun on her shoulders. The sky was now a bird's-egg blue scattered with small, pillowy clouds, which reminded her of lying on her back among the vines on dreamy childhood days, seeing the shapes of animals frolicking above her. This was where she belonged.

"Papa, you didn't have to come," she cried out as she stepped off the stairway and onto the tarmac.

"Monty, my child, come here." He wrapped her in his big, comforting arms and she felt tears prickle her eyes.

He pushed her back gently and beamed at her. "Look at you, my beautiful daughter. The very picture of your mother, God rest her sweet soul. Come, come, get in."

A liveried driver got out and tipped his hat to her. "Good morning, Ms. De Leon. I'll get your bags."

Papa climbed in after her, took the facing seat, and pulled a bottle of cava from an iced bucket. "This is our latest sparkling, darling girl, it's sublime, and worthy of this celebration!"

She watched as this uncharacteristically effusive man deftly filled two waiting flutes, feeling guilty that she hadn't visited sooner; that he'd had to charter a plane and command her to come. Perhaps his confrontation with mortality had changed him; softened him. She had to bite her tongue to keep from lecturing him on the sugar in wine, and how bad it was for him. He already knew anyhow, and she didn't want to ruin this extraordinary reunion. "This is wonderful, Papa, but isn't a bit early?"

"Don't you tell me it's too early to rejoice!"

They clinked glasses and she marveled at the soft, moussy bubbles and light notes of fruit. It was like drinking silk. "This is wonderful, Papa. Armand's outdone himself."

He smiled approvingly as he held up his flute and examined the contents with a critical eye. "Indeed, he has. It really is so good to see you, Montserrat. I have breakfast waiting for us at the winery, and another of Armand's triumphs. A very special bottle I've been saving."

She was already feeling lightheaded. "I do have jet lag, Papa. I might not be able to walk if I have much more."

"Ach, that's because you live in a country full of barbarians who don't drink wine every day. You'll slip back into the old ways soon enough."

* * *

They lingered over the vast spread of all her favorite foods, savoring Armand's exquisite tempranillo while they got reacquainted and shared stories of their lives apart. The conversation was punctuated by frequent laughter, and she couldn't remember the last time she'd felt so happy—not just generally, but here particularly. She was exhausted, and on her way to becoming legitimately drunk, but the exhilaration she felt supplanted that.

And perhaps that had been his plan all along, ensuring her guard was fully down before he became taciturn and broached the topic she'd been dreading.

"It's time to discuss your sister. Have you heard from her?"

She drained the last bit of wine in her glass, vamping for a few extra seconds. "Not since yesterday."

His expression was implacable as he drummed his fingers on the table. "You're holding something back."

You have to tell him. You knew that all along.

"I never hold anything back from you, Papa, I just didn't want to address unpleasantries until it was absolutely necessary. We were having such a nice time."

He splashed more wine into her glass, eyes boring into hers. "Yes, it's been very nice, but it's now time for business. Tell me what you know."

"The police called me on the flight here. A Los Angeles homicide detective. They're looking for her." The rage that transformed his face was terrifying and she shrank a little in her chair.

"And why is that?"

"To question her about a murder and a kidnapping. I told them it was ridiculous."

"Did they believe you?"

"I don't know, Papa. Do police ever believe anything?"

He pushed back from the table and tossed his napkin over his plate. "I told you she was making a mess of things."

"But this? Surely not."

"Haven't I told you time and again that you've always given her too much credit? *I've* given her too much credit."

"Do you know something about this?" she asked incredulously.

"Of course I do, you don't think I watch her with the eyes of a falcon?"

"Why didn't you tell me? Maybe I could have helped."

He scoffed bitterly. "She's beyond help. And I've always kept you insulated from the details of her work and failures out of necessity. It gives you plausible deniability."

Montserrat felt the blood drain to her feet as a horrible clarity began to seep in. She wasn't doing charity work. "This all has to do with Peppy Pets, doesn't it?"

"Why did you think I sent you to Wilder? Suggested you discourage the deal if it was appropriate? With your research, I gave her a perfect blueprint to give me interest in the company so I could resume operations."

She was stunned speechless for a moment. "*That's* what the paperwork was about?"

He smiled cruelly. "She couldn't control Messane any more than she can control herself, and she went rogue. How foolish I was to think she could execute a simple task without causing a disaster." His eyes narrowed and he pinned her in place with his gaze. "If the police get their hands on her, she will ruin this family."

"She wouldn't do that!"

He scoffed bitterly. "She would do anything to save her own hide. She's been a liability for most of her life, but now she's become one we can no longer afford. It all stops now."

"Papa, what are you saying?" she whispered.

"I'm saying she is no longer a De Leon. Don't ever speak her name in this house again. Don't ever speak to her again. She'll call you for help because I'm freezing her accounts, but don't you dare answer, and don't you dare give her money."

Montserrat lowered her head. "She'll be more dangerous with nowhere to turn."

His anger subsided, and his eyes drifted to a place and time far beyond her. "You still see her as a little girl who lost her mother, but you were a little girl then, too. Look at her, look at you. She's a woman now, and there are consequences for her actions."

"Give me a chance to fix this—"

"It's too late for that, Montserrat. I'm sorry." He pushed away from the table abruptly. "Go to bed and get some rest."

Chapter Sixty-Two

NOLAN SIGNED OFF WITH TROY CHAPMAN, the man she'd verbally abused earlier. "Pull up to the terminal, he'll meet us outside and take us to the tarmac. Private passengers are brought directly to the planes by ground transport, so we'll have a great view."

"Must be nice," Crawford said. "No security checkpoints and you get dropped off at the front door. A great place for celebrities and drug dealers to sneak out of the city unseen. Burbank should put that in their promotional pamphlets."

"Maybe they have a suggestion box."

"Anybody get taken to Cabral's plane yet?"

"No, Chapman's on top of it. He pulled the pilots, airport security is watching, and the squads are on site."

"DEA?"

"Two agents on the ground waiting for us."

"You ready?"

"Al, I am so ready."

"Yeah, me, too."

Troy Chapman was a squat man, wearing a rumpled uniform and a worried expression when they pulled up. Nolan opened her window. "Mr. Chapman?"

He looked at her warily, as if she might bite. "You must be Detective Nolan."

The way he said it made her want to smile, but she didn't. "And this is my partner, Detective Crawford. Do we drive to the tarmac?"

"Yes."

"Hop in and show us the way."

He settled into the backseat. "This is quite a callout. I certainly hope this doesn't come to violence."

Nolan turned around and saw him rubbing his thumbs together anxiously. "We hope so, too, but this is a very violent woman."

All the color leached from his face. "Oh," he whispered to his thumbs.

Out of generosity and maybe a little guilt about how she'd handled him on the first phone call, she tried to reassure him. "I'm sure we'll resolve this peacefully. She's not expecting us, so we have the element of surprise."

His head bobbed up and down, as if the action would make it true. "Just follow this road to the stop sign and make a right, Detective Crawford. That takes us to the private gates."

As they turned the corner, they saw two squads parked on the far side of the strip, and four sleek white jets of varying sizes. Their pristine skins gleamed under the runway lights as they awaited their pampered passengers.

"The smallest one is Cabral's charter. Pull up to the first hangar, Agents McCaffrey and Rilke are inside."

After Chapman introduced them, he excused himself and returned to his safe office inside his safe airport to continue coordinating and monitoring. Nolan didn't feel safe at all, even in the hangar with two formidable feds decked out in full tactical gear with automatic weapons.

"Thanks for coming, guys," Crawford said.

McCaffrey nodded. "Justin said you were on the trail of a very nasty woman we might be interested in. An associate of Jaime Cabral was all he had time to tell us. Who are we after?"

Nolan gave them the abridged version, because the sun would rise before she would be able to finish the full story. McCaffrey and Rilke both listened attentively, then exchanged stunned looks.

"She wouldn't happen to be related to Sebastian De Leon, would she?" McCaffrey asked.

"She's his daughter. You know of him?"

He looked at his partner and whistled. "Hell, yes, he's an evil son of a bitch, but nobody has been able to prove it."

Crawford's eyes expanded. "What do you mean?"

"He's one of the richest men in Europe, hell, maybe even the world. A Spanish nobleman, philanthropist, winemaker, totally legit on paper. But by all accounts, he's also the most powerful underworld figure on the continent. Every agency over there has been looking at him for over a decade—drugs, weapons, human trafficking, you name it. But if any law enforcement gets within a country mile of him, they suddenly get shut down."

Crawford and Nolan were both gaping.

"Pull some things together for you?"

She nodded. "Very much so. You know a lot about him."

"Interpol briefed the DEA a while back and we all got the memo. They thought they had something to connect him to the States, LA in particular, but it fell through."

"Or maybe somebody made sure it fell through."

"You get the picture, the wheels of corruption never stop turning." McCaffrey frowned as he searched his memory. "His daughter was never mentioned in the brief, though. I didn't know he had one."

"He has two. One is a rock-star lawyer in New York City, but Magdalena disappeared ten years ago. Literally vanished off the map. We only caught a break with a surveillance photo and facial recognition."

"You want my opinion, she probably went underground so she

could expand Daddy's operations to the US while the other daughter stays clean and handles any fallout. Sebastian's brother and nephews are lawyers, too, big firm in Madrid. Very connected."

Crawford grunted. "I'm sure that comes in handy."

"Being a nobleman probably does, too. Pardon my cynicism, but I'm sure he enjoys some protection from the Spanish government."

Rilke finally spoke up. "This could really break something open, which makes this situation a hell of a lot more dangerous than it was five minutes ago. No offense, but we'd like to take point, we're geared up for this and we deal with these people every day."

"You'll get no argument from me," Crawford said.

Nolan nodded her assent. The game had changed in the eleventh hour, and they weren't equipped to deal with an arrest that could march them straight into an international cartel firing squad. "No offense taken. How do you want to play this?"

McCaffrey's radio squawked, startling them all. It was Chapman. "Heads up, transport is heading your way in five. Single passenger, female, requested that her bags be loaded into the cabin before she boards."

"It's just her and the driver?"

"Yes."

"Tell the driver to stay in the cabin until we give the all clear."

Chapter Sixty-Three

"THIS IS IDEAL," MCCAFFREY SAID. "NO bodyguards with her, and if she asked for the bags to be loaded before she boards, I'm guessing she wants to keep an eye on them. Once the driver is safely inside, I'll approach her. Rilke, get out there and shelter on the blind side of the plane in case there are friendly eyes or we need fast action on the ground."

"Friendly eyes?" Nolan asked.

"Guards out of view. She might be transporting something. You and Detective Crawford stay in the hangar until things are secure, then you can make your arrest."

Crawford puffed out an anxious sigh. "So, you do all the scary stuff and we just waltz up and put her in cuffs?"

Rilke liked that. "This is yours. You get all the glory, we just risk getting our balls shot off."

"Well, don't."

"It's not my intention. In position, Godspeed everybody."

Godspeed. It was something Nolan had heard her father say dozens of times before. It was an archaic saying that had never gone out of style in the lexicon of danger, because there were no atheists in foxholes.

* * *

She felt and heard her respiration accelerate in tandem with Al's as two orbs of light pierced the night in advance of a limousine. It stopped at the deployed stairway and the driver got out and opened the back passenger door.

Mimi stepped out of the car, and it was like gazing on a mythical creature you didn't really believe existed. But she was very real, flesh and blood, mortal like everybody else. She was no longer a fake platinum blond, or a woman in a black watch cap, but an elegant figure in a cream silk skirt suit. Her hair was wavy and dark, gathered in a ponytail that reached the middle of her back. The visage was new to them, but the face was unmistakable.

The suit was snug enough to show a weapon if she'd been wearing one. That would be in the Louis Vuitton tote slung over her shoulder. Nolan tensed when she dug into the bag, but she didn't pull a gun, just a phone she regarded with irritation before redepositing it.

Sorry, honey, Jaime won't be calling you back.

They watched breathlessly as the driver unloaded two large suitcases, also Louis Vuitton, from the limo's trunk. They were obviously heavy, and he struggled to haul them up the plane's narrow stairs. Mimi watched him, serene as Buddha, then gazed upward, maybe looking for stars beyond the bright lights of the airport and the city. She didn't seem particularly concerned about Jaime or anything else.

When the driver disappeared into the plane, McCaffrey emerged from the shadows, weapon raised. "Magdalena De Leon, turn around and put your hands on the car! Now!"

Nolan and Crawford raised their own guns, but she obeyed calmly.

"And who might you be, ruining my vacation?" Her voice was low and smooth and laced with mockery.

McCaffrey gave the signal and they stepped out of the hangar as the two squads sped across the runway toward them. Nolan was suspicious that such an intense chase would end so anticlimactically, but most cases closed with a whimper, not a bang. And Mimi was too arrogant to fight—she had the backing of a seemingly invincible father, and probably thought immunity was a birthright.

"LAPD Homicide," Nolan said steadily, even though the adrenaline load made her body quiver. "You're under arrest for murder and kidnapping."

She chuckled. "How very theatrical! But you're sorely misguided. I haven't done anything wrong."

"Trust me, Ms. De Leon," Crawford snapped, "you're going to be in prison for the rest of your life. And your father and sister might be there to keep you company."

Mimi tensed visibly, but didn't move. Nolan approached, gun in one hand, cuffs in the other. Crawford and McCaffrey flanked her, and Rilke emerged from his post behind the plane. She was steps away when a sharp crack blistered the air.

In a frantic, stuttering cinema of noise and confusion, Nolan felt her partner's bulk knock her to the ground and cover her; heard McCaffrey and Rilke shouting, their boots stomping past them; the squeal of tires as the squads peeled away in pursuit. Then more gunshots. She was face-down and couldn't see anything but pavement, and she couldn't breathe. Whether it was Al's weight crushing her lungs, or simply pure terror, she would never know.

Minutes passed—or had it been hours? Eventually, Al whispered, "They got him, Mags," and rolled off her. The adrenaline was still surging and it felt like acid in her veins. She inhaled a shaky breath of jet fuel fumes and looked up.

Mimi was crumpled on the ground, her cream suit turning crimson, her beautiful face ruined. She wouldn't be in prison for the rest of her life after all.

Chapter Sixty-Four

ON THE DRIVE HOME FROM ANAHEIM, Sam checked in with Melody. Her voice bounced up and down the scale of excitement as she told him about the news coverage of the raid and the cocktail she'd just invented to celebrate the occasion. He smiled, thinking of how considerate she was and how very domestic she'd become. Did she realize it?

The epiphany that he was becoming domestic right along with her was sudden and stunning. He took great care of his lawn now; he'd built out a sundeck and bought new outdoor furniture; painted the whole interior of the house in cheerful colors that reflected his newfound optimism. All things that added a sense of permanence. They were both nesting.

More significantly, he now looked forward to going home when he knew she would be there; loved sharing the biggest and littlest things with her, and feeling the weight and warmth of her body in his bed. They hadn't been together long, but they already had a private language of inside jokes and physical tells. She had become an integral part of his life and his happiness, and the transformation had been so gradual, he hadn't even seen it.

He called his mother next, and she was equally happy to hear from him. The unflappable Vivian Easton got very emotional when he told her the good news about the Bechtolds. The women in his life had nothing to worry about anymore. He tried calling Maggie and Al again, which was foolish and probably extremely annoying. It's not like they were just sitting around with nothing to do but chat on the phone. Still, the stakeout at Burbank airport would be dangerous and it troubled him, even though they were beyond competent in the field and had DEA there for backup.

With only the schuss of his tires on the pavement to keep him company, his thoughts wandered into the incomprehensible. What was the connection between drugs in pet food boxes, Rome's kidnapping, and Bruce Messane's murder? He knew there had to be one, but Maggie and Al were the only ones who could decipher it for him.

He was still amped from the raid as he let himself into the house, anxious for a cocktail and a piece of Melody's coffee cake. Normally, she greeted him at the door, but she was sitting on the sofa, fixated on the television where a breaking news report played.

"Sam, look at this, there was a shooting at Burbank airport."

His heart was racing as he sank next to her. "That's where Maggie and Al are, did they say if anyone was hurt?"

"The details are sketchy, but they're reporting that two criminal suspects were killed. I just saw Maggie and Al in an aerial shot. They're okay, Sam."

He hadn't realized he'd been holding his breath. "Thank God, I was worried."

She leaned over and kissed him on the cheek. "Come into the kitchen while I mix our drinks."

"Does this new drink have a name?"

"Not yet, there are so many cocktails, everything I think of has been taken."

Sam settled into a chair at his pathetic, secondhand dinette table, a holdover from his separation from Yuki. Why hadn't he replaced it? He watched her measure and shake and pour, then garnish the drinks with Griottines—French, brandy-soaked cherries he hadn't known existed until she'd come into his life. It was delicious.

"This is the best cocktail in the world, Melody. I could drink a gallon of this."

"Well, don't, there's a lot of booze in it. Now tell me what your first SWAT operation was like."

"I pretty much told you everything on the phone—"

"You told me what happened, but I want to know what it felt like to you."

"You sound like Dr. Frolich."

"I'm a licensed psychologist now. Do you want to lie on the sofa?"

"Not alone."

She stifled a smile. "Be serious, Sam."

"It was terrifying. Exciting. Slow, and then so fast, my head felt like it was going to spin off my neck. I liked it, Melody. I don't know if that's good or bad, but I liked it."

"No flashbacks?"

"I thought about Afghanistan, there were a lot of similarities, but I wasn't back there."

She smiled. "Then it's good."

"Margolis offered me the job. I accepted."

"That's even better! Is this a full-time gig?"

He gestured to their cozy tableau. "No, but I'd like this to be a full-time gig."

"What?" she asked warily.

"Us. I was thinking on the way home. You're paying exorbitant rent for an apartment you're hardly ever at. We're best friends and lovers and I miss you when you're not here, and I hope you miss me, too. This house is empty without you in it."

Her mouth and eyes formed three astonished circles. "Are you asking me to move in with you?"

"If it's what you want. It's what I want."

"This isn't just about saving me money?"

"God, no, Melody. Well . . . without rent, you could afford a practice space with a working elevator." The levity would have normally brought a smile to her face, but she remained expressionless as she held his gaze for a moment, then looked down into her drink.

"I definitely wasn't expecting this."

"Neither was I. It just came out."

"It's a nice thought . . . no, a wonderful thought."

"But?"

She looked up. A sheen of tears transformed her green eyes into a vivid shade of emerald. "My apartment is the first real place I've ever had on my own. It represents my independence from addiction."

Sam quelled his disappointment—he wasn't finished making his case. "A real, committed relationship also represents freedom from addiction. Listen, maybe it's too soon to talk about this, and I understand. We both have a lot of baggage that makes it hard for us to trust. But I do trust you, and I think you trust me. All I ask is that you think about it. No pressure, the offer stands, and if you don't accept it, it won't change anything between us."

She started twisting a blond curl around her finger nervously. "I do trust you, Sam, I trust you with my life. But the bottom has always dropped out on anything good in my world. I don't want to ruin things by changing what we have now."

The reservoir of tears finally spilled over, and Sam took her into his arms. "Neither of us expect good to last because of what we've been through, but don't you think we deserve it?" He tipped her chin up, forcing her to look at him. "Melody, I love you. I've loved you since the day I met the smartest, sweetest, sexiest bartender in LA. Whatever you decide, you need to know that."

She bit her trembling lip. "I love you, too, Sam Easton."

He smiled and kissed her chastely. "Well, I'd say we covered some ground tonight. Let's drink to that."

Melody refilled their glasses and they sat in thoughtful silence, minds too busy processing the seismic shift to speak. Besides, any further words were unnecessary.

Eventually, she looked up. Her eyes were dry and Sam was elated to see that the spark of mischief had returned along with the crooked smile and the dimple in her cheek. "*If* I did move in with you, could I buy a new kitchen table? It's a little . . . tired."

Sam's entire body shook with laughter. "It's ugly as hell! But we would buy a new one together, something we both loved."

"That sounds nice."

"S and M."

"What are you talking about?"

He raised his glass. "This drink. That's the name. Sam and Melody."

"Sam, that's so . . . so . . ."

"Warped? I know, but it suits our sense of humor."

"I was going to say perfect."

Another inside joke to add to the roster. Sam had no doubt the list would continue to grow.

Chapter Sixty-Five

NOLAN AND CRAWFORD SAT IN THEIR sedan, numbed witnesses to the bedlam of emergency vehicles and LAPD, DEA, and FBI personnel swarming the runway. The world was strobing red and blue, and it made Nolan's head hurt. Media helicopters were trolling the skies, shifting their focus from LAPD's successful resolution of a kidnapping and a record-breaking drug bust to an even more dramatic story. And they didn't know the half of it.

"You okay, Mags?"

After having killed someone in the line of duty and witnessing a self-immolation over the past year, she had learned that stoicism was not a productive way to process trauma. "I'm shell-shocked. I can't wrap my head around any of this right now."

"It's a lot to handle."

"How are you?"

"Same. Trying to stop myself from thinking about what could have happened. The worst didn't, so why am I torturing myself?"

"Remember when the bridge in Minneapolis collapsed and all those cars went into the Mississippi?"

"Hard to forget. Thirteen people died."

"I have a friend who was behind the last car that went in. Ten feet and a few minutes saved her life. She still has nightmares about what would have happened if she hadn't run back into the house for her glasses. I think it's hardwired."

"Mimi was the target. That saved *our* lives."

She touched his arm. "Thanks, Al."

"For what?"

"Tackling me. I think you broke one of my ribs."

He grinned. "Hey, I'm a knight in shining armor, protecting my damsel. It's another hardwired thing."

She looked out her window and opened it when she saw McCaffrey approaching.

"You guys okay?"

"We're okay. And grateful you were here. Thanks for that."

"Thank *you*. This might unravel a big syndicate, which would make us look really good. Still blows my mind that a businessman's death led you to this."

"In the end it was all about greed."

He nodded. "We positively identified the vic as Magdalena De Leon, so you're good to notify. We don't know who the killer is yet, but he used a sniper rifle and he was a distance away. She was obviously a high-value target."

"Thank God he was a good shot. Did he make it?" Crawford asked.

"He's resting peacefully in the morgue now."

"A sniper is pretty slick for cartel work, isn't it?"

"The cartels can't hang people from bridges in this country, so they've been known to employ more elegant assassination practices. This is going to end up as a joint task force effort, and I'm sure the DEA will take over the investigation. One less murder on your hands."

"They can have it. Did you find anything good in her bags?"

"Very good stuff—computer, a couple of guns, phones. A lot of cash and some fake passports. The rest were clothes and shoes and jewelry."

"That could help tie up our murder."

"You'll have full access. Interdepartmental love." He folded his beefy arms across his chest and gazed at the controlled chaos. "This is messy, but we'll get it sorted. Gotta run, but good luck wrapping things up on your end."

After he left, Nolan stared out the windshield, watching but not really seeing. Her brain was on strike. She was amazed it had held out this long. "This is the end, but it's really only the beginning."

"We have a shitload of work ahead of us," he agreed. "All we need is the gun that killed Messane and we can tie a bow on this thing; let the feds handle the financial crimes and international intrigue. God, the debriefings are going to suck."

She stretched out in her seat and rubbed her throbbing temples. "Cynthia Jackson was a big part of untangling this. I hope Peppy Pets doesn't go under."

"With Messane out of the picture, I'm sure it will survive one way or the other. Didn't you tell Ross it was too big to fail?"

"I hope it is, otherwise he has to cook a chicken every week."

Crawford looked over her shoulder, out the passenger window, and smiled.

"Speaking of knights in shining armor."

Chapter Sixty-Six

NOLAN TURNED AND SAW REMY JOGGING toward them, his curly black hair disheveled, his expression intense and grim. Her addled mind instinctively went to the dark side—something was wrong.

She jumped out of the car. "Remy, what are you doing here?"

He stopped just short of her, catching his breath. "Justin called to tell me what was going down, and on the way over here, I heard there were shots fired."

"But why would Justin—"

He closed the distance between them in one long stride and took her into his arms. "I told you we were the worst kept secret in LAPD," he whispered.

She suddenly felt boneless, and sagged against him as she held on tight, finding release from agonizing hours of stress, exhaustion, frustration, and more recently, the trauma of seeing the aftermath of a hunter with a sniper rifle.

"You said we were the worst kept secret in *Homicide*."

Remy cupped her chin and tucked a wayward strand of strawberry blond behind her ear. "I guess word travels fast. God, I'm glad you're okay."

"Are you glad I'm okay?" Crawford was leaning across the seat, smirking at him.

"I'm very glad you're okay, too, Al."

He receded with a look of alarm. "Captain at your four thirty, moving fast."

Nolan quickly disengaged from Remy's embrace, but it was too late. Mendoza was just a few feet away. Of course, he would be here. She should have thought of that. *Too late.*

His broad russet face was unreadable. "Good evening, Detectives. I'm relieved to see you're alright. And congratulations—your murder investigation has uncovered quite a conspiracy from what I'm hearing. We'll have full federal assistance, and I'm coordinating with them now. Expect debriefings in the near future."

Nolan was completely unprepared to confront a moment she'd been dreading for months, and wanted to crawl under the car. Instead, she nodded calmly. "We'll have our updated reports on your desk by morning. Solving Mr. Messane's murder remains our first priority."

"As it should be, and I imagine that will be forthcoming."

Crawford joined them, hoping to deflect attention away from his crimson-faced partner and her forbidden beau. "Yes, sir, there are several weapons that haven't been looked at yet, from Grady Raab's scene and this one. We're confident one of them will match our bullet, because we know Magdalena De Leon was behind the murder."

"Very good." He regarded Remy with bland curiosity. "I'm surprised to see you here, Detective Beaudreau. Do you have an interest in this case?"

Nolan cringed inwardly.

"Very much so, sir. I have been investigating a possible connection between Dr. Kang's case, and I believe I've found one. I wanted to inform them."

"Personally, I see."

"I'm here personally because I was very concerned for Maggie and Al's safety."

Crawford knew the captain was playing a game of cat and mouse, so once again, he interjected himself. "Remy, what connection did you find?"

"There was an empty Peppy Pets box in Kang's apartment, but I didn't think anything of it because he owned a cat. I put it together when I talked to Justin."

"So Messane probably *was* providing him with drugs. Drugs he stole from the cartel, which is always a horrible idea." He looked at Nolan. "The missing box in his wine cellar. Mimi knew and she found his stash. I'm sure he kept some loot in Malibu, too."

"I have no doubt your reports are going to be very compelling. I look forward to reading them." Mendoza looked anxiously over his shoulder. "I have to get back to it, but you all go home and get some sleep. It's going to be a long day tomorrow."

"Will you be doing a presser tonight, sir?" Nolan asked.

"A brief interagency one. The media rumor mill is already churning out wild speculations, and we need to curtail that. It could hamper the investigation. Gossip is the pettiest tendency of human nature, and I loathe it."

Nolan didn't discount hallucinations at this point, but she could swear she saw a smile quiver on his lips that he extinguished by sheer force of will.

"That's why I never listen to it, sir," Crawford offered a little too enthusiastically.

"Neither do I." His eyes slid from Nolan to Remy. "Of course, gossip often has some basis in truth. That's why we have to be especially careful when handling it. Have a good night, Detectives."

Crawford shook his head as he watched him get reabsorbed by the melee. "That was scary."

"It was a gracious warning," Remy said quietly. "He can't ignore this forever, it's his job on the line, too. Maggie and I are officially on notice."

Chapter Sixty-Seven

MONTSERRAT STOOD ON A BROAD STONE terrace that overlooked orderly rows of vines in muted shades of green and gold—botanical soldiers marching toward the mountains on an undulating field. She'd always thought the vineyard was most beautiful when it was slumbering for the winter, especially in the fading light of day. But it all seemed ugly to her now.

Her hands were still shaking after her call from Detective Nolan, but with monumental effort, she'd managed to curb the tears. She had to regain her composure before she delivered the news to Papa. There was no way to predict his reaction, but she knew it would be painful to watch. Mimi was his biggest failure, and whatever anger he carried would clash violently with the sorrow of losing a child.

"Montserrat, my beautiful angel, I'm so offended you didn't come to me immediately when you arrived!"

She jumped at the booming voice, and turned to see Armand stepping out onto the terrace, his white smile slashing a brown face leathered and burnished by decades spent in the vineyard. She tried to return it, but it was impossible. "Armand, it's wonderful to see you. Papa said you were out today, otherwise I would have."

His smile vanished behind compressed lips. "Oh, my dearest,

you're so sad, come here. Tell me what's wrong, Armand will fix it. I make wine that will fix any heartache."

"Not this one." She felt like a child again, crying into a chest almost as big as the barrels he tended. But she hadn't just lost a toy this time. "Magdalena is dead. I don't know how to tell Papa."

"*Dios mío*, no, no, no! You must sit, this is a burden you shouldn't carry standing up." He led her to the heavy oak table, scarred by generations of De Leons, then crouched before her and took her hands. "How did this happen?"

"She was shot."

"*Dios mío*," he murmured again, crossing himself. "I told your father not to send her to Los Angeles, such a dangerous place, but he only listens to me about wine."

"You knew she was in Los Angeles?" she sniffled.

He rose from his crouch and took the chair next to her. "He said he found work for her there with a charity of his. Certainly nothing that would get her killed."

"The police were looking for her. For murder and kidnapping. Did he tell you?"

Armand lowered his eyes. "Of course, he's my oldest friend. I've never seen him so angry. I told him she wouldn't do such things, but he called me an old fool and ranted about her destroying the family. I think he will be sorry for saying such things when he hears."

She's been a liability for most of her life, but now she's become one we can no longer afford. It all stops now.

Montserrat felt a terrible weight settle over her; a violent chill racking her body. No. No, it was impossible. Her father might be ruthless, maybe even a monster, but even he wouldn't be capable of . . . "Where is Papa?"

"The last time I saw him, he was in the barrel room. Do the police know who killed her, Monty?"

"Not yet, but he's dead, so they'll be able to identify him eventually."

"There's no justice in that, he deserves to suffer a lifetime in prison!" He put his head in his hands and began to weep. "It's the last time she will break his heart. I doubt it will heal this time."

*   *   *

She found her father sitting on a wine crate, drinking a red and smoking a cigar. He looked up and greeted her with empty eyes.

"From the looks of you, you've heard about your sister," he said woodenly.

Montserrat had to lock her knees to keep them from buckling. "So have you. How?"

He wagged his head. "There was no saving her this time. No other way."

She felt cold and brittle, like she might shatter into a million pieces on the ancient stone floor. "Did you . . ." She couldn't finish the sentence.

He pitched his cigar in disgust. "She killed herself. My only job is to protect this family. To protect you. Any threat must be eliminated."

"Even if that threat is your own *daughter*?"

His face flamed red. "She is not my daughter!"

Montserrat felt something flee from her soul as she sank to the floor. "My God, Papa. How could you do this? Why didn't you give her another chance?"

He spat on the floor. "You're very intelligent, Montserrat, but you sound so stupid now. How many more chances would you have me give her while she destroyed everything? Belonging to this family requires great sacrifices. You know that, she never did."

"I will never forgive you," she mumbled, her voice sounding very far away.

"I'll be gone soon, so you don't have to worry about it."

Chapter Sixty-Eight

NOLAN EMERGED SLOWLY FROM A DREAMLESS sleep, then jolted up in panic when she saw the clock. It was five a.m. and she'd set her alarm for an hour earlier. At least she thought she had. She registered the smell of coffee and her brain fog cleared sluggishly. Remy had driven her home while she called Maya Lucerno and worked on her report. He'd forced her to eat a banana, then put her to bed. She didn't remember her head hitting the pillow.

She slipped a robe on over her pajamas and padded down the hall. Remy greeted her before she'd turned the corner into the kitchen. He was at the table by the window, laptop open in front of him. His hair was a tangle, and his eyes were cradled by dark pouches.

"Why didn't you wake me up?" she grumped.

He smiled up at her. "You're particularly beautiful when you're annoyed. Sit down, I'll get you some coffee."

"No time, I need to shower and finish my report."

"I've finished it for you. Well, mostly."

She gaped at him, then sank into a chair. "What do you mean?"

He placed a mug of coffee in front of her and kissed her sweetly. "I took some liberties with your computer. Your reports and notes are impressively detailed and concise; it was actually quite easy. But you'll have to fill in some blanks."

"That's . . . incredible. Did you even sleep?"

"No."

She felt a wash of guilt. "But why?"

He tipped his head and pinned her with his dark eyes. "You're going to be spending the day with the captain and the feds, you need it more than I do."

Nolan's stomach squirmed at the mention of the captain. "You really are Prince Charming."

"Prince Charming would have solved Messane's murder, too. Ross—who adores you almost as much as I do—spent half the night in the lab, and none of the guns from Raab's house or Mimi's luggage match your bullet."

"Dammit. We have to start all over."

"Go shower, Maggie. I'll forage for something for us to eat. From the looks of your fridge, it might be ketchup soup."

She shrugged apologetically. "There's cereal."

"And no milk. We have to have a conversation about your shopping habits. And other things, but we'll save that for later."

* * *

She had Remy drop her down the street at Benji's. Everybody knew his Porsche, and after last night, a sighting could be catastrophic. She bought *fresh* scones and jumbo coffees, then slunk down the sidewalk like a naughty teenager, eyes busy as she scoped for potential enemies.

Crawford was already at his desk, typing furiously from his notes. He looked up and his eyes widened when he saw breakfast. "Holy manna from an angel."

"I wouldn't go that far, but the scones are still warm."

He helped himself and grunted in pleasure. The scone hardly crumbled at all. "Did you sleep, Mags?"

"I can't remember."

He chuckled. "Likewise. How's the report coming along?"

She tossed a flash drive on his desk. "Remy pulled an all-nighter and finished it for me. I just had to flesh it out."

He leaned back in his chair and steepled his fingers. "That is some real chivalry. Did you send it to the captain?"

"Yep. Lucerno, too. She brought the Bechtolds home last night and between the hospital and car ride, she got a full accounting. She's madder than a Tasmanian devil, though. The media were waiting for them, and they had to cordon off the whole block."

"Sick bastards. They don't have a single shred of decency between the lot of them."

"It's under control now, and patrols will be posted there until this dies down."

"Does she know why Mimi didn't just kill them after he signed away everything?"

"The document was postdated two years ago when Bechtold left Peppy Pets. She wanted them alive so they would verify their charitable intentions—air quotes—if it was challenged. Bechtold has a long history of donating millions of dollars to animal welfare charities, so in concept, it worked, but it would have fallen apart completely under scrutiny."

"Totally insane. Like Mimi."

"She also mentioned Messane to the Bechtolds. Said he'd betrayed her, and that there was a funny story behind his murder. She didn't share it, though."

"That's sick."

"As sick as she was. Is Ike in? I got him his weird coffee."

"Not yet, but he called. Animal Rescue International is a shell corp, like we figured. I told him it was in the feds' hands now, and to stay sober for debriefings. He thought that was hilarious. I'm not sure why."

"Did you hear about the lab reports on the guns?"

"Yeah, I talked to Ross, too. But he said they haven't tested all the guns from the Anaheim bust, there were a shitload of them. I have my hopes pinned on Jaime Cabral or one of his henchmen being good for Messane."

Nolan nodded thoughtfully. "That makes sense. Where's the captain? I figured he'd be sniffing around here first thing."

"He's with the feds right now. Speaking of our fearless leader, how are you feeling about last night?"

"Like shit."

"Did you talk about it?"

"Not yet."

He sighed. "It'll work out, Mags."

"I don't know how, that's the scary thing." She dug her ringing phone out of her bag. She raised a quizzical brow at Al. "It's Lucerno. Good morning again, Detective."

"Sorry to bother you, but I just arrived at the Bechtolds' to check in with them."

"How are they?"

"From what I'm seeing, great. They're unloading some boxes and suitcases, so it looks like they're back together. Kind of unsettling to see them acting so normally, because I know they're still in shock."

"Temporary mania, running from the bad thing as fast as they can."

"I'm afraid of what will happen when they come down."

"They have each other, that will help. I know of an excellent psychiatrist who specializes in PTSD. I'll text you her name."

"Thank you."

"What can we do for you?" Nolan thought her sigh sounded pained.

"I just finished reading your latest report front to back, which is mind-blowing. Have you found Messane's shooter yet?"

"No, unfortunately."

"They were driving a black Escalade, and you have a witness, correct?"

"That's right, but he didn't see the plates or who was driving."

"Well, right now, I'm looking at a black Escalade, and it belongs to Rome Bechtold. This is probably crazy, there are a million of them in the city, but given his past connection with Messane and his wife's affair . . . I know that was a long time ago, but I thought it was worth a mention."

She was momentarily distracted by Crawford, who'd spilled his coffee all over his desk. "That is worth a mention. Does he own a gun?"

"No, I checked. And Rome is the kindest man I've ever met, I don't believe he could ever take a life, human or otherwise. But this case is so screwed up, I don't think we can overlook anything."

Nolan knew Lucerno was emotionally invested in the Bechtolds, but bonded to Rome in a way most people would never experience in a lifetime. The fact that she'd called was a testament to her devotion to the job. Good cop. "It seems doubtful to us, too. Mimi had that kidnapping planned a long time ago. She knew about Bechtold's controlling shares and had paperwork drawn up. You don't do that on a whim just in case someone gets killed."

"I didn't think about that. You're absolutely right."

"We'll keep it on our radar, though. We appreciate the call, Detective Lucerno."

"God, I hope this is nothing, they are very dear people. Rome especially."

Nolan heard her voice break. "We hope so, too."

Chapter Sixty-Nine

"NO WAY IT'S HIM," CRAWFORD REMARKED as he mopped up his desk. "We never thought it was."

"No, but we have to look at it."

"Look at what? Rome Bechtold owns a black Escalade. So does Reggie Blattner and a thousand other people in this city. We don't have a gun, video footage, a credible motive, or a witness. Except for Ty Mattison, who was pretty much worthless."

For the past twenty-four hours, Nolan had been plagued by a sense that there had to be answers buried in all the oddities of this case. But whenever a thought prickled the back of her mind, a new development flushed it away like a startled bird. But one finally settled and perched. "Ty Mattison wasn't completely worthless. He said Mimi showed up, saw Messane was dead, and started laughing her ass off."

Crawford shrugged. "Yeah, so? She was a certified nutjob who was happy her hit man accomplished his task."

"Or she could have been happily surprised because she was on her way to do it herself and somebody beat her to the punch. Maybe that was the funny story."

He pushed his lips out as he thought about it. "I see what you're saying, but it's pure speculation about the emotional state of a psychopath."

"Don't forget the recent calls between Messane and Nicole Bechtold. If they rekindled the affair and he found out about it, that's solid motive. Crime of passion, just not what we were thinking."

"We can't prove that. We can never prove that. Even if we could, it doesn't put a gun in Bechtold's hand. And how the hell would he know Messane would be in the shittiest neighborhood in Culver City at that exact time?"

"He'd know if he was the one who put the tracker on his car. The software would be on his computer if he did."

"Good luck finding a judge who would give us a subpoena. And so what if he had eyes on Messane? It still doesn't put a gun in his hand." Crawford pressed his palms to his forehead. "I know you want to solve this yesterday, but this is all conjecture, vague at best. Short of a confession, this is a big, fat, dead end. And seriously, Messane was in bed with a cartel, for God's sake. That's one sure way to get yourself killed, and they had a crystal-clear motive." He poked at the remainder of his coffee-soaked scone. "I came up under Bob Sandburg, a crusty, old son of a bitch with a clearance rate you wouldn't believe. You're way too young to remember him."

"But I've heard of him. Kind of a legend."

"He was that, for a lot of reasons, some good, some bad. He always told me, 'If you hear hoofbeats, don't look for a zebra.' Rome Bechtold is a zebra."

Nolan nodded. She knew he was right. "It's just hard to let go of a new angle when there's nothing else."

"I'm not saying let it go, I'm just saying let this whole mess roll out, see if we get a hit from Anaheim. I'm betting on it."

Fifteen minutes later, Ross called. The single twenty-two at the scene didn't match their bullet. A zebra was all they had.

Chapter Seventy

MAYA LUCERNO STEPPED OUT OF HER car and into a glorious Southern California morning—the kind that made you feel like the luckiest person in the world to live here. Yesterday's rain had freshened the air, winter blooms had recovered from their battering, and the lush greenery of the Bechtolds' yard seemed to glow in the sun.

Rome and Nicole paused in their moving labors when they noticed her walking up the drive. "Good morning, Maya! What a nice surprise to see you here."

They still looked tired and drawn, and their eyes were guarded and very sad—that might never change—but they radiated emotional and physical strength that she didn't believe was solely an effect of mania. She'd learned last night that they were both tougher than they looked, and she didn't doubt they were going to get through this together. "I just wanted to see how you were doing, or if there's anything you need."

Nicole clasped her hands together thankfully. "That's so kind of you. Please come in for a coffee or espresso or anything else you'd like. Rome picked up croissants from my favorite bakery, Fleur on Montana, have you been? It's positively divine, the best outside Paris, but you have to get there very early."

Lucerno smiled. Nicole was back in LA hostess mode, and even if it was a temporary anomaly related to shock, she was thrilled to see it. No reason to spoil the moment by confessing that her favorite bakery was Dunkin' Donuts on Crenshaw. "That sounds lovely. Here, let me help you. You two should be resting."

Rome set his box down, put his arm around his wife, and kissed the top of her head tenderly. "You go in, sweetheart, we'll take care of the rest." Once the door had closed behind her, he turned with misted eyes. "Maya, thank you for everything. We owe you our lives."

You owe the sociopath who kidnapped you for your lives, because she let you go, we weren't even close. And don't forget, I'm the one who lost you in the first place. My fault.

Lucerno tried to shake the unrelenting guilt out of her mind, but it would always be with her. Her father had made sure of that. "Seeing you two safe and happy is all the thanks I need." She was startled when he folded her into his arms, but not surprised. Strong attachments between victim and rescuer always formed after traumatic events—it was normal and healthy. It was also normal and healthy that the connection fade over time. Both parties had to distance themselves eventually so they could move on in their real lives.

She hugged him back tightly, swallowing the sticky lump of emotion in her throat. She needed him as much as he needed her right now. It was going to be hard to let go this time.

He pushed her away gently and looked at her with eyes no longer veiled by sadness or tears. "You saved us. You saved everything."

"I can't take credit for that—there were so many people involved. We're all proud of the strength you and Nicole showed, and grateful for a happy ending. It means everything to us. Truly."

"Will you pass along our sincerest thanks?"

"You know I will. I'll grab these last two boxes. Go inside and be with Nicole. I know that's never going to get old."

He chuckled. "You're right about that. Thank you."

She pulled out one box and set it on the driveway, then bent to retrieve the second. That's when she noticed a crumpled rag lodged beneath the passenger seat, out of place in the otherwise pristine interior. She reached for it and felt something hard beneath her fingers; knew what it was without seeing it. Her heart started to hammer and sweat oozed from her forehead.

"Is everything okay, do you need help?" Rome called from the porch.

"No, no, I'm fine, but I just got a call," she lied, brandishing her phone. "I'll be in shortly."

"I'll get those for you, then."

Her eyes flared in panic and she hoped he hadn't noticed. "You march right back in there and dote on your wife. That's a police order."

Rome grinned. "Well, I certainly won't disobey a police order."

She swallowed down bile and kept the silent phone to her ear, pretending to talk while she tugged on the rag.

Don't look don't look don't look . . .

It was a KelTec twenty-two, a cheap gun that was beat to hell, like it had been on the street for a while. The kind you would get in a back-alley deal for twenty bucks. She leaned over, sniffed the muzzle, and her heart plummeted. It had been fired very recently.

Maya Lucerno's mind careened back in time. She was ten again, playing spy with herself, because she didn't have any siblings or a mother. Or a father for that matter, not really. She tiptoed into the hallway and saw that his office door was open just a crack. He was still wearing his police uniform, and he looked so handsome in it. But she was scared, because he was holding a gun that wasn't his— and she knew guns, because all good spies did. A few moments later, he put it in a bottom desk drawer, locked it, then drained the glass he was holding in the other hand. When he saw her, he stripped his belt from the loops of his pants.

How many times do I have to tell you to keep your nose out of adult business?

Years later, as the bastard was dying from drink in the hospital, she confronted him, because she was an adult and it *was* her business now. She hadn't anticipated a deathbed confession, and it devastated her. But it didn't surprise her.

He was a bad man, a child killer who should have rotted in prison. But the case was thrown out on a technicality because the prosecutor wasn't old enough to wipe his own ass. I kept that damn gun all these years to remind me that the system fails sometimes, and justice isn't always black-and-white. You'll find it in the drawer. You have a choice to make, Maya. I hope it's the right one.

She hadn't made the right choice. After his funeral, she drove to the desert, and as far as she knew, the gun had never been found. She'd been paying penance ever since, but the past was back now. The past always came back. And once you stepped over a line, it was easier to do the next time.

You have a choice to make.

With a shuddering breath, she tucked the gun in her waistband, buttoned her jacket over it, and hauled the boxes into the house, where she was greeted with the warmth of family. In a twisted way, she felt like she was balancing the scales by righting a wrong: saving a good man instead of the name of a dead son of a bitch who hadn't deserved her protection.

Justice wasn't always black-and-white.

Chapter Seventy-One

NOLAN SPEARED THE LAST SUCCULENT CHUNK of lobster and popped it in her mouth with a contented sigh. The food, the champagne, the sybaritic atmosphere of the Bel-Air, being with Remy in an environment where they could let their guard down—it was such a stark contrast to the last thirty-eight hours, she felt like she was inhabiting somebody else's body. Somebody else's life. Or maybe she *had* been killed at Burbank airport and this was heaven.

She looked up and met his intense black gaze; eyes that barely contained a storm, she'd always thought. Her stomach fluttered like it did on a downward plunge of a roller coaster. "You're watching me eat, Remy. It's weird. Or do I have spinach in my teeth?"

He gave her a lazy smile and gestured to Micah for another bottle. "Everything you do fascinates me."

"You don't have to get me drunk to sleep with me, you know."

"I understand that, but this is a celebration. You made it through a day of debriefings, uncovered a cabal of epic proportions, possibly saved the world—what better reasons to open another bottle?"

"Solving my case would be the best reason."

"I think you understand that there is a distinct possibility you may never solve it. Cartels are rather skilled at getting away with murder."

She nodded reluctantly. "But I won't stop trying."

"The zebra?"

"It's all we have right now."

"Then chase it. In the meantime, you're going to put a lot of very evil people away, Maggie. That's a victory, so enjoy it."

She smiled and regarded her empty flute. "I am. Too much, I think."

"There is no such thing as too much Krug." He poured the last of the bottle into her glass. "I've decided to leave Homicide Special Section. It's the only way we can be together."

She knew it would come up eventually; still, she choked on her champagne because she hadn't expected a decisive statement on the matter without even a pretense of discussion. "No, Remy!"

"There isn't an alternative."

"Yes, there is. I'll leave. I'm a junior, I'll just transfer to another—"

He shook his head. "Your career is brilliant and it's just beginning. I won't let you walk away from that."

"And I won't let you walk away. This is what you do and I know you can't live without it."

He reached across the table and took her hands. "I have recently come to realize that I can live without anything except you."

It was the second shock in a space of a few seconds, and a rush of tears burned her eyes.

"Oh my, I hope that doesn't make you sad. Are you going to break my heart?"

"No, it makes me very, very happy. But . . . I'm afraid if you leave, you'll end up resenting me, and I can't live with that."

"And if you left, would you end up resenting me?"

"No, of course not. I would feel better."

"And I would feel worse."

Nolan blotted her eyes daintily with a napkin, hoping she'd put on the waterproof mascara this morning. "We have choices and none of them are good."

"My choice is very good. For you and for me. Maggie, I'm burned out, and that's the truth."

"I don't believe you. You're at the top of your game—"

"The perfect time to drop the mic."

"Even a move to Narc would be a downgrade."

"Actually, I'm not considering a downgrade, I'm considering leaving the LAPD entirely. I hope that convinces you of my sincerity."

Her jaw slid open. The third shock. "You can't be serious."

"I'm very serious. This isn't a snap decision, it's been percolating for a while. This job I love is starting to feel like a prison, and that's wrong."

"I had no idea."

"Neither did I. Not until I fell in love with you."

The fourth shock. Her heart wouldn't survive another. "But . . . what would you do?" she sputtered, feeling panicky because cutting ties with a significant part of his life might make it easier to sever other connections, no matter what he thought now.

He released her hands and relaxed in his chair. "Life is filled with unlimited opportunity. I could go private—Malachai Dubnik has been trying to headhunt me for years. I could buy a vineyard. I could raise miniature ponies."

In spite of her distress, she giggled, albeit nervously. "Miniature ponies?"

"You have to admit, they're cute."

She took a large swallow of champagne simply because it was a distraction; and getting drunk didn't sound like the worst idea at this point. "Remy, this is a lot to process. It's our lives." *Our* lives. That had slipped out without a single reservation and she felt her cheeks burn.

"It's the right decision at the right time. I've never been maudlin about the past. The future is what excites me now."

Nolan was stunned to realize that she rarely thought about the

future, at least not seriously. A job that required such meticulous attention to the present gave you tunnel vision. Her career was her life, and
that was that. She'd always thought it was the same for Remy. But either
she'd been wrong, or he was making a great sacrifice for her, which was
unacceptable. "Tell me the truth—are you really burned out?"

"Even more so than I'm sharing right now. If the captain hadn't
confronted us, I would have likely stayed in a place that wasn't making me happy, simply out of habit, and inertia is a waste of life. And
how can I make you happy if I'm not? It's a win-win, Maggie."

She looked down at her empty plate, afraid to meet those tempest
eyes. "Did you mean what you said earlier?"

"I assume you're referencing my comments about loving you and
not being able to live without you. Look at me, Maggie."

It wasn't a command, but her eyes took it as one. The roller-coaster
feeling was back.

"Yes, I meant it. I never lie, and I always say what I mean. Those
are two very different things by the way, so you may properly infer
that I am a man of my word always."

He didn't ask her if she felt the same way. Because he knew. "Does
that mean I'm still invited to New Orleans for Christmas?"

For the first time all night, his eyes lightened to a paler shade of
black. "You'll come with me?"

Nolan once again became aware of the lively sounds of the lounge,
like somebody had just pressed play on a paused TV show. Life was
moving on, and she would try to keep up. There was a new future
to explore, filled with possibilities, whatever they might be. "I won't
have to eat alligator or anything, will I?"

"Just on Christmas morning, along with eye of newt and sparrow
tongues. All very tasty once you get used to them."

She desperately wanted to toss her napkin at him, but there was
something about the Bel-Air that inspired decorum. "I'll come, Remy.
Gladly."

Micah arrived at their table with an iced bucket and two fresh glasses. "Your Krug, Detectives."

Nolan smiled up at him and touched his hand as he was about to unwrap the foil. "Thank you, Micah, but on second thought, we'll just take the check."

Acknowledgments

A BILLION-DECIBEL SHOUT-OUT TO ALL THE dear, amazing people in my life who carried me through an impossibly difficult year. I am blessed to have a legion of heroes watching my six. Eternal gratitude.

Many thanks to Kelley Ragland, Hector DeJean, Sara Beth Haring, and the many others at St. Martin's/Minotaur Books for the stellar job they do bringing books to life. It's a joy to work with you all.

To Ellen Geiger, my agent and dear friend—love you. Matt Mc-Gowan, Sam Stoloff, Tess Weitzner, and Jade Wong-Baxter, you're the best.

I don't think I've ever mentioned this in acknowledgments before because you all know that fiction allows you to take Machiavellian liberties in service of the greater good. You can make up whatever you want, which is why I don't write nonfiction. Therefore, any exaggerations or outright lies are completely intentional.

About the Author

Pamela Stege

P. J. Tracy is the pseudonym of Traci Lambrecht, bestselling and award-winning author of the Monkeewrench series. Lambrecht and her mother, P. J., wrote eight novels together as P. J. Tracy before P. J. passed away in 2016. Traci continues the Monkeewrench series solo, as well as writing the Margaret Nolan series and working on film and television adaptations of her work. She spent most of her childhood painting and showing Arabian horses, and graduated with a Russian Studies major from St. Olaf College in Northfield, Minnesota, where she also studied voice. After ten years in Los Angeles, she now lives outside Minneapolis.